Edward Everett Hale

Stories of Invention told by Inventors and their Friends

Edward Everett Hale

Stories of Invention told by Inventors and their Friends

ISBN/EAN: 9783744750271

Printed in Europe, USA, Canada, Australia, Japan

Cover: Foto ©Andreas Hilbeck / pixelio.de

More available books at **www.hansebooks.com**

STORIES OF INVENTION

TOLD BY INVENTORS AND
THEIR FRIENDS.

By EDWARD E. HALE.

BOSTON:
ROBERTS BROTHERS.
1889.

PREFACE.

THIS little book closes a series of five volumes which I undertook some years since, in the wish to teach boys and girls how to use for themselves the treasures which they have close at hand in the Public Libraries now so generally opened in the Northern States of America. The librarians of these institutions are, without an exception, so far as I know, eager to introduce to the young the books at their command. From these gentlemen and ladies I have received many suggestions as the series went forward, and I could name many of them who could have edited or prepared such a series far more completely than I have done. But it is not fair to expect them, in the rush of daily duty, to stop and tell boys or girls what will be "nice books" for them to read. If they issue frequent bulletins of information in this direction, as is done so admirably by the librarians at Providence and at Hartford, they do more than any one has a right to ask them for. Such bulletins must be confined principally to helping young people read about the current events of the day. In that case it will only be indirectly that they send the young readers back into older literature, and make them acquainted with the best work of earlier times.

I remember well a legend of the old Public Library at Dorchester, which describes the messages sent to the hard-pressed librarian from the outlying parts of the town on the afternoon of Saturday, which was the only time when the Library was open.

"Mother wants a sermon book and another book." This was the call almost regularly made by the messengers.

I think that many of the most accomplished librarians of to-day have demands not very dissimilar, and that they will be glad of any assistance that will give to either mother or messenger any hint as to what this "other book" shall be.

It is indeed, of course, almost the first thing to be asked that boys and girls shall learn to find out for themselves what they want, and to rummage in catalogues, indexes, and encyclopædias for the books which will best answer their necessities. Mr. Emerson's rule is, "Read in the line of your genius." And the young man or maiden who can find out, in early life, what the line of his or her genius is, has every reason to be grateful to the teacher, or the event, or the book that has discovered it. I have certainly hoped, in reading and writing for this series, that there might be others of my young friends as sensible and as bright as Fergus and Fanchon, who will be found to work out their own salvation in these matters, and order their own books without troubling too much that nice Miss Panizzi or that omniscient Mrs. Bodley who manages the Library so well, and knows so well what every one in the town has read, and what he has not read.

I had at first proposed to publish with each book a little bibliography on the subjects referred to, telling particularly where were the available editions and the prices at which they could be bought by young collectors. But a little experiment showed that no such supplement could be made, which should be of real use for most readers for whom these books are made. The same list might be too full for those who have only small libraries at command, and too brief for those who are fortunate enough to use large ones. Indeed, I should like to say to such young readers of mine as have the pluck and the sense to read a preface, that the sooner they find out how to use the received guides in such matters, — the very indexes and bibliographies which I should use in making such a list for them, — why, the better will it be for them.

Such books as Poole's Index, Watt's and Brunet's Bibliographies, and the New American Indexes, prepared with such care by the Librarians' Association, are at hand in almost all the Public Libraries; and the librarians will always be glad to encourage intelligent readers in the use of them.

I should be sorry, in closing the series, not to bear my testimony to the value of the Public Library system, still so new to us, in raising the standard of thought and education. For thirty years I have had more or less to do with classes of intelligent young people who have met for study. I can say, therefore, that the habit of thought and the habit of work of such young people now is different from what it was thirty years ago. Of course it ought to be. You can say to a young learner now, " This book says thus and so, but you must learn for yourself whether this author is prejudiced or ill-informed, or not."

You can send him to the proper authorities. On almost any detail in general history, if he live near one of the metropolitan libraries, you can say to him, " If you choose to study a fortnight on this thing, you will very likely know more about it than does any person in the world." It is encouraging to young people to know that they can thus take literature and history at first hand. It pleases them to know that "the book" is not absolute. With such resources that has resulted which such far-seeing men as Edward Everett and George Ticknor and Charles Coffin Jewett hoped for, — the growth, namely, of a race of students who do not take anything on trust. As Professor Agassiz was forever driving up his pupils to habits of original observation in natural history, the Public Library provokes and allures young students to like courage in original research in matters of history and literature.

EDWARD E. HALE.

Roxbury, April 1, 1885.

CONTENTS.

STORIES OF INVENTION

TOLD BY INVENTORS.

———◆———

I.

INTRODUCTION.

THERE is, or is supposed to be, somewhere in Nor-
folk County in Massachusetts, in the neighborhood
of the city of Boston, a rambling old house which in its
day belonged to the Oliver family. I am afraid they
were most of them sad Tories in their time ; and I am not
sure but these very windows could tell the story of one or
another brick-bat thrown through them, as one or another
committee of the people requested one or another Oliver,
of the old times, to resign one or another royal commission. But a very peaceful Rowland has taken the place
of those rebellious old Olivers.

This comfortable old house is now known to many
young people as the home of a somewhat garrulous old
gentleman whom they call Uncle Fritz. His real name
is Frederick Ingham. He has had a checkered life,
but it has evidently been a happy one. Once he was in
the regular United States Navy. For a long time he was
a preacher in the Sandemanian connection, where they
have no ordained ministers. In Garibaldi's time he was a

colonel in the patriot service in Italy. In our civil war he held a command in the national volunteer navy; and his scientific skill and passion for adventure called him at one time across "the Great American Desert," and at another time across Siberia, in the business of constructing telegraphs. In point of fact, he is not the relation of any one of the five-and-twenty young people who call him Uncle Fritz. But he pets them, and they pet him. They like to make him a regular visit once a week, as the winter goes by. And the habit has grown up, of their reading with him, quite regularly, on some subject selected at their first meeting after they return from the country. Either at Lady Oliver's house, as his winter home is called, or at Little Crastis, where he spends his summers, those selections for reading have been made, which have been published in a form similar to that of the book which the reader holds in his hand.

The reader may or may not have seen these books, — so much the worse for him if he have not, — but that omission of his may be easily repaired. There are four of them: STORIES OF WAR told by Soldiers; STORIES OF THE SEA told by Sailors; STORIES OF ADVENTURE told by Adventurers; STORIES OF DISCOVERY told by Discoverers.

Since the regular meetings began, of which these books are the history, the circle of visitors has changed more or less, as most circles will, in five years. Some of those who met are now in another world. Some of the boys have grown to be so much like men, that they are "subduing the world," as Uncle Fritz would say, in their several places, and that they write home, from other latitudes and longitudes, of the Discoveries and Adventures in which they have themselves been leaders. But younger sisters and brothers take the places of older brothers and sisters.

The club — for it really is one — is popular, Lady Oliver's house is large, and Uncle Fritz is hospitable. He says himself that there is always room for more; and Ellen Flaherty, or whoever else is the reigning queen in the kitchen, never complains that the demand is too great for her "waffles."

Last fall, when the young people made their first appearance, the week before Thanksgiving day, after the new-comers had been presented to Uncle Fritz, and a chair or two had been brought in from the dining-room to make provision for the extra number of guests, it proved that, on the way out, John Coram, who is Tom Coram's nephew, had been talking with Helen, who is one of the old Boston Champernoons, about the change of Boston since his uncle's early days.

"I told her," said he to Uncle Fritz, "that Mr. Allerton was called 'the last of the merchants,' and he is dead now."

"That was a pet phrase of his," said Uncle Fritz. "He meant that his house, with its immense resources, simply bought and sold. He was away for many years once. When he returned, he found that the chief of his affairs had made an investment, from motives of public spirit, in a Western railroad. 'I thought we were merchants,' said the fine old man, disapproving. As he turned over page after page of the account, he found at last that the whole investment had been lost. 'I am glad of that,' said he; 'you will remember now that we are merchants.'"

"But surely my father is a merchant," said Julius. "He calls himself a merchant, he is put down as a merchant in the Directory, and he buys and sells, if that makes a man a merchant."

"All that is true," said Uncle Fritz. "But your father also invests money in railroads; so far he is engaged in transportation. He is a stockholder and a director in the Hecla Woollen Mills at Bromwich; so far he is a manufacturer. He told me, the other day, that he had been encouraging my little friend Griffiths, who is experimenting in the conservation of electric power; so far he. is an inventor, or a patron of inventions.

"In substance, what Mr. Allerton meant when he said 'I thought we were merchants,' was this: he meant that that firm simply bought from people who wished to sell, and sold to people who wished to buy.

"The fact, that almost every man of enterprise in Massachusetts is now to a certain extent a manufacturer, shows that a great change has come over people here since the beginning of this century."

"Those were the days of Mr. Cleveland's adventures, and Mr. Forbes's," said Hugh.

He alluded to the trade in the Pacific, in which these gentlemen shared, as may be read in Stories of Adventure.

Uncle Fritz said, "Yes." He said that the patient love of Great Britain for her colonies forbade us here from making so much as a hat or a hob-nail while we were colonies, as it would gladly do again now. He said that the New Englanders had a great deal of adventurous old Norse blood in their veins, that they had plenty of ship-timber and tar. If they could not make hob-nails they could make ships; and they made very good ships before they had been in New England ten years.

Luckily for us, soon after the country became a country, near a hundred years ago, the quarrels of Europe were such, that if an English ship carried produce of the West

Indies or China to Europe, France seized, if she could, ship and cargo ; if a French ship carried them, English cruisers seized ship and cargo, if they could. So it happened that the American ships and the American sailors, who were not at war with England and were not at war with France, were able to carry the stores which were wanted by all the world. The wars of Napoleon were thus a steady bounty for the benefit of the commerce of America. When they were well over, we had become so well trained to commerce here, that we could build the best ships in the world ; and we thought we had the best seamen in the world, — certainly there were no better. Under such a stimulus, and what followed it, our commerce, as measured by the tonnage of our ships, was as large as that of any nation, and, if measured by the miles sailed, was probably larger.

All this prosperity to merchants was broken up by the War of 1812, between the United States and Great Britain. For two years and a half, then, our intercourse with Europe was almost cut off ; for the English cruisers now captured our vessels whenever they could find them. At last we had to make our own hob-nails, our guns, our cannon, our cotton cloth, and our woollen cloth, if we meant to have any at all. The farmers' wives and daughters had always had the traditions of spinning and weaving.

When Colonel Ingham said this, Blanche nodded to Mary and Mary to Blanche.

" That means," said the Colonel, " that you have brought dear old mother Tucker's spinning-wheel downstairs, and have it in the corner behind your piano, does it not ? "

Blanche laughed, and said that was just what she meant.

" It does very well in ' Martha,' " said the Colonel. "And can you spin, Blanche ? "

Blanche rather surprised him by saying that she could, and the Colonel went on with his lecture. Fergus, who is very proud of Blanche, slipped out of the room, but was back after a minute, and no one missed him.

Here in Massachusetts some of the most skilful merchants — Appletons, Perkinses, and Lawrences — joined hand with brave inventors like Slater and Treadwell, and sent out to England for skilful manufacturers like Crompton and Boott; thus there sprung up the gigantic system of manufacture, which seems to you children a thing of course. Oddly enough, the Southern States, which had always hated New England and New England commerce, and had done their best to destroy it when they had a chance, were very eager to secure a home-market for Southern cotton; and thus, for many years after the war, they kept up such high protective duties that foreign goods were very dear in America, and the New England manufacturers had all the better prices.

While Uncle Fritz was saying this in substance, Ransom, the old servant, appeared with a spinning-wheel from Colonel Ingham's music-room. The children had had it for some charades. Kate Fogarty, the seamstress of the Colonel's household, followed, laughing, with a great hank of flax; and when the Colonel stopped at the interruption, Fergus said, —

" I thought, Uncle Fritz, they would all like to see how well Blanche spins; so I asked Ransom to bring in the wheel."

And Blanche sat down without any coaxing, and made her wheel fly very prettily, and spun her linen thread as well as her great-grandmamma would have done. Colonel Ingham was delighted; and so were all the children, half of whom had never seen any hand-spinning before. All of them had seen cotton and wool spun in factories ; in fact, half of them had eaten their daily bread that day, from the profit of the factories that for ten hours of every day do such spinning.

"Now, you see," said the well-pleased Colonel, "Blanche spins that flax exactly as her grandmother nine generations back spun it. She spins it exactly as Mrs. Dudley spun it in the old house where Dr. Paterson's church stands. It is strange enough, but for one hundred and fifty years there seems to have been no passion for invention among the New Englanders. Now they are called a most *inventive* people, and that bad word has been coined for them and such as they.

"But all this is of the last century. It was as soon as they were thrown on their own resources that they began to invent. Eli Whitney, a Worcester County boy, graduated at Yale College in 1791. He went to Georgia at once, to be a tutor in a planter's family ; but before he arrived, the planter had another tutor. This was a fortunate chance for the world ; for poor Whitney, disappointed, went to spend the winter at the house of Mrs. General Greene. One day, at dinner, some guests of hers said that cotton could never be exported with profit unless a machine could be made to separate the seeds from the 'wool.' 'If you want anything invented,' said Mrs. Greene, 'ask my young friend Mr. Whitney ; he will invent anything for you.' Whitney had then never seen cotton unmanufactured. But he went to work ; and before he was one year out of college, he had invented the cotton-gin, which created an enormous product of cotton, and, in fact, changed the direction of the commerce of the world.

"Well, you know about other inventions. Robert

Fulton, who built the first effective steamboat, was born in Pennsylvania the same year Whitney was born in Massachusetts.

"Hector, you are fond of imaginary conversations: write one in which Whitney and Fulton meet, when each is twenty-one; let Daniel Boone look in on them, and prophesy to them the future of the country, and how much it is to owe to them and to theirs."

"I think Blanche had better write it—in a ballad," said Hector, laughing. "It shall be an old crone spinning; and as she turns her wheel she shall describe the Ætna Factory at Watertown."

"There shall be a *refrain*," said Wallace, —

> "'Turn my wheel gayly;
> Spin, flax, spin.'"

"No," said Hatty; "the refrain shall be

> 'Four per cent in six months,
> Eight per cent in twelve.'

We are to go to Europe if the Vesuvius Mills pay a dividend. But if they *pass*, I believe I am to scrub floors in my vacation."

"Very well," said Uncle Fritz, recalling them to the subject they had started on. "All this is enough to show you how it is that you, who are all New Englanders, are no longer seafaring boys or girls, exclusively or even principally. Your great-grandmother, Alice, saved the lives of all the crew of a Bristol trader, by going out in her father's boat and taking her through the crooked passage between the Brewsters. You would be glad to do it, but I am afraid you cannot."

"I should rather encourage those who go to do it," said Alice, demurely, repeating one of their familiar jokes.

"And your great-grandfather, Seth, is the Hunt who discovered Hunt's Reef in the Philippines. I am afraid you cannot place it on the map."

"I know I cannot," said Seth, bravely.

"No," said the old gentleman. "But all the same the reef is there. I came to an anchor in the 'Calypso,' waiting for a southwest wind, in sight of the breakers over it. And I wish we had the pineapples the black people sold us there.

"All the same the New Englanders are good for something. Ten years hence, you boys will be doing what your fathers are doing, — subduing the world, and making it to be more what God wants it to be. And you will not work at arms' length, as they did, nor with your own muscles."

"We have Aladdin's lamp," said Mary, laughing.

"And his ring," said Susie. "I always liked the ring one better than the lamp one, though he was not so strong."

"He is prettier in the pictures," said George.

"Yes," said the Colonel; "we have stronger Genii than Aladdin had, and better machinery than Prince Camaralzaman."

"I heard some one say that Mr. Corliss had added twenty-seven per cent to the working power of the world by his *cut-off*," said Fergus.

The Colonel said he believed that was true. And this was a good illustration of what one persevering and intelligent man can do in bringing in the larger life and nobler purpose of the Kingdom of Heaven. Such a man makes men cease from *labor*, which is always irksome, and *work* with God. This is always ennobling.

"I am ashamed to say that I do not know what a

cut-off is," said Alice, who, like Seth, had been trained to "confess ignorance."

" I was going to say so," said John Rodman.

" And I, — and I, — and I," said quite a little chorus.

"We must make up a party, the first pleasant day, and go and see the stationary engine which pumps this water for us." So the Colonel met their confessions. " But does not all this indicate that we might spend a few days in looking up inventions ? "

" I think we ought to," said Hatty. "Certainly we ought, if the Vesuvius pays. Imagine me at Manchester. Imagine John Bright taking me through his own mill, and saying to me, ' This is the rover we like best, on the whole. Do you use this in America ? ' Imagine me forced to reply that I do not know a rover when I see one, and could not tell a ' slubber ' from a ' picker.' "

The others laughed, and confessed equal ignorance. " Only, John Bright has no mills in Manchester, Hatty."

" Well, they are somewhere ; and I must not eat the bread of the Vesuvius slubbers, and not know something of the way in which slubbers came to be."

" Very well," said Uncle Fritz, as usual recalling the conversation to sanity. " Whom shall we read about first ? "

" Tubal Cain first," said Fergus. " He seems to have been the first of the crew."

" It was not he who found out witty inventions," said Fanchon, in a mock *aside*.

" I should begin with Archimedes," said Uncle Fritz.

" Excellent ! " said Fergus ; " and then may we not burn up old Fogarty's barn with burning-glasses ? "

The children dislike Fogarty, and his barn is an eyesore to them. It stands just beyond the hedge of the Lady Oliver garden.

"I thank Archimedes every time I take a warm bath. Did he not invent hot baths?"

"What nonsense! He was killed by Caligula in one."

"You shall not talk such stuff. — Uncle Fritz, what books shall I bring you?"

It would seem as if, perhaps, Uncle Fritz had led the conversation in the direction it had taken. At least it proved that, all together on the rolling book-rack which Mr. Perkins gave him, were the account of Archimedes in the Cyclopædia Britannica, the account in the French Universal Biography, the life in La Rousse's Cyclopædia, Plutarch's Lives, and a volume of Livy in the Latin. From these together, Uncle Fritz, and the boys and girls whom he selected, made out this little history of Archimedes.

II.

ARCHIMEDES.

ARCHIMEDES was born in Syracuse in the year 287 B. C., and was killed there in the year 212 B. C. He is said to have been a relation of Hiero, King of Syracuse; but he seems to have held no formal office known to the politicians. Like many other such men, however, from his time down to Ericsson, he came to the front when he was needed, and served Syracuse better than her speech-makers. While he was yet a young man, he went to Alexandria to study; and he was there the pupil of Euclid, the same Euclid whose Geometry is the basis of all the geometry of to-day.

While Archimedes is distinctly called, on very high authority, "the first mathematician of antiquity," and while we have nine books which are attributed to him, we do not have — and this is a great misfortune — any ancient biography of him. He lived seventy-five years, for most of that time probably in Syracuse itself; and it would be hard to say how much Syracuse owed to his science. At the end of his life he saved Syracuse from the Romans for three years, during a siege in which, by his ingenuity, he kept back Marcellus and his army. At the end of this siege he was killed by a Roman soldier when the Romans entered the city.

The books of his which we have are on the " Sphere and Cylinder," " The Measure of the Circle," " Conoids and Spheroids," "On Spirals," "Equiponderants and Centres of Gravity," "The Quadrature of the Parabola," "On Bodies floating in Liquids," "The Psammites," and "A Collection of Lemmas." The books which are lost are "On the Crown of Hiero;" "Cochleon, or Water-Screw;" "Helicon, or Endless Screw;" "Trispaston, or Combination of Wheels and Axles;" "Machines employed at the Siege of Syracuse;" "Burning Mirror;" "Machines moved by Air and Water;" and "Material Sphere."

As to the story of the bath-tub, Uncle Fritz gave to Hector to read the account as abridged in the "Cyclopædia Britannica."

"Hiero had set him to discover whether or not the gold which he had given to an artist to work into a crown for him had been mixed with a baser metal. Archimedes was puzzled by the problem, till one day, as he was stepping into a bath, and observed the water running over, it occurred to him that the excess of bulk occasioned by the introduction of alloy could be measured by putting the crown and an equal weight of gold separately into a vessel filled with water, and observing the difference of overflow. He was so overjoyed when this happy thought struck him that he ran home without his clothes, shouting, 'I have found it, I have found it,' — Εὕρηκα, Εὕρηκα.

"This word has been chosen by the State of California for its motto."

To make the story out, it must be supposed that the crown was irregular in shape, and that the precise object was to find how much metal, in measurement, was used in its manufacture. Suppose three cubic inches of gold were used, Archimedes knew how much this would cost. But if three cubic inches of alloy were used, the king had been cheated.   What the overflow of the water taught was the precise cubic size of the various ornaments of the crown.   A silver crown or a lead crown would displace as much water as a gold crown of the same shape and ornament.   But neither silver nor lead would weigh so much as if pure gold were used, and at that time pure gold was by far the heaviest metal known.

Fergus, who is perhaps our best mathematician, pricked up his ears when he heard there was a treatise on the relation of the Circle to the Square.   Like most of the intelligent boys who will read this book, Fergus had tried his hand on the fascinating problem which deals with that proportion.   Younger readers will remember that it is treated in "Swiss Family."   Jack — or is it perhaps Ernest? — remembers there, that for the ribbon which was to go round a hat the hat-maker allowed three times the diameter of the hat, and a little more.   This "little more" is the delicate fraction over which Archimedes studied; and Fergus, after him.   Fergus knew the proportion as far as thirty-three figures in decimals.   These are 3.141, 592,653,589,793,238,462,643,383,279,502.   When Uncle Fritz asked Fergus to repeat these, the boy did it promptly, somewhat to the astonishment of the others.   He had committed it to memory by one of Mr. Gouraud's "analogies," which are always convenient for persons who have mathematical formulas to remember.

When those of the young people who were interested in mathematics looked at Archimedes's solution of the problem, they found it was the same as that they had themselves tried at school.   But he carried it so far as to inscribe a circle between two polygons, each of ninety-six sides; and his calculation is based on the relation between the two.

Taking the "Swiss Family Robinson" statement again,

Archimedes shows that the circumference of a circle exceeds three times its diameter by a small fraction, which is less than $\frac{10}{70}$ and greater than $\frac{10}{71}$, and that a circle is to its circumscribing square nearly as 11 to 14. Those who wish to carry his calculations farther may be pleased to know that he found the figures 7 to 22 expressed the relation more correctly than 1 to 3 does. Metius, another ancient mathematician, used the proportion 113 to 355. If you reduce that to decimals, you will find it correct to the sixth decimal. Remember that Archimedes and Metius had not the convenience of the Arabic or decimal notation. Imagine yourselves doing Metius's sum in division when you have to divide CCCLV by CXIII. Archimedes, in fact, used the Greek notation,—which was a little better than the Roman, but had none of the facility of ours. For every *ten*, from 20 to 90, they had a separate character, and for every *hundred*, and for every *thousand*. The *thousands* were the units with a mark underneath. Thus *a* meant 1, and *ͺa* meant 1,000. To express 113, Archimedes would have written ριγ. To express 355, he would have written τνε ; and the place which these signs had in the order would not have affected their value, as they do with us.

We cannot tell how the greater part of Archimedes's life was spent. But whether he were nominally in public office or not, it is clear enough that he must have given great help to Syracuse and her rulers, as an engineer, long before the war in which the Romans captured that great city. At that time Syracuse was, according to Cicero, " the largest and noblest of the Greek cities." It was in Sicily ; but, having been built by colonists from Greece, who still spoke the Greek language, Cicero speaks of it among Greek cities, as he would have spoken of Thurii, or Sybaris, or the cities of "Magna Græcia," — "great Greece," as they called the Greek settlements in southern Italy. In the Second Punic War Syracuse took sides against Rome with the Carthaginians, though her old king, Hiero, had been a firm ally of the Romans. The most interesting accounts that we have of Archimedes are in Livy's account of this war, and in Plutarch's Life of Marcellus, who carried it on on the Roman side. Livy says of Archimedes that he was —

"A man of unrivalled skill in observing the heavens and the stars, but more deserving of admiration as the inventor and constructor of warlike engines and works, by means of which, with a very slight effort, he turned to ridicule what the enemy effected with great difficulty.

" The wall, which ran along unequal eminences, most of which were high and difficult of access, some low and open to approach along level vales, was furnished by him with every kind of warlike engine, as seemed suitable to each particular place. Marcellus attacked from the quinqueremes [his large ships] the wall of the Achradina, which was washed by the sea. From the other ships the archers and slingers and light infantry, whose weapon is difficult to be thrown back by the unskilful, allowed scarce any person to remain upon the wall unwounded. These soldiers, as they required some range in aiming their missiles upward, kept their ships at a distance from the wall. Eight more quinqueremes joined together in pairs, the oars on their inner sides being removed, so that side might be placed to side, and which thus formed ships [of double width], and were worked by the outer oars, carried turrets built up in stories, and other battering-engines.

" Against this naval armament Archimedes placed, on different parts of the walls, engines of various dimensions.

Against the ships which were at a distance he discharged stones of immense weight; those which were nearer he assailed with lighter and more numerous missiles. Lastly, in order that his own men might heap their weapons upon the enemy without receiving any wounds themselves, he perforated the wall from the top to the bottom with a great number of loop-holes, about a cubit in diameter, through which some with arrows, others with scorpions of moderate size, assailed the enemies without being seen. He threw upon their sterns some of the ships which came nearer to the walls, in order to get inside the range of the engines, raising up their prows by means of an iron grapple attached to a strong chain, by means of a *tolleno* [or derrick], which projected from the wall and overhung them, having a heavy counterpoise of lead which forced the line to the ground. Then, the grapple being suddenly disengaged, the ship, falling from the wall, was by these means, to the utter consternation of the seamen, so dashed against the water that even if it came back to its true position it took in a great quantity of water."

" Fancy," cried Bedford, " one of their double quinque-remes, when she had run bravely in under the shelter of the wall. Just as the men think they can begin to work, up goes the prow, and they all are tumbled down into the steerage. Up she goes, and fifty rowers are on each other in a pile ; when the old pile-driver claw lets go again, and down she comes, splash into the sea. And then Archimedes pokes his head out through one of the holes, and says in Greek, ' How do you like that, my friends?' I do not wonder they were discouraged."

The bold cliff of the water front of Syracuse gave Archimedes a particular advantage for defensive operations of this sort. They are described in more detail in Plutarch's

Life of Marcellus, who was the Roman general employed against Syracuse, and who was held at bay by Archimedes for three years.

Here is Plutarch's account : —

Marcellus, with sixty galleys, each with five rows of oars, furnished with all sorts of arms and missiles, and a huge bridge of planks laid upon eight ships chained together,[1] upon which was carried the engine to cast stones and darts, assaulted the walls. He relied on the abundance and magnificence of his preparations, and on his own previous glory ; all which, however, were, it would seem, but trifles for Archimedes and his machines.

These machines he had designed and contrived, not as matters of any importance, but as mere amusements in geometry, — in compliance with King Hiero's desire and request, some little time before, that he should reduce to practice some part of his admirable speculations in science, and by accommodating the theoretic truth to sensation and ordinary use, bring it more within the appreciation of people in general. Eudoxus and Archytas had been the first originators of this far-famed and highly prized art of mechanics, which they employed as an elegant illustration of geometrical truths, and as a means of sustaining experimentally, to the satisfaction of the senses, conclusions too intricate for proof by words and diagrams. As, for example, to solve the problem so often required in constructing geometrical figures, "Given the two extremes to find the two mean lines of a proportion," both these mathematicians had recourse to the aid of instruments, adapting to their purpose certain curves and sections of lines. But what with Plato's indignation

---

[1] These are the quinqueremes, fastened together, of the other account.

at it, and his invectives against it as the mere corruption and annihilation of the one good of geometry, which was thus shamefully turning its back upon the unembodied objects of pure intelligence, to recur to sensation, and to ask help (not to be obtained without base subservience and depravation) from matter; so it was that mechanics came to be separated from geometry, and when repudiated and neglected by philosophers, took its place as a military art.

Archimedes, however, in writing to King Hiero, whose friend and near relative he was, had stated that, given the force, any given weight might be moved; and even boasted, we are told, relying on the strength of demonstration, that if there were another earth, by going into it he could move this.

Hiero being struck with amazement at this, and entreating him to make good this assertion by actual experiment, and show some great weight moved by a small engine, he fixed upon a ship of burden out of the king's arsenal, which could not be drawn out of the dock without great labor by many men. Loading her with many passengers and a full freight, sitting himself the while far off, with no great endeavor, but only holding the head of the pulley in his hand and drawing the cord by degrees, he drew the ship in a straight line, as smoothly and evenly as if she had been in the sea.

The king, astonished at this, and convinced of the power of the art, prevailed upon Archimedes to make him engines accommodated to all the purposes, offensive and defensive, of a siege. These the king himself never made use of, because he spent almost all his life in a profound quiet and the highest affluence. But the apparatus was, in a most opportune time, ready at hand for the Syracusans, and with it also the engineer himself.

When, therefore, the Romans assaulted the walls in two places at once, fear and consternation stupefied the Syracusans, believing that nothing was able to resist that violence and those forces. But when Archimedes began to ply his engines, he at once shot against the land forces all sorts of missile weapons, with immense masses of stone that came down with incredible noise and violence, against which no man could stand; for they knocked down those upon whom they fell in heaps, breaking all their ranks and files. In the mean time huge poles thrust out from the walls over the ships [these were the derricks, or *tollenos*, of Livy] sunk some by the great weights which they let down from on high upon them; others they lifted up into the air by an iron hand or beak like a crane's beak, and when they had drawn them up by the prow, and set them on end upon the poop, they plunged them to the bottom of the sea. Or else the ships, drawn by engines within, and whirled about, were dashed against the steep rocks that stood jutting out under the walls, with great destruction of the soldiers that were aboard them. A ship was frequently lifted up to a great height in the air (a dreadful thing to behold), and was rolled to and fro and kept swinging, until the mariners were all thrown out, when at length it was dashed against the rocks, or let fall.

At the engine that Marcellus brought upon the bridge of ships, — which was called *Sambuca* from some resemblance it had to an instrument of music of that name, — while it was as yet approaching the wall, there was discharged a piece of a rock of ten talents' weight,[1] then a second and a third, which, striking upon it with immense force and with a noise like thunder, broke all its

---

[1] The estimates of a talent vary somewhat, but ten talents made about seven hundred pounds.

foundation to pieces, shook out all its fastenings, and completely dislodged it from the bridge. So Marcellus, doubtful what counsel to pursue, drew off his ships to a safer distance, and sounded a retreat to his forces on land. They then took a resolution of coming up under the walls, if it were possible, in the night; thinking that as Archimedes used ropes stretched at length in playing his engines, the soldiers would now be under the shot, and the darts would, for want of sufficient distance to throw them, fly over their heads without effect. But he, it appeared, had long before framed for such occasion engines accommodated to any distance, and shorter weapons; and had made numerous small openings in the walls, through which, with engines of a shorter range, unexpected blows were inflicted on the assailants. Thus, when they, who thought to deceive the defenders, came close up to the walls, instantly a shower of darts and other missile weapons was again cast upon them. And when stones came tumbling down perpendicularly upon their heads, and, as it were, the whole wall shot out arrows against them, they retired.

And now, again, as they were going off, arrows and darts of a longer range inflicted a great slaughter among them, and their ships were driven one against another, while they themselves were not able to retaliate in any way. For Archimedes had provided and fixed most of his engines immediately under the wall; whence the Romans, seeing that infinite mischiefs overwhelmed them from no visible means, began to think they were fighting with the gods.

Yet Marcellus escaped unhurt, and, deriding his own artificers and engineers, " What," said he, " must we give up fighting with this geometrical Briareus, who plays pitch and toss with our ships, and with the multitude of darts which he showers at a single moment upon us, really outdoes the hundred-handed giants of mythology?" And doubtless the rest of the Syracusans were but the body of Archimedes's designs, one soul moving and governing all; for, laying aside all other arms, with his alone they infested the Romans and protected themselves. In fine, when such terror had seized upon the Romans that if they did but see a little rope or a piece of wood from the wall, instantly crying out that there it was again, that Archimedes was about to let fly some engine at them, they turned their backs and fled, Marcellus desisted from conflicts and assaults, putting all his hope in a long siege. Yet Archimedes possessed so high a spirit, so profound a soul, and such treasures of scientific knowledge, that though these inventions had now obtained him the renown of more than human sagacity, he yet would not deign to leave behind him any commentary or writing on such subjects; but, repudiating as sordid and ignoble the whole trade of engineering, and every sort of art that lends itself to mere use and profit, he placed his whole affection and ambition in those purer speculations where there can be no reference to the vulgar needs of life, — studies the superiority of which to all others is unquestioned, and in which the only doubt can be whether the beauty and grandeur of the subjects examined or the precision and cogency of the methods and means of proof most deserve our admiration.

It is not possible to find in all geometry more difficult and intricate questions, or more simple and lucid explanations. Some ascribe this to his natural genius; while others think that incredible toil produced these, to all appearance, easy and unlabored results. No amount of investigation of yours would succeed in attaining the proof; and yet, once seen, you immediately believe you would have discovered it, — by so smooth and so rapid a path he leads you to the conclusion required. And thus it ceases to be incredible that (as is commonly told of him) the charm of his familiar and domestic science made him forget his food and neglect his person to that degree that when he was occasionally carried by absolute violence to bathe, or have his body anointed, he used to trace geometrical figures in the ashes of the fire, and diagrams in the oil on his body, being in a state of entire preoccupation, and, in the truest sense, divine possession, with his love and delight in science. His discoveries were numerous and admirable; but he is said to have requested his friends and relations that when he was dead they would place over his tomb a sphere containing a cylinder, inscribing it with the ratio which the containing solid bears to the contained.

The boys were highly edified by this statement of the difficulty which Archimedes's friends found in making him take a bath, and chaffed Jack, who had asked if he were not the inventor of bath-tubs.

When the reading from Plutarch was over, Fergus asked if that were all, and was disappointed that there was nothing about the setting of ships on fire by mirrors. It is one of the old stories of the siege of Syracuse, that he set fire to the Roman ships by concentrating on them the heat of the sun from a number of mirrors. But this story is not in Livy, nor is it in Plutarch, though, as has been seen, they were well disposed to tell what they knew which was marvellous in his achievements. It is told at length and in detail by Zonaras and Tzetzes, two Greek writers of the twelfth century, who must have found it in some ancient writers whose works we do not now have.

" Archimedes," says Zonaras,[1] " having received the rays of the sun on a mirror, by the thickness and polish of which they were reflected and united, kindled a flame in the air, and darted it with full violence upon the ships, which were anchored within a certain distance, in such a manner that they were burned to ashes."

The same writer says that Proclus, a celebrated " mathematician " of Constantinople, in the sixth century, at the siege of Constantinople set fire to the Thracian fleet by means of brass mirrors. Tzetzes is yet more particular. He says that when the Roman galleys were within a bow-shot of the city walls, Archimedes brought together hexagonal specula (mirrors) with other smaller ones of twenty-four facets, and caused them to be placed each at a proper distance ; that he moved these by means of hinges and plates of metal ; that the hexagon was bisected by the meridian of summer and winter ; that it was placed opposite the sun ; and that a great fire was thus kindled, which consumed the ships.

Now, it is to be remembered that these are the accounts of writers who were not so good mechanics as Archimedes. It should be remembered, also, that in the conditions of war then, the distance at which ships would be anchored in a little harbor like that of Syracuse was not great. By " bow-shot " would be meant the distance at which a bow would do serious damage. Doubtful as the story of Zonaras and Tzetzes seems, it received unexpected confirmation in the year 1747 from a celebrated experiment tried by the naturalist Buffon.

<hr>

[1] Quoted in Fabricius's Greek fragments.

After encountering many difficulties, which he had foreseen with great acuteness, and obviated with equal ingenuity, Buffon at length succeeded in repeating Archimedes's performance. In the spring of 1747 he laid before the French Academy a memoir which, in his collected works, extends over upwards of eighty pages. In this paper he described himself as in possession of an apparatus by means of which he could set fire to planks at the distance of 200 and even 210 feet, and melt metals and metallic minerals at distances varying from 25 to 40 feet. This apparatus he describes as composed of 168 plain glasses, silvered on the back, each six inches broad by eight inches long. These, he says, were ranged in a large wooden frame, at intervals not exceeding the third of an inch, so that, by means of an adjustment behind, each should be movable in all directions independent of the rest; the spaces between the glasses being further of use in allowing the operator to see from behind the point on which it behooved the various disks to be converged.

In this last statement there is a parallel with that of Tzetzes, who speaks of the division of Archimedes's mirrors.

At the present moment naturalists are paying great attention to plans for the using of the heat of the sun. It is said that on any county in the United States, twenty by thirty miles square, there is wasted as much heat of the sun as would drive, if we knew how to use it, all the steam-engines in the world.

Fergus asked Uncle Fritz if he believed that Archimedes threw seven hundred pounds of stone from one of his machines. The largest modern guns throw shot of one thousand pounds, and it is only quite recently that any such shot have been used.

Uncle Fritz told him that in the museum at St. Germain-en-Laye he would one day see a modern catapult, made by Colonel de Reffye from the design of a Roman catapult on Trajan's Column. This is supposed to be of the same pattern which is called an "Onager" in the Latin books. This catapult throws, when it is tested, a shot of twenty-four pounds, or it throws a sheaf of short arrows. In one catapult the power is gained by twisting ox-hide very tightly, and suddenly releasing it. Another is a very stout bow, worked with a small windlass. Of course this will give a great power.

Seven hundred pounds, however, seems beyond the ability of any such machines as this; but from his higher walls Archimedes could, of course, have rolled such stones down on the decks of the ships below. And if he were throwing other stones or leaden balls to a greater distance with his *Onagers,* it may well be that Plutarch or Livy did not take very accurate account of the particular engine which threw one stone or another.

Archimedes was killed by a Roman soldier, to the great grief of Marcellus, when the Romans finally took Syracuse. The city fell through drunkenness, which was, and is, the cause of more failure in the world than anything else which can be named. Marcellus, in some conversations about the exchange or redemption of a prisoner, observed a tower somewhat detached from the wall, which was, as he thought, carelessly guarded. Choosing the night of a feast of Diana, when the Syracusans were wholly given up to wine and sport, he took the tower by surprise, and from the tower seized the wall and made his way into the city. In the sack of the city by the soldiers, which followed, Archimedes was killed. The story is told in different ways. Plutarch says that he was working out some problem by a diagram, and never noticed the incursion of the Romans, nor that the city was taken. A soldier, unexpectedly coming up to him in this transport of study and meditation, commanded him to follow him to Marcellus ; which he declining to do before he had worked out his problem to a demonstration, the soldier, enraged, drew his sword, and ran him through. "Others write that a Roman soldier, running upon him with a drawn sword, offered to kill him, and that Archimedes, looking back, earnestly besought him to hold his hand a little while, that he might not leave what he was then at work upon inconsequent and imperfect; but the soldier, not moved by his entreaty, instantly killed him. Others, again, relate that as Archimedes was carrying to Marcellus mathematical instruments, dials, spheres, and angles by which the magnitude of the sun might be measured to the sight, some soldiers, seeing him, and thinking that he carried gold in a vessel, slew him.

"Certain it is, that his death was very afflicting to Marcellus, and that Marcellus ever after regarded him that killed him as a murderer, and that he sought for the kindred of Archimedes and honored them with signal honors."

Archimedes, as has been said, had asked that his monument might be a cylinder bearing a sphere, in commemoration of his discovery of the proportion between a cylinder and a sphere of the same diameter. A century and a half after, when Cicero was quæstor ·of Sicily, he found this monument, neglected, forgotten, and covered with a rank growth of thistles and other weeds.

"It was left," he says, "for one who came from Arpinas, to show to the men of Syracuse where their greatest countryman lay buried."

III.

FRIAR BACON.

" **A**LL the world seems to have known of Columbus's discoveries as soon as he came home, but all the world did not know at once of Archimedes's inventions; indeed, I should think the world did not know now what all of them are."

Hester Van Brunt was saying this in the hall, as the girls laid off their waterproofs, when they next met the Colonel.

" I think that may often be said of what we call Inventions and what we call Discoveries," he said, "till quite recent times. When a man invented a new process, it was supposed that if he could keep the secret, it might be to him a very valuable secret. But when one discovered an island or a continent, it was almost impossible to keep the secret. They tried it sometimes, as you know. But there must be a whole ship's crew who know something of the new-found land, and from some of them the secret would leak out.

" But there has been many a process in the arts lost, because the man who discovered the new quality in nature or invented the new method in manufacture kept it secret, so that he might do better work than his competitors. This went so far that boys were apprenticed to masters to learn ' the secrets of their trades.' "

Fergus said that in old times inventors were not always treated very kindly. If people thought they were sorcerers, or in league with the Devil, they did not care much for the invention.

Uncle Fritz said they would find plenty of instances of the persecution of inventors, even to quite a late date. It is impossible, of course, to say how many good things were lost to the world by the pig-headedness which discouraged new inventions. It is marvellous to think what progress single men made, who had to begin almost at the beginning, and learn for themselves what every intelligent boy or girl now finds ready for him in the Cyclopædia. It is very clear that the same beginnings were made again and again by some of the early inventors. Then, what they learned had been almost forgotten. There was no careful record of their experiments, or, if any, it was in one manuscript, and that was not accessible to people trying to follow in their steps.

"I have laid out for you," said Uncle Fritz, "some of the early accounts of Friar Bacon, — Roger Bacon. He is one of the most distinguished of the early students of what we now call natural philosophy in England. It was in one of the darkest centuries of the Dark Ages.

"But see what he did.

"There are to be found in his writings new and ingenious views of Optics, — as, on the refraction of light, on the apparent magnitude of objects, on the magnified appearance of the sun and moon when on the horizon. He describes very exactly the nature and effects of concave and convex lenses, and speaks of their application to the purposes of reading and of viewing distant objects, both terrestrial and celestial; and it is easy to prove from his writings that he was either the inventor or the improver of

the telescope.   He also gives descriptions of the camera
obscura and of the burning-glass.   He made, too, several
chemical discoveries.   In one place he speaks of an inex-
tinguishable fire, which was probably a kind of phosphorus.
In another he says that an artificial fire could be prepared
with saltpetre and other ingredients which would burn at
the greatest distance, and by means of which thunder and
lightning could be imitated.   He says that a portion of this
mixture of the size of an inch, properly prepared, would
destroy a whole army, and even a city, with a tremendous
explosion accompanied by a brilliant light.   In another
place he says distinctly that thunder and lightning could
be imitated by means of saltpetre, sulphur, and charcoal.
As these are the ingredients of gunpowder, it is clear that
he had an adequate idea of its composition and its power.
He was intimately acquainted with geography and astronomy.   He had discovered the errors of the calendar
and their causes, and in his proposals for correcting them
he approached very nearly to the truth.   He made a cor-
rected calendar, of which there is a copy in the Bodleian
Library in Oxford.   In moral philosophy, also, Roger
Bacon has laid down some excellent precepts for the
conduct of life.[1]

" Now, if you had such a biography of such a man now,
you would know that without much difficulty you could
find all his more important observations in print.   So soon
as he thought them important, he would communicate
them to some society which would gladly publish them.
In the first place, he would be glad to have the credit of
an improvement, an invention, or a discovery.   If the invention were likely to be profitable, the nation would secure
the profit to him if he fully revealed the process.   They

---

[1] Encyclopædia Americana : art. " Roger Bacon."

would give him, by a ' patent,' the right to the exclusive profit for a series of years. The nation thus puts an end to the old temptation to secrecy, or tries to do so.

" But if you will read some of the queer passages from the old lives of Bacon, you will see how very vague were the notions which the people of his own time had of what he was doing."

Then Hester read some passages which Colonel Ingham had marked for her.

•

OF THE PARENTS AND BIRTH OF FRYER BACON, AND HOW HE ADDICTED HIMSELF TO LEARNING.

In most men's opinions he was born in the West part of *England* and was son to a wealthy Farmer, who put him to School to the Parson of the Town where he was born : not with intent that he should turn Fryer (as he did), but to get so much understanding, that he might manage the better that wealth he was to leave him. But young *Bacon* took his learning so fast, that the Priest could not teach him any more, which made him desire his Master that he would speak to his father to put him to *Oxford*, that he might not lose that little learning that he had gained : his Master was very willing so to do : and one day, meeting his father, told him, that he had received a great blessing of God, in that he had given him so wise and hopeful a Child as his son *Roger Bacon* was (for so was he named) and wished him withal to doe his duty, and to bring up so his Child, that he might shew his thankfulness to God, which could not better be done than in making him a Scholar ; for he found by his sudden taking of his learning, that he was a child likely to prove a very great Clerk :

hereat old *Bacon* was not well pleased (for he desired to bring him up to Plough and to the Cart, as he himself was brought) yet he for reverence sake to the Priest, shewed not his anger, but kindly thanked him for his paines and counsel, yet desired him not to speak any more concerning that matter, for he knew best what best pleased himself, and that he would do : so broke they off their talk and parted.

So soon as the old man came home, he called to his son for his books, which when he had, he locked them up, and gave the Boy a Cart Whip in place of them, saying to him : " Boy, I will have you no Priest, you shall not be better learned than I, you can tell by the Almanack when it is best sowing Wheat, when Barley, Peas and Beans : and when the best libbing is, when to sell Grain and Cattle I will teach thee ; for I have all Fairs and Markets as perfect in my memory, as Sir *John*, our Priest, has Mass without Book : take me this Whip, I will teach the use of it. It will be more profitable to thee than this harsh Latin : make no reply, but follow my counsel, or else by the Mass thou shalt feel the smart hand of my anger." Young *Bacon* thought this but hard dealing, yet he would not reply, but within six or eight days he gave his Father the slip, and went to a Cloister some twenty miles off, where he was entertained, and so continued his Learning, and in small time came to be so famous, that he was sent for to the University of Oxford, where he long time studied, and grew so excellent in the secrets of Art and Nature, that not England only, but all Christendom, admired him.

HOW FRYER BACON MADE A BRAZEN HEAD TO SPEAK, BY THE WHICH HE WOULD HAVE WALLED ENGLAND ABOUT WITH BRASS.

Fryer *Bacon*, reading one day of the many conquests of England, bethought himself how he might keep it hereafter from the like conquests, and so make himself famous hereafter to all posterity. This (after great study) he found could be no way so well done as one; which was to make a head of Brass, and if he could make this head to speak (and hear it when it speaks) then might he be able to wall all England about with Brass. To this purpose he got one Fryer *Bungy* to assist him, who was a great Scholar and a Magician, (but not to be compared to Fryer *Bacon*), these two with great study and pains so framed a head of Brass, that in the inward parts thereof there was all things like as in a natural man's head: this being done, they were as far from perfection of the work as they were before, for they knew not how to give those parts that they had made motion, without which it was impossible that it should speak: many books they read, but yet could not find out any hope of what they sought, that at the last they concluded to raise a spirit, and to know of him that which they could not attain to by their own studies. To do this they prepared all things ready and went one Evening to a wood thereby, and after many ceremonies used, they spake the words of conjuration, which the Devil straight obeyed and appeared unto them, asking what they would? "Know," said Fryer *Bacon*, "that we have made an artificial head of Brass, which we would have to speak, to the furtherance of which we have raised thee, and being raised, we will keep thee here, unless thou tell to us the way and manner how to make this Head to speak." The Devil told him that he had not that power of himself: "Beginner of lies," said Fryer *Bacon*, "I know that thou wouldst dissemble, and therefore tell it us quickly, or else we will here bind thee to remain during our pleasures." At these threatenings the Devil consented to do it, and told them, that with a continual fume of the six hottest simples it should have motion, and in one month space speak, the Time of the month or day he knew not: also he told them, that if they heard it not before it had done speaking, all their labour should be lost: they being satisfied, licensed the Spirit for to depart.

Then went these two learned Fryers home again, and prepared the Simples ready, and made the fume, and with continual watching attended when this Brazen-head would speak: thus watched they for three weeks without any rest, so that they were so weary and sleepy, that they could not any longer refrain from rest: then called Fryer *Bacon* his man *Miles*, and told him, that it was not unknown to him what pains Fryer *Bungy* and himself had taken for three weeks space, only to make, and to hear the Brazen-head speak, which if they did not, then had they lost all their labour, and all England had a great loss thereby: therefore he entreated Miles that he would watch whilst that they slept, and call them if the Head speake. "Fear not, good Master," said Miles, "I will not sleep, but hearken and attend upon the head, and if it do chance to speak, I will call you: therefore I pray take you both your rests and let me alone for watching this head." After Fryer *Bacon* had given him a great charge the second time, Fryer *Bungy* and he went to sleep, and *Miles*, alone to watch the Brazen-head. *Miles* to keep himself from sleeping, got a Tabor and Pipe, and being merry disposed sang him many a merry Song ; and thus with his own Music and his Songs spent he his time, and kept from sleeping at last. After some noise the Head spake these two words: " *Time is.*" Miles hearing it to speak no more, thought his Master would be angry if he waked him for that, and therefore he let them both sleep, and began to mock the Head in this manner : " Thou Brazen-faced Head, hath my Master took all this pains about thee, and now dost thou requite him with two words, *Time is ?* had he watched with a Lawyer so long as he hath watched with thee, he would have given him more, and better words than thou hast yet. If thou canst speak no wiser, they shall sleep till doom's day for me. *Time is :* I know *Time is*, and that thou shall hear, good man Brazen face." And with this he sang him a song to his own music as to times and seasons, and went on, " Do you tell us, Copper-nose, when Time is? I hope we Scholars know our Times, when to drink drunk, when to kiss our hostess, when to go on her score, and when to pay it, that time comes seldom." After half an hour had passed, the Head did speak again, two words, which were these : " *Time was.*" *Miles* respected these words as little as he did the former, and would not wake them, but still scoffed at the Brazen head, that it had learned no better words, and have such a Tutor as his Master : and in scorn of it sung a Song to the tune of " A Rich Merchant man," beginning as follows :

> Time was when thou a kettle
> Wert filled with better matter :
> But Fryer *Bacon* did thee spoil,
> When he thy sides did batter,

with more to the same purpose. " *Time was*," said he, " I know that, Brazen face, without your telling, I know

Time was, and I know what things there was when Time was, and if you speak no wiser, no Master shall be waked for me." Thus *Miles* talked and sung till another half hour was gone, then the Brazen head spake again these words, " *Time is past :* " and therewith fell down, and presently followed a terrible noise, with strange flashes of fire, so that *Miles* was half dead with fear. At this noise the two Fryers awaked, and wondered to see the whole room so full of smoke, but that being vanished they might perceive the Brazen head broken and lying on the ground : at this sight they grieved, and called *Miles* to know how this came. Miles half dead with fear, said that it fell down of itself, and that with the noise and fire that followed he was almost frighted out of his wits : Fryer *Bacon* asked him if he did not speak? "Yes," quoth *Miles*, " it spake, but to no purpose. I 'll have a Parrot speak better in that time than you have been teaching this Brazen head." "Out on thee, villain," said Fryer *Bacon*, " thou hast undone us both, hadst thou but called us when it did speak, all England had been walled round about with Brass, to its glory, and our eternal fames : what were the words it spake?" "Very few," said *Miles*, "and those none of the wisest that I have heard neither : first he said, ' *Time is.*' " "Hadst thou called us then," said Fryer *Bacon*, "we had been made for ever." "Then," said *Miles*, "half an hour after it spake again and said ' *Time was.*' " "And wouldst thou not call us then?" said *Bungy*. "Alas !" said *Miles*, "I thought he would have told me some long Tale, and then I purposed to have called you : then half an hour after, he cried ' *Time is past,*' and made such a noise, that he hath waked you himself, methinks." At this Fryer *Bacon* was in such a rage, that he would have beaten his man, but he was restrained by *Bungy:* but nevertheless for his punishment, he with his Art struck him dumb for one whole month's space. Thus that great work of these learned Fryers was overthrown (to their great griefs) by this simple fellow.

HOW FRYER BACON BY HIS ART TOOK A TOWN, WHEN THE KING HAD LAIN BEFORE IT THREE MONTHS, WITHOUT DOING IT ANY HURT.

In those times when Fryer *Bacon* did all his strange tricks, the Kings of *England* had a great part of *France* which they held a long time, till civil wars at home in this Land made them to lose it. It did chance that the King of England (for some cause best known to himself) went into *France* with a great Army, where after many victories, he did besiege a strong Town, and lay before it full three months, without doing to the Town any great damage, but rather received the hurt himself. This did so vex the King, that he sought to take it in any way, either by policy or strength: to this intent he made Proclamation, that whosoever could deliver this Town into his hand, he should have for his pains ten thousand Crowns truly paid. This was proclaimed, but there was none found that would undertake it: at length the news did come into *England* of this great reward that was promised. Fryer *Bacon* hearing of it, went into *France*, and being admitted to the King's presence, he thus spake unto him: "Your Majesty I am sure hath not forgot your poor servant *Bacon*, the love that you showed to me being last in your presence, hath drawn me for to leave my Country and my Studies, to do your Majesty service: I beseech your Grace, to command me so far as my poor Art or life may do you pleasure." The King thanked him for his love, but told him that he had now more need of Arms than Art, and wanted brave Soldiers rather than learned Scholars. Fryer *Bacon* answered, "Your Grace saith well; but let me (under correction) tell you, that Art oftentimes doth these things that are impossible to Arms, which I will make good in few examples. I will speak only of things performed by Art and Nature, wherein there shall be nothing Magical: and first by the figuration of Art, there may be made Instruments of Navigation without men to row in them, as great ships, to brook the Sea, only with one man to steer them, and they shall sail far more swiftly than if they were full of men : Also Chariots that shall move with an unspeakable force, without any living creature to stir them.   Likewise, an Instrument may be made to fly withal, if one sit in the midst of the Instrument, and do turn an engine, by which the wings being Artificially composed, may beat air after the manner of a flying Bird. By an Instrument of three fingers high, and three fingers broad, a man may rid himself and others from all Imprisonment: yea, such an Instrument may easily be made, whereby a man may violently draw unto him a thousand men, will they, nill they, or any other thing. By Art also an Instrument may be made, wherewith men may walk in the bottom of the Sea or Rivers without bodily danger: this *Alexander* the Great used (as the Ethnic philosopher reporteth) to the end he might behold the Secrets of the Seas. But Physical Figurations are far more strange : for by that may be framed Perspects and Looking-glasses, that one thing shall appear to be many, as one man shall appear to be a whole Army, and one Sun or Moon shall seem divers. Also perspects may be so framed, that things far off shall seem most nigh unto us: with one of these did *Julius Cæsar* from the

Sea coasts in *France* marke and observe the situation of the Castles in *England*. Bodies may also be so framed, that the greatest things shall appear to be the least, the highest lowest, the most secret to be the most manifest, and in such like sort the contrary. Thus did *Socrates* perceive, that the Dragon which did destroy the City and Country adjoining with his noisome breath, and contagious influence, did lurk in the dens between the Mountains : and thus may all things that are done in Cities or Armies be discovered by the enemies. Again, in such wise may bodies be framed, that venemous and infectious influences may be brought whither a man will : In this did *Aristotle* instruct *Alexander;* through which instruction the poyson of a Basiliske, being lifted up upon the wall of a City, the poyson was conveyed into the City, to the destruction thereof : Also perspects may be made to deceive the sight, as to make a man believe that he seeth great store of riches when there is not any. But it appertaineth to a higher power of Figuration, that beams should be brought and assembled by divers flections and reflections in any distance that we will, to burne anything that is opposite unto it, as is witnessed by those Perspects or Glasses that burn before and behind. But the greatest and chiefest of all figurations and things figured, is to describe the heavenly bodies, according to their length and breadth in a corporal figure, wherein they may corporally move with a daily motion. These things are worth a kingdom to a wise man. These may suffise, my royal Lord, to shew what Art can do : and these, with many things more, as strange, I am able by Art to perform. Then take no thought for winning this Town, for by my Art you shall (ere many days be past) have your desire."

The King all this while heard him with admiration : but

hearing him now, that he would undertake to win the Town, he burst out in these speeches: " Most learned *Bacon*, do but what thou hast said, and I will give thee what thou most desirest, either wealth or honour, choose what thou wilt, and I will be as ready to perform, as I have been to promise."

" Your Majesty's love is all that I seek," said the Fryer, "let me have that, and I have honour enough, for wealth, I have content, the wise should seek no more : but to the purpose. Let your Pioneers raise up a mount so high, (or rather higher), than the wall, and then you shall see some probability of that which I have promised."

This Mount in two days was raised : then Frier *Bacon* went with the King to the Top of it, and did with a perspect shew to him the Town, as plainly as if he had been in it : at this the King did wonder, but Fryer *Bacon* told him, that he should wonder more, ere next day noon : against which Time, he desired him to have his whole Army in readiness, for to scale the wall upon a signal given by him, from the Mount. This the King promised to do, and so returned to his Tent full of Joy, that he should gain this strong Town. In the morning Fryer *Bacon* went up to the Mount and set his Glasses, and other Instruments up : in the meantime the King ordered his Army, and stood in a readiness for to give the assaults : when the signal was given which was the waving of a flag. Ere nine of the clock Fryer *Bacon* had burnt the State-house of the Town, with other houses only by his Mathematical Glasses, which made the whole Town in an uproar, for none did know how it came : whilst that they were quenching of the same, Fryer *Bacon* did wave his flag : upon which signal given, the King set upon the Town, and took it with little or no resistance. Thus through the Art of this learned man the King got this strong Town, which he could not do with all his men without Fryer *Bacon's* help.

HOW FRYER BACON BURNT HIS BOOKS OF MAGIC AND GAVE HIMSELF TO THE STUDY OF DIVINITY ONLY; AND HOW HE TURNED ANCHORITE.

Now in a time when Fryer *Bacon* kept his Chamber (having some great grief) he fell into divers meditations: sometimes into the vanity of Arts and Sciences: then would he condemn himself for studying of those things that were so contrary to his Order and Soul's health; and would say that Magic made a Man a Devil; sometimes would he meditate on Divinity; then would he cry out upon himself for neglecting the study of it, and for studying Magic: sometime would he meditate on the shortness of man's life, then would he condemn himself for spending a time so short, so ill as he had done his: so would he go from one thing to another and in all condemn his former studies.

And that the world should know how truly he did repent his wicked life, he caused to be made a great fire; and sending for many of his Friends, Scholars, and others, he spake to them after this manner: "My good Friends and fellow Students, it is not unknown unto you, how that through my Art I have attained to that credit, that few men living ever had. Of the wonders that I have done, all England can speak, both King and Commons: I have unlocked the secret of Art and Nature, and let the world see those things, that have layen hid since the death of Hermes, that rare and profound Philosopher: My Studies have found the secrets of the Stars; the Books that I have made of them, do serve for Precedents to our greatest

Doctors, so excellent hath my Judgement been therein. I likewise have found out the secrets of Trees, Plants and Stones, with their several uses ; yet all this knowledge of mine I esteem so lightly, that I wish that I were ignorant, and knew nothing : for the knowledge of these things, (as I have truly found) serveth not to better a man in goodness, but only to make him proud and think too well of himself.   What hath all my knowledge of nature's secrets gained me ?   Only this, the loss of a better knowledge, the loss of divine Studies, which makes the immortal part of man (his Soul) blessed.   I have found, that my knowledge has been a heavy burden, and has kept down my good thoughts : but I will remove the cause which are these Books : which I do purpose here before you all to burn." They all intreated him to spare the Books, because in them there were those things that after-ages might receive great benefit by.   He would not hearken unto them but threw them all into the fire, and in that flame burnt the greatest learning in the world.   Then did he dispose of all his goods ; some part he gave to poor Scholars, and some he gave to other poor folks : nothing he left for himself : then caused he to be made in the Church-wall a Cell, where he locked himself in, and there remained till his death.   His time he spent in Prayer, Meditation and such Divine Exercises, and did seek by all means to persuade men from the study of Magic.   Thus lived he some two years space in that Cell, never coming forth : his meat and drink he received in at a window, and at that window he did discourse with those that came to him ; His grave he digged with his own nails, and was laid there when he dyed. Thus was the Life and Death of this famous Fryer, who lived the most part of his life a Magician, and died a true penitent sinner and an Anchorite.

When Hester had finished reading, one of the boys said that if people believed such things as that, he thought the wonder was that they made any progress at all. Uncle Fritz said that in matters which make up what we call science, they did not make much progress. The arts of the world do not seem to have advanced much between the days of Solomon and those of William the Conqueror.

"As you see," said Uncle Fritz, "an inventor was set down as a magician. I think you can remember more instances."

Yes. Almost all the young people remember that in Marco Polo's day there was a distinguished Venetian engineer with the armies of Genghis Khan, whose wonderful successes gave rise, perhaps, to the story of Aladdin.[1] The scene of his successes was Pekin ; and it is to be remembered that the story of Aladdin is not properly one of the Arabian Nights, and that the scene is laid in China.

This led them to trying to match the wonders of Aladdin and of the Arabian Nights by the wonders of modern invention ; and they pleased themselves by thinking of marvels they could show to unlearned nations if they had the resources of Mr. Edison's laboratory.

"Aladdin rubbed his lamp," said Blanche. "You see, the lamp was his electrical machine ; and when he rubbed it, the lightnings went flying hither and thither, and said, 'Here we are.'"

"That is all very fine," said Jack Withers ; "but I stand by the Arabian Nights, after all, and I think I shall, till Mr. Edison or the Taunton locomotive shop will make for me some high-stepper on whose back I may rise above the clouds, pass over the length and breadth of Massachusetts, descend in the garden where Blanche is

[1] See "Stories of Adventure."

confined by the hated mistress of a boarding-school in Walpole, and then, winning her ready consent, can mount again with her, and before morning descend in the garden of a beautiful cottage at Newport. We will spend six weeks in playing tennis in the daytime, dancing in the Casino in the evenings, and in sailing in Frank Shattuck's yacht between whiles. Then, and not till then, would I admit that the Arabian Nights have been outdone by modern science."

They all laughed at Jack's extravaganza, which is of a kind to which they are beginning to be accustomed. But Mabel stuck to her text, and said seriously, that Uncle Fred had said that what people now called science sprung from the workshops of these very magicians. "The magicians then had all the science there was. And if magic had not got a bad name, should we not call the men of science magicians now?"

Uncle Fritz said yes to all her questions, but he said that they did not cover the whole matter. The difference between a magician and a man of science involves these habits: the magician keeps secret what he knows, while the man of science discloses all he learns. Then the magician affected to have spiritual power at command, while the man of science only affects to use what he calls physical powers. Till either of them tell us how to distinguish spiritual forces from physical forces, the second distinction is of the less importance. But the other has made all the difference in the world between the poor magic-men and the science-men. For, as they had seen with Friar Bacon, the magic-men have had their stories told by most ignorant people, seeing they did not generally leave any records behind them; but the men of modern science, having chosen to tell their own stories, have had them told, on the whole, reasonably well, though generally stupidly.

"What a pity we have not Solomon's books of science!" said John Tolman.

"It is one of the greatest of pities that such books as those were not kept. It seems as if people would have built on such foundations, and that Science would have marched from step to step, instead of beginning over and over again. But we do have Pliny's Natural History, as he chose to call it. Far from building on that as a foundation, the Dark Ages simply accepted it. And there are blunders or sheer lies in that book, and in Aristotle's books, and Theophrastus's, and other such, which have survived even to our day."

The children were peeping into the collection from which the Friar Bacon stories had been read, and they lighted on these scraps about the supposed life of Virgil. To the people of the Dark Ages Virgil was much more a man of magic than a poet.

HOW VIRGILIUS WAS SET TO SCHOOL.

As Virgilius was born, then the town of Rome quaked and trembled: and in his youth he was wise and subtle, and was put to school at Tolentin, where he studied diligently, for he was of great understanding. Upon a time the scholars had licence to go to play and sport them in the fields after the usance of the old time ; and there was also Virgilius thereby also walking among the hills all about : it fortuned he spied a great hole in the side of a great hill wherein he went so deep that he could not see no more light, and then he went a little further therein, and then he saw some light again, and then went he forth straight : and within a little while after, he heard a voice that called, " Virgilius, Virgilius ; " and he looked about, and he could not see no body ; then Virgilius spake and asked, " Who calleth me ? " Then heard he the voice again, but he saw nobody : then said he, " Virgilius, see ye not that little board lying beside you there, marked with that word ? " Then answered Virgilius, " I see that board well enough." The voice said, " Do away that board, and let me out thereat." Then answered Virgilius to the voice that was under the little board, and said, " Who art thou that talkest me so ! " Then answered the devil : " I am a devil, conjured out of the body of a certain man, and banished till the day of judgement, without I be delivered by the hands of men. Thus, Virgilius, I pray you to deliver me out of this pain, and I shall shew unto thee many books of necromancy, and how thou shalt come by it lightly and know the practise therein, that no man in the science of necromancy shall pass thee ; and moreover I shall shew and inform you so that thou shalt have all thy desire, whereby methinks it is a great gift for so little a doing, for ye may also thus all your friends helpen, and make · your enemies unmighty." Through that great promise was Virgil tempted ; he bad the fiend shew the books to him that he might have and occupy them at his will. And so the fiend shewed him, and then Virgilius pulled open a board, and there was a little hole, and thereat crawled the devil out like an eel, and came and stood before Virgilius like a big man ; thereat Virgilius was astonished and marvelled greatly thereof that so great a man might come out at so little a hole ; then said Virgilius, " should ye well pass into the hole that ye came out of ? " " Yea, I shall well," said the devil. — " I hold the best pledge that I have, ye shall not do it." " Well," said the devil, " thereto I consent." And then the devil crawled into the little hole again, and as he was therein, Virgilius covered the hole again, and so was the devil beguiled, and might not there come out again, but there abideth still therein. Then called the devil dreadfully to Virgilius and said, " What have ye done?" Virgilius answered, " Abide there still to your day appointed." And from thenceforth abideth he there. And so Virgilius became very cunning in the practise of the black science.

HOWE THE EMPEROR ASKED COUNSEL OF VIRGILIUS, HOW THE NIGHT RUNNERS AND ILL DOERS MIGHT BE RID-OUT OF THE STREETS.

The emperor had many complaints of the night runners and thieves, and also of the great murdering of people in the night, in so much that the emperor asked counsel of Virgilius, and said : " That he hath great complaints of the thieves that runneth by night for they kill many men ; what counsel, Virgilius, is best to be done?" Then answered Virgilius to the emperor, " Ye shall make a horse of copper and a copper man upon his back, having in his hands a flail of iron, and that horse, ye shall so bring afore the towne house, and ye shall let cry that a man from henceforth at ten of the clock should ring a bell, and he that after the bell was rung in the streets should be slain, no work thereof should be done." And when this cry was made the ruffians set not a point, but kept the streets as they did afore and would not let therefor ; and as soon as the bell was rung at ten of the clock, then leaped the horse of copper with the copper man through the streets of Rome, insomuch that he left not one street in Rome unsought; and as soon as he found any man or woman in the street he slew them stalk dead, insomuch that he slew above two hundred persons or more. And this seeing, the thieves and night-runners how they might find a remedy therefor, thought in their minds to make a drag with a ladder thereon; and as they would go out by night they took their ladders with them, and when they heard the horse come, then cast they the drag upon the houses, and so went up upon their ladders to the top of the houses, so that the copper man might not touch them; and so abide they still in their wicked doing. Then came they again to the emperor and complained, and then the emperor asked counsel of Virgilius; and Virgilius answered and said, "that then he must get two copper hounds and set them of either side of the copper horse, and let cry again that no body after the bell is rung should depart out of their house that would live." But the night walkers cared not a point for that cry; but when they heard the horse coming, with their ladders climbed upon the houses, but the dogs leaped after and tore them all in pieces; and thus the noise went through Rome, in so much that nobody durst in the night go in the street, and thus all the night-walkers were destroyed.

HOW VIRGILIUS MADE A LAMP THAT AT ALL TIMES BURNED.

For profit of the common people, Virgilius on a great mighty marble pillar, did make a bridge that came up to the palace, and so went Virgilius well up the pillar out of the palace; that palace and pillar stood in the midst of

Rome; and upon this pillar made he a lamp of glass that always burned without going out, and nobody might put it out; and this lamp lightened over all the city of Rome from the one corner to the other, and there was not so little a street but it gave such light that it seemed two torches there had stand; and upon the walls of the palace made he a metal man that held in his hand a metal bow that pointed ever upon the lamp for to shoot it out; but always burned the lamp and gave light over all Rome. And upon a time went the burgesses' daughters to play in the palace and beheld the metal man; and one of them asked in sport, why he shot not? And then she came to the man and with her hand touched the bow, and then the bolt flew out, and brake the lamp that Virgilius made; and it was wonder that the maiden went not out of her mind for the great fear she had, and also the other burgesses' daughters that were in her company, of the great stroke that it gave when it hit the lamp, and when they saw the metal man so swiftly run his way; and never after was he no more seen; and this foresaid lamp was abiding burning after the death of Virgilius by the space of three hundred years or more.

It is on the wrecks and ruins recorded in such fables as these that modern science is builded.

IV.

BENVENUTO CELLINI.

" NOW we will leave the fairy tales," said Uncle Fritz,
" and begin on modern times."

" Modern times means since 1492," said Alice, — " the
only date in history I am quite sure of, excepting 1866."

" Eighteen-hundred and sixty-six," said John Good-
rich, — " the *Annus Mirabilis*, celebrated for the birth of
Miss Alice Francis and Mr. J. G."

" Hush, hush ! Uncle Fritz wants to say something."

" We will leave the fairy tales," said poor chicken-
pecked Uncle Fritz, " and begin with Benvenuto Cellini.
Who has seen any of his work ? "

Several of the girls who had been in Europe remembered seeing gold and silver work of Benvenuto Cellini's
in the museums. Uncle Fritz told them that the little
hand-bell used on his own tea-table was modelled at
Chicopee, in Massachusetts, from a bell which was the
design of Benvenuto Cellini ; and he sent for the bell that
the children might see how ingenious was the ornamenta-
tion, and how simply the different designs were connected
together.

He told Alice she might read first from Vasari's account of him. Vasari's book, which the children now
saw for the first time, is a very entertaining one. Vasari
was himself an artist, of the generation just following

Michael Angelo. He was, indeed, the contemporary of Raphael. But he is remembered now, not for his pictures, nor for his work in architecture, both of which were noted in his time, but for his lives of the most excellent painters, sculptors, and architects, which was first published in 1550. Benvenuto Cellini was born ten years before Vasari, and here is a part of Vasari's life of him.

LIFE OF BENVENUTO CELLINI.

Benvenuto Cellini, citizen of Florence, born in 1500, at present a sculptor, in his youth cultivated the goldsmith's business, and had no equal in that branch. He set jewels, and adorned them with diminutive figures, exquisitely formed, and some of them so curious and fanciful that nothing finer or more beautiful can be conceived. At Rome he made for Pope Clement VII. a button to be worn upon his pontifical habit, fixing a diamond to it with the most exquisite art. He was employed to make the stamps for the Roman mint, and there never have been seen finer coins than those that were struck in Rome at that period.

After the death of Pope Clement, Benvenuto returned to Florence, where he made stamps with the head of Duke Alessandro, for the mint, wonderfully beautiful. Benvenuto, having at last devoted himself to sculpture and casting statues, made in France many works, while he was employed at the Court of King Francis I. He afterwards came back to his native country, where he executed in metal the statue of Perseus, ·who cut off Medusa's head. This work was brought to perfection with the greatest art and diligence imaginable.

Though I might here enlarge on the productions of Benvenuto, who always shewed himself a man of great spirit and vivacity, bold, active, enterprising, and formidable to his enemies, — a man, in short, who knew as well how to speak to princes as to exert himself in his art, — I shall add nothing further, since he has written an account of his life and works, and a treatise on goldsmith's work as well as on casting statues and many other subjects, with more art and eloquence than it is possible for me to imitate. I shall therefore content myself with this account of his chief performances.

Benvenuto was quite proud of his own abilities as a writer. Very fortunately for us he has left his own memoirs. Here is the introduction.

BENVENUTO'S AUTOBIOGRAPHY.

" It is a duty incumbent on upright and credible men of all ranks, who have performed anything noble or praiseworthy, to record, in their own writing, the events of their lives; yet they should not commence this honorable task before they have passed their fortieth year. Such at least is my opinion, now that I have completed my fifty-eighth year, and am settled in Florence.

" Looking back on some delightful and happy events of my life, and on many misfortunes so truly overwhelming that the appalling retrospect makes me wonder how I reached this age, in vigor and prosperity, through God's goodness, I have resolved to publish an account of my life.

" My grandfather, Andrea Cellini, was still living when

I was about three years of age, and he was then above a hundred. As they were one day removing a water-pipe, a large scorpion, which they had not perceived, came out of it. The scorpion descended upon the ground and had got under a great bench, when I, seeing it, ran and caught it in my hand. This scorpion was of such a size that whilst I held it in my little hand, it put out its tail on one side, and on the other darted its two mouths. I ran overjoyed to my grandfather, crying out, ' Grandfather, look at my pretty little crab ! ' The good old man, who knew it to be a scorpion, was so frightened, and so apprehensive for my safety, that he seemed ready to drop down dead, and begged me with great eagerness to give the creature to him ; but I grasped it the harder and cried, for I did not choose to part with it. My father, who was in the house, ran to us upon hearing the noise, and, happening just at that instant to espy a pair of scissors, he laid hold of them, and, by caressing and playing with me, he contrived to cut off the head and tail of the scorpion. Then, finding I had received no harm from the venomous reptile, he pronounced it a happy omen."

His father taught him to play upon the flute, and wished him to devote himself to music; but his own inclinations were different.

" Having attained the age of fifteen, I engaged myself, against my father's inclinations, with a goldsmith named Antonio di Sandro, an excellent artist and a very worthy man. My father would not have him allow me any wages ; for this reason, that since I voluntarily applied myself to this art, I might have an opportunity to withdraw whenever I thought proper. So great was my inclination to improve, that in a few months I rivalled the most skilful journeyman in the business, and began to reap some fruits from my labor. I continued, however, to play sometimes, through complaisance to my father, either upon the flute or the horn ; and I constantly drew tears and deep sighs from him every time he heard me. From a feeling of filial piety, I often gave him that satisfaction, endeavoring to persuade him that it gave me also particular pleasure.

"Once when I was staying at Pisa, my father wrote to me in every letter exhorting me not to neglect my flute, in which he had taken so much pains to instruct me. Upon this, I entirely lost all inclination to return to him ; and to such a degree did I hate that abominable flute, that I thought myself in a sort of paradise in Pisa, where I never once played upon that instrument."

At the age of twenty-three (in 1523), Cellini went to Rome, where he did much work for the Pope, Clement VII.

"About this time so dreadful an epidemic disease prevailed in Rome, that several thousands died every day. Somewhat terrified at this calamity, I began to indulge myself in certain recreations, as the fancy took me. On holidays I amused myself with visiting the antiquities of that city, and sometimes took their figures in wax ; at other times, I made drawings of them. As these antiquities are all ruinous edifices, where a number of pigeons build their nests, I had a mind to divert myself among them with my fowling-piece, and often returned home laden with pigeons of the largest size. But I never chose to put more than a single ball into my piece, and in this manner, being a good marksman, I procured a considerable quantity of game. The fowling-piece was, both on the inside and the outside, as bright as a looking-glass. I likewise made the powder as fine as the minutest dust, and in the use of it I discovered some of the most admirable secrets that ever were known till this time. When I had charged my piece with a quantity of powder equal in weight to the fifth part of the ball, it carried two hundred paces, point blank.

" While I was enjoying these pleasures, my spirits suddenly revived. I no longer had my usual gloom, and I worked to more purpose than when my attention was wholly engrossed by business; on the whole, my gun turned rather to my advantage than the contrary.

" All Italy was now up in arms, and the Constable Bourbon, finding there were no troops in Rome, eagerly advanced with his army towards that capital. Upon the news of his approach, all the inhabitants took up arms. I engaged fifty brave young men to serve under me, and we were well paid and kindly treated.

" The army of the Duke of Bourbon having already appeared before the walls of Rome, Alessandro del Bene requested that I would go with him to oppose the enemy. I complied, and, taking one of the stoutest youths with us, — we were afterwards joined by another, — we came up to the walls of Campo Santo, and there descried that great army which was employing every effort to enter the town at that part of the wall to which we had approached. Many young men were slain without the walls, where they fought with the utmost fury; there was a remarkably thick mist.

" Levelling my arquebuse where I saw the thickest crowd of the enemy, I discharged it with a deliberate aim at a person who seemed to be lifted above the rest; but the mist prevented me from distinguishing whether he were on horseback or on foot. I then cautiously approached the walls, and perceived that there was an extraordinary confusion among the assailants, occasioned by our having shot the Duke of Bourbon; he was, as I understood afterwards, that chief personage whom I saw raised above the rest."

The Pope was induced by an enemy of Benvenuto, the Cardinal Salviati, to send for a rival goldsmith, Tobbia, to come to Rome. On his arrival both were summoned into the Pope's presence.

" He then commanded each of us to draw a design for setting a unicorn's horn, the most beautiful that ever was seen, which had cost 17,000 ducats. As the Pope proposed making a present of it to King Francis, he chose to have it first richly adorned with gold; so he employed us to draw the designs. When we had finished them we carried them to the Pope. Tobbia's design was in the form of a candlestick; the horn was to enter it like a candle, and at the bottom of the candlestick he had represented four little unicorns' heads, — a most simple invention. As soon as I saw it, I could not contain myself so as to avoid smiling at the oddity of the conceit. The Pope, perceiving this, said, 'Let me see that design of yours.' It was the single head of a unicorn, fitted to receive the horn. I had made the most beautiful sort of head conceivable, for I drew it partly in the form of a horse's head, and partly in that of a hart's, adorned with the finest sort of wreaths and other devices; so that no sooner was my design seen but the whole Court gave it the preference."

Benvenuto continued to make many beautiful things for Pope Clement VII. up to the time of his death. That Pope was succeeded in the papal chair by Cardinal Farnese (Paul III.), on the 13th of October, 1534.

"I had formed a resolution to set out for France, as well because I perceived that the Pope's favor was withdrawn from me by means of slanderers who misrepresented my services, as for fear that those of my enemies who had most influence might still do me some greater injury. For these reasons I was desirous to remove to some other country, and see whether fortune would there prove more favorable to me. Leaving Rome, I bent my course to Florence, whence I travelled on to Bologna, Venice, and Padua."

He reached Paris, with two workmen whom he took with him from Rome, "without meeting any ill accident, and travelling on in uninterrupted mirth." But being dissatisfied with his reception there, he returned instantly to Rome, where his fears were realized; for he was arrested by order of the Pope, and made a prisoner in the Castle of St. Angelo.

"This was the first time I ever knew the inside of a prison, and I was then in my thirty-seventh year. The constable of the Castle of St. Angelo was a countryman of mine, a Florentine, named Signor Giorgio Ugolini. This worthy gentleman behaved to me with the greatest politeness, permitting me to walk freely about the castle on my parole of honor, and for no other reason but because he saw the severity and injustice of my treatment.

"Finding I had been treated with so much rigor in the affair, I began to think seriously about my escape. I got my servants to bring me new thick sheets, and did not send back the dirty ones. Upon their asking me for them, I answered that I had given them away to some of the poor soldiers. I pulled all the straw out of the tick of my bed, and burned it; for I had a chimney in the room where I lay. I then cut those sheets into a number of slips each about one third of a cubit in width; and when I thought I had made a sufficient quantity to reach from the top to the bottom of the lofty tower of the Castle of St. Angelo, I told my servants that I had given away as much of my linen as I thought proper, and desired they would take care to bring me clean sheets, adding that I would constantly return the dirty ones.

"The constable of the castle had annually a certain disorder which totally deprived him of his senses; and when the fit came upon him, he was talkative to excess. Every year he had some different whim: one time he fancied himself metamorphosed into a pitcher of oil; another time he thought himself a frog, and began to leap as such; another time he imagined he was dead, and it was found necessary to humor his conceit by making a show of burying him; thus he had every year some new frenzy. This year he fancied himself a bat, and when he went to take a walk, he sometimes made just such a noise as bats do; he likewise used gestures with his hands and body, as if he were going to fly. His physicians and his old servants, who knew his disorder, procured him all the pleasures and amusements they could think of, and as they found he delighted greatly in my conversation, they frequently came to me to conduct me to his apartment, where the poor man often detained me three or four hours chatting with him.

" He asked me whether I had ever had a fancy to fly. I answered that I had always been very ready to attempt such things as men found most difficult; and that with regard to flying, as God had given me a body admirably well calculated for running, I had even resolution enough to attempt to fly. He then proposed to me to explain how I could contrive it. I replied that when I attentively considered the several creatures that fly, and thought of effecting by art what they do by the force of nature, I did not find one so fit to imitate as the bat. As soon as the poor man heard mention made of a bat, he cried out aloud, ' It is very true ! a bat is the thing.' He then addressed himself to me, and said, ' Benvenuto, if you had the opportunity, would you have the heart to make an attempt to fly?' I answered that if he would give me leave, I had courage enough to attempt to fly by means of a pair of wings waxed over. He said thereupon, ' I should like to see you fly ; but as the Pope has enjoined me to watch over you with the utmost care, I am resolved to keep you locked up with a hundred keys, that you may not slip out of my hands.' I said, before all present, ' Confine me as close as you please, I will contrive to make my escape, notwithstanding.' "

At night, with a pair of pincers which he had secured, he removed the nails which fastened the plates of iron fixed upon the door, imitating with wax the heads of the nails he took out, so that their absence need not be seen.

" One holiday evening, the constable being very much disordered, he scarce said anything else but that he was become a bat, and desired his people that if Benvenuto should happen to escape, they should take no notice of it, for he must soon catch me, as he should doubtless be better able to fly by night than I ; adding, ' Benvenuto is only a counterfeit bat, but I am a bat in real earnest.'

" As I had formed a resolution to attempt my escape that night, I began by praying fervently to Almighty God that it would please him to assist me in the enterprise. Two hours before daybreak, I took the iron plates from the door with great trouble. I at last forced the door, and having taken with me my slips of linen, which I had rolled up in bundles with the utmost care, I went out and got upon the right side of the tower, and leaped upon two tiles of the roof with the greatest ease. I was in a white doublet, and had on a pair of white half-hose, over which I wore a pair of little light boots, that reached half-way up my legs, and in one of these I put my dagger. I then took the end of one of my bundles of long slips, which I had made out of the sheets of my bed, and fastened it to one of the tiles of the roof that happened to jut out. Then letting myself down gently, the whole weight of my body being sustained by my arm, I reached the ground. It was not a moonlight night, but the stars shone with resplendent lustre. When I had touched the ground, I first contemplated the great height which I had descended with so much courage, and then walked away in high joy, thinking I had recovered my liberty. But I soon found myself mistaken, for the constable had caused two pretty high walls to be erected on that side. I managed to fix a long pole against the first wall, and by the strength of my arms to climb to the top of it. I then fastened my other string of slips, and descended down the steep wall.

" There was still another one ; and in letting myself down, being unable to hold out any longer, I fell, and, striking my head, became quite insensible. I continued in that state about an hour and a half, as nearly as I can guess. The day beginning to break, the cool breeze that precedes the rising of the sun brought me to my senses; but I conceived a strange notion that I had been beheaded, and was then in purgatory. I recovered by degrees my strength and powers, and, perceiving that I had got out of the castle, I soon recollected all that had befallen me. Upon attempting to rise from the ground, I found that my right leg was broken, three inches above the heel, which threw me into a terrible consternation. Cutting with my dagger the part of my string of slips I had left, I bandaged my leg as well as I could. I then crept on my hands and knees towards the gate with my dagger in my hand, and effected my egress. It was about five hundred paces from the place where I had had my fall to the gate by which I entered the city. It was then broad daylight. As I happened to meet with a water-carrier, who had loaded his ass, and filled his vessels with water, I called to him, and begged he would put me upon the beast's back, and carry me to the landing-place of the steps of St. Peter's Church. I offered to give him a gold crown, and, so saying, I clapped my hand upon my purse, which was very well lined. The honest waterman instantly took me upon his back, and carried me to the steps before St. Peter's Church, where I desired him to leave me and run back to his ass.

" Whilst I was crawling along upon all four, one of the servants of Cardinal Cornaro knew me, and, running immediately to his master's apartment, awakened him out of his sleep, saying to him, ' My most reverend Lord, here is your jeweller, Benvenuto, who has made his escape out of the castle, and is crawling along upon all four, quite besmeared with blood.'   The cardinal, the moment he heard this, said to his servants, ' Run, and bring him hither to my apartment upon your backs.'   When I came into his presence the good cardinal bade me fear nothing, and immediately sent for an excellent surgeon, who set the bone, bandaged my leg, and bled me.   The cardinal then caused me to be put into a private apartment, and went directly to the Vatican, in order to intercede in my behalf with the Pope.

" Meanwhile the report of my escape made a great noise all over Rome ; for the long string of sheeting fastened to the top of the lofty tower of the castle had excited attention, and the inhabitants ran in crowds to behold the sight.   By this time the frenzy of the constable had reached its highest pitch ; he wanted, in spite of all his servants, to fly from the same tower himself, declaring there was but one way to retake me, and that was to fly after me.   He caused himself to be carried into the presence of his Holiness, and began a terrible outcry, saying that I had promised him, upon my honor, that I would not fly away, and had flown away notwithstanding."

The Cardinal Cornaro, however, and others interceded for Benvenuto with the Pope, on account of his courage, and the extraordinary efforts of his ingenuity, which seemed to surpass human capacity.   The Pope said he had intended to keep him near his person, and to prevent him from returning to France, adding, " I am concerned to hear of his sufferings, however.   Bid him take care of his health ; and when he is thoroughly recovered, it shall be my study to make him some amends for his past troubles."   He was visited by young and old, persons of all ranks.

After this, Benvenuto went once more to France, where he was received with high consideration by Francis I., who gave him, for his home and workshop in Paris, a large old castle called the Nesle, of a triangular form, close to the walls of the city. Here, with workmen brought with him from Italy, he began many great works.

" Being thus become a favorite of the king, I was universally admired. As soon as I had received silver to make it of, I began to work on the statue of Jupiter, and took into my service several journeymen. We worked day and night with the utmost assiduity, insomuch that, having finished Jupiter, Vulcan, and Mars in earth, and Jupiter being pretty forward in silver, my shop began to make a grand show. Just about this time the king made his appearance at Paris, and I went to pay my respects to him. When his Majesty saw me, he called to me in high spirits, and asked me whether I had anything curious to show him at my shop, for he intended to call there. I told him of all I had done, and he expressed an earnest desire to see my performances ; and after dinner that day, all the nobility belonging to the Court of France repaired to my shop.

" I had just come home, and was beginning to work, when the king made his appearance at my castle gate. Upon hearing the sound of so many hammers, he commanded his retinue to be silent. All my people were at work, so that the king came upon us quite unexpectedly. As he entered the saloon, the first object he perceived was myself with a large piece of plate in my hand, which was to make the body of Jupiter ; another was employed on the head, another again on the legs, so that the shop resounded with the beating of hammers. His Majesty was highly pleased, and returned to his palace, after having conferred so many favors on me that it would be tedious to enumerate them.

" Having with the utmost diligence finished the beautiful statue of Jupiter, with its gilt pedestal, I placed it upon a wooden socle, which scarce made any appearance, and within that socle I fixed four little globes of wood, which were more than half hidden in their sockets, and so contrived that a little child could with the utmost ease move this statue of Jupiter backwards and forwards, and turn it about. I took it with me to Fontainebleau, where the King then resided. I was told to put it in the gallery, — a place which might be called a corridor, about two hundred paces long, adorned and enriched with pictures and pieces of sculpture, amongst them some of the finest imitations of the antique statues of Rome. Here also I introduced my Jupiter; and when I saw this great display of the wonders of art, I said to myself, ' This is like passing between the pikes of the enemy ; Heaven protect me from all danger ! '

" This figure of Jupiter had a thunderbolt in his right hand, and by his attitude seemed to be just going to throw it ; in his left I had placed a globe, and amongst the flames I had with great dexterity put a piece of white torch. On the approach of night I lighted the torch in the hand of Jupiter ; and as it was raised somewhat above his head, the light fell upon the statue, and caused it to appear to much greater advantage than it would otherwise have done. When I saw his Majesty enter with several great lords and noblemen, I ordered my boy to push the statue before him, and this motion, being made with admirable contrivance, caused it to appear alive ; thus the other figures in the gallery were left somewhat behind, and the eyes of all the beholders were first struck with my performance.

" The king immediately cried out : ' This is one of the finest productions of art that ever was beheld. I, who take pleasure in such things and understand them, could never have conceived a piece of work the hundredth part so beautiful ! ' "

Cellini, however, who was exacting and sensitive, became dissatisfied with the treatment of the King of France ; and, leaving his workmen at his tower of the Nesle, he returned to Italy, and engaged in the service of Cosmo de' Medici, Grand Duke of Tuscany, who assigned him a house to work in.

His chief performance here was a bronze statue of Perseus for the fine square before the Palazzo Vecchio. After many drawbacks, doubts, and difficulties, —

" I now took courage, resolving to depend on myself, and banished all those thoughts which from time to time occasioned me great inquietude, and made me sorely repent my ever having quitted France. I still flattered myself that if I could but finish my statue of Perseus, all my labors would be converted to delight, and meet with a glorious and happy reward.

" This statue was intended to be of bronze, five ells in height, of one piece, and hollow. I first formed my model of clay, more slender than the statue was intended to be. I then baked it, and covered it with wax of the thickness of a finger, which I modelled into the perfect form of the statue. In order to effect in concave what the wax represented in convex, I covered the wax with clay, and baked this second covering. Thus, the wax dissolving, and escaping by fissures left open for the purpose, I obtained, between the first model and the second covering, a space for the introduction of the metal. In order to introduce the bronze without moving the first model, I placed the model in a pit dug under the furnace, and by means of pipes and apertures in the model itself, I meant to introduce the liquid metal.

"After I had made its coat of earth, covered it well, and bound it properly with irons, I began by means of a slow fire to draw off the wax, which melted away by many vent-holes, — for the more of these are made, the better the moulds are filled; and when I had entirely stripped off the wax, I made a sort of fence round my Perseus, that is, round the mould, of bricks, piling them one upon another, and leaving several vacuities for the fire to exhale at. I next began gradually to put on the wood, and kept a constant fire for two days and two nights, till, the wax being quite off and the mould well baked, I began to dig a hole to bury my mould in, and observed all those fine methods of proceeding that are proscribed by our art. When I had completely dug my hole, I took my mould, and by means of levers and strong cables directed it with care, and suspended it a cubit above the level of the furnace, so that it hung exactly in the middle of the hole. I then let it gently down to the very bottom of the furnace, and placed it with all the care and exactness I possibly could. After I had finished this part of my task I began to make a covering of the very earth I had taken off; and in proportion as I raised the earth, I made vents for it, of a sort of tubes of baked earth, generally used for conduits, and other things of a similar nature.

"I had caused my furnace to be filled with several pieces of brass and bronze, and heaped them upon one another in the manner taught us by our art, taking particular care to leave a passage for the flames, that the metal might the sooner assume its color, and dissolve into a fluid. Thus, with great alacrity, I excited my men to lay on the pine-wood, which, because of the oiliness of the resinous matter that oozes from the pine-tree and that my furnace was admirably well made, burned at such a rate that I was continually obliged to run to and fro, which greatly fatigued me. I, however, bore the hardship; but, to add to my misfortune, the shop took fire, and we were all very much afraid that the roof would fall in and crush us. From another quarter, that is, from the garden, the sky poured in so much rain and wind that it cooled my furnace.

"Thus did I continue to struggle with these cross accidents for several hours, and exerted myself to such a degree that my constitution, though robust, could no longer bear such severe hardship, and I was suddenly attacked by a most violent intermitting fever; in short, I was so ill that I found myself under a necessity of lying down upon my bed. This gave me great concern, but it was unavoidable. I thereupon addressed myself to my assistants, who were about ten in number, saying to them: 'Be careful to observe the method which I have shown you, and use all possible expedition; for the metal will soon be ready. You cannot mistake; these two worthy men here will quickly make the orifices. With two such directors you can certainly contrive to pour out the hot metal, and I have no doubt but my mould will be filled completely. I find myself extremely ill, and really believe that in a few hours this severe disorder will put an end to my life.' Thus I left them in great sorrow, and went to bed. I then ordered the maids to carry victuals and drink into the shop for all the men, and told them I did not expect to live till the next morning. In this manner did I continue for two hours in a violent fever, which I every moment perceived to increase, and I was incessantly crying out, ' I am dying, I am dying.'

" My housekeeper was one of the most sensible and affectionate women in the world. She rebuked me for giving way to vain fears, and at the same time attended me with the greatest kindness and care imaginable ; however, seeing me so very ill, and terrified to such a degree, she could not contain herself, but shed a flood of tears, which she endeavored to conceal from me. Whilst we were both in this deep affliction, I perceived a man enter the room, who in his person appeared to be as crooked and distorted as a great S, and began to express himself in these terms, in a dismal and melancholy voice : ' Alas, poor Benvenuto, your work is spoiled, and the misfortune admits of no remedy.'

" No sooner had I heard the words uttered by this messenger of evil, but I cried out so loud that my voice might be heard to the skies, and got out of bed. I began immediately to dress, and, giving plenty of kicks and cuffs to the maidservants and the boy as they offered to help me on with my clothes, I complained bitterly in these terms : ' Oh, you envious and treacherous wretches, this is a piece of villany contrived on purpose ; but I will sift it to the bottom, and before I die give such proofs who I am as shall not fail to astonish the whole world.' Having huddled on my clothes, I went, with a mind boding evil, to the shop, where I found all those whom I had left so alert and in such high spirits, standing in the utmost confusion and astonishment. I thereupon addressed them thus : ' Listen, all of you, to what I am going to say ; and since you either would not or could not follow the method I pointed out, obey me now that I am present. My work is before us; and let none of you offer to oppose or contradict me, for such cases as this require activity and not counsel.' Hereupon one of them had the assurance to say to me, ' Look you, Benvenuto, you have undertaken a work which our art cannot compass, and which is not to be effected by human power.'

" Hearing these words, I turned round in such a passion, and seemed so bent upon mischief, that both he and all the rest unanimously cried out to me, ' Give your orders, and we will all second you in whatever you command ; we will assist you as long as we have breath in our bodies.' These kind and affectionate words they uttered, as I firmly believe, in a persuasion that I was upon the point of expiring. I went directly to examine the furnace, and saw all the metal in it concreted. I thereupon ordered two of the helpers to step over the way to a butcher for a load of young oak which had been above a year drying, which had been already offered to me.

" Upon his bringing me the first bundles of it, I began to fill the grate. This sort of oak makes a brisker fire than any other wood whatever ; but the wood of elder-trees and pine-trees is used in casting artillery, because it makes a mild and gentle fire. As soon as the concreted metal felt the power of this violent fire, it began to brighten and glitter. In another quarter I made them hurry the tubes with all possible expedition, and sent some of them to the roof of the house to take care of the fire, which through the great violence of the wind had acquired new force ; and towards the garden I had caused some tables with pieces of tapestry and old clothes to be placed in order to shelter me from the rain. As soon as I had applied the proper remedy to each evil, I with a loud voice cried out to my men to bestir themselves and lend a helping hand ; so that when they saw that the concreted metal began to melt again, the whole body obeyed me with such zeal and alacrity that every man did the work of three.   Then I caused a mass of pewter weighing about sixty pounds to be thrown upon the metal in the furnace, which, with the other helps, as the brisk wood-fire, and stirring it sometimes with iron and sometimes with long poles, soon became completely dissolved. Finding that, contrary to the opinion of my ignorant assistants, I had effected what seemed as difficult to raise as the dead, I recovered my vigor to such a degree that I no longer percéived whether I had any fever, nor had I the least apprehension of death.

"Suddenly a loud noise was heard, and a glittering of fire flashed before our eyes, as if it had been the darting of a thunderbolt.   Upon the appearance of this extraordinary phenomenon terror seized upon all present, and none more than myself.   This tremendous noise being over, we began to stare at each other, and perceived that the cover of the furnace had burst and flown off, so that the bronze began to run.

" I immediately caused the mouths of my mould to be opened ; but, finding that the metal did not run with its usual velocity, and apprehending that the cause of it was that the fusibility of the metal was injured by the violence of the fire, I ordered all my dishes and porringers, which were in number about two hundred, to be placed one by one before my tubes, and part of them to be thrown into the furnace ; upon which all present perceived that my mould was filling : they now with joy and alacrity assisted and obeyed me.   I, for my part, was sometimes in one place, sometimes in another, giving my directions and assisting my men, before whom I offered up this prayer: 'O God, I address myself to thee. I acknowledge in gratitude this mercy, that my mould has been filled. I fall prostrate before thee, and with my whole heart return thanks to thy divine majesty.'

"My prayer being over, I took a plate of meat which stood upon a little bench, and ate with a great appetite. I then drank with all my journeymen and assistants, and went joyful and in good health to bed; for there were still two hours of night, and I rested as well as if I had been troubled with no disorder.

"My good housekeeper, without my having given any orders, had provided a good capon for my dinner. When I arose, which was not till about noon, she accosted me in high spirits, and said merrily, 'Is this the man that thought himself dying? It is my firm belief that the cuffs and kicks you gave us last night when you were quite frantic and possessed, frightened away your fever, which, apprehending you should fall upon it in the same manner, took to flight.' So my whole poor family, having got over such panics and hardships, without delay procured earthen vessels to supply the place of the pewter dishes and porringers, and we all dined together very cheerfully; indeed, I do not remember having ever in my life eaten a meal with greater satisfaction or a better appetite. After dinner, all those who had assisted me in my work came and congratulated me upon what had happened, returned thanks to the Divine Being for having interposed so mercifully in our behalf, and declared that they had in theory and practice learnt such things as were judged impossible by other masters. I thereupon thought it allowable to boast a little of my knowledge and skill in this fine art, and, pulling out my purse, satisfied all my workmen for their labor.

" Having left my work to cool during two days after it was cast, I began gradually to uncover it. I first of all found the Medusa's head, which had come out admirably by the assistance of the vents. I proceeded to uncover the rest, and found that the other head — I mean that of Perseus — was likewise come out perfectly well. I went on uncovering it with great success, and found every part turn out to admiration, till I reached the foot of the right leg, which supports the figure. I found that not only the toes were wanting, but part of the foot itself, so that there was almost one half deficient. This occasioned me some new trouble; but I was not displeased at it, as I had expected this very thing.

"It pleased God that as soon as ever my work, although still unfinished, was seen by the populace, they set up so loud a shout of applause, that I began to be somewhat comforted for the mortifications I had undergone; and there were sonnets in my praise every day upon the gate, the language of which was extremely elegant and poetical. The very day on which I exhibited my work, there were above twenty sonnets set up, containing the most hyperbolical praises of it. Even after I had covered it again, every day a number of verses, with Latin odes and Greek poems, were published on the occasion, — for it was then vacation at the University of Pisa, and all the learned men and scholars belonging to that place vied with each other in writing encomiums on my performance. But what gave me the highest satisfaction was that even those of the profession — I mean statuaries and painters — emulated each other in commending me. In fact, I was so highly praised, and in so elegant a style, that it afforded me some alleviation for my past mortification and troubles, and I made all the haste I could to put the last hand to my statue.

"At last, as it pleased the Almighty, I completely finished my work, and on a Thursday morning exhibited it fully. Just before the break of day so great a crowd gathered about it, that it is almost impossible for me to give the reader an idea of their number; and they all seemed to vie with each other who should praise it most. The duke stood at a lower window of the palace, just over the gate, and, being half concealed within side, heard all that was said concerning the work. After he had listened several hours, he left the window highly pleased, and sent me this message: 'Go to Benvenuto, and tell him from me that he has given me higher satisfaction than I ever expected. Let him know at the same time that I shall reward him in such a manner as will excite his surprise.'"

The manuscript of Benvenuto's Life is not carried much farther. The narrative breaks off abruptly in 1562, when Cellini was in the sixty-second year of his age. He does not appear from this time to have been engaged in any work of much importance. After the execution of his grand achievement of the Perseus, the narrative of his life seems to have been the most successful of all the labors of his declining years.

On the 15th day of February, 1570, this extraordinary man died. He was buried, by his own direction, with great funeral pomp. A monk who had been charged to compose the funeral sermon, in praise both of his life and works and of his excellent moral qualities, mounted the pulpit and delivered a discourse which was highly approved by the whole academy and by the people. They struggled to enter the chapter, as well to see the body of Benvenuto as to hear the commendation of his good qualities.

V.

BERNARD PALISSY.

TWO or three of the girls had dabbled a little in painting on porcelain, and several of them had become interested in various sorts of pottery. Mabel had been at Newburyport, on a visit with some friends who had a potter's wheel of their own; and she had turned for herself, and had had baked, some vases and dishes which she had brought home with her.

This tempted them all to make a party, in which several of the boys joined, to go to the Art Museum and see the exquisite pottery there, of different sorts, ancient and modern. There they met one of the gentlemen of a large firm of dealers in keramics; and he asked them to go through their magnificent establishment, and see the collection, which is one of great beauty. It shows several of the finest styles of manufacture in very choice specimens.

This prepared them to see Japanese work. And when Uncle Fritz heard of this, he asked Professor Morse, of Salem, if he would show them his marvellous collection of Japanese pottery. Professor Morse lived in Japan under very favorable auspices, and he made there a wonderful collection of the work of the very best artists. So five or six of the young people went down to Salem, at his very kind invitation, and saw there what is one of the finest collections in the world.

All this interested them in what now receives a great deal of attention, the manufacture and ornament of pottery. The word *keramics* is a word recently added to the English language to express the art of making pottery and of ornamenting it.

When Uncle Fritz found that they really wanted to know about such things, he arranged that for one afternoon they should read about

BERNARD PALISSY THE POTTER.

Bernard Palissy was born, about 1510, in the little town of Biron, in Périgord, France. He became not only a great artist, but a learned physician, and a writer of merit.

Born of poor parents of the working-class, he had to learn some trade, and early applied himself to working glass, not as a glazier, but staining it and cutting it up in little bits, to be joined together with lead for the colored windows so much used in churches. This was purely mechanical work ; but Bernard's ambition led him to study drawing and color, that he might himself design and execute, in glass, scenes from the Bible and lives of the saints, such as he saw done by his superiors.

When he was old enough, curious to see the world and learn new things, he took a journey on foot through several provinces of France, by observation thus supplying the defects of his early education, and reaping a rich harvest of facts and ideas, which developed the qualities of his intelligence.

It was at this time that the Renaissance in Art was making itself felt throughout Europe. Francis I. of France encouraged all forms of good work by his patronage ;

and wherever he went the young Palissy was animated and inspired by the sight of beautiful things.

Faience, an elegant kind of pottery, attracted his attention. This appeared first in the fourteenth century. The Arabs had long known the art of making tiles of clay, enamelled and richly ornamented. They brought it into Spain, as is shown in the decorations of the Alhambra at Seville and elsewhere. Lucca della Robbia in Italy first brought the art to perfection, by making figures and groups of figures in high relief, of baked clay covered with shining enamel, white, tinted with various colors. The kind of work called *majolica* differed from the earlier faience by some changes in the material used for the enamel. In the middle of the sixteenth century remarkable historical paintings were executed in faience, upon huge *plaques*. All the cities of Italy vied with each other in producing wonders in this sort of work; it is from one of them, Faenza, that it takes its name. The method of making the enamel was a deep secret; but Bernard Palissy, with long patience and after many failures, succeeded in discovering it, — or, rather, in inventing for himself a new method, which in some respects excelled the old.

Palissy was the author of several essays, or " Discourses;" and from one of these, written in quaint old French, we have his own account of his invention.

He married and settled down in the year 1539 with a good income from his intelligent industry. He had a pleasant little house in the country, where, as he says, " I could rejoice in the sight of green hills, where were feeding and gambolling lambs, sheep, and goats."

An incident, apparently slight, disturbed this placid domestic happiness. He came across a cup of enamelled pottery, doubtless from Italy. "This cup," he says, "was of such beauty, that, from the moment I saw it, I entered into a dispute with myself as to how it could have been made."

Enamel is nothing more than a kind of glaze colored with metallic acids, and rendered opaque by the mixture of a certain quantity of tin. It is usually spread upon metal, when only it is properly called enamel; but this glaze can also be put upon earthenware. It makes vessels water-tight, and gives them brilliancy of surface. To find out how to do this was to make a revolution in the keramic art.

In France, in the sixteenth century, the only vessels, such as jugs or vases, were made either of metal, wood, or coarse porous pottery, through which water could penetrate; like the goulehs of the Arabs, or the cantaras of the Moors, which are still used for fresh water to advantage, since the evaporation of the drops keeps the water cold.

Many attempts had been made to imitate the beautiful and costly vases of China; but no one succeeded until the potters of Italy found out how to make faience. The discovery was hailed as a most valuable one. The princes who owned the works guarded their secret with jealous care, — to betray it would have been punished by death; so that Bernard Palissy had no hope of being taught how it was done, even if he should go to the places in Italy where the work was carried on.

"But," he says, "what others had found out, I might also discover; and if I could once make myself master of the art of glazing, I felt sure I could elevate pottery to a degree of perfection as yet unknown. What a glory for my name, what a benefit to France, if I could establish this industry here in my own land!"

He turned and turned the cup in his fingers, admiring the brilliant surface. "Yes," he said at last; "it shall be so, for I choose! I have already studied the subject. I will work still harder, and reach my aim at last."

Exceptional determination of character was needed for such an object. Palissy knew nothing about the component parts of enamels; he had never even seen the process of baking clay, and he had to begin with the very simplest investigations. To study the different kinds of earth and clay, to acquire the arts of moulding and turning, and to gain some knowledge of chemistry, all these were necessary. But he did not flinch, and pursued his idea with indomitable perseverance.

"Moving only by chance," he says, "like a man groping in the dark, I made a collection of all the different substances which seemed at all likely to make enamel, and I pounded them up fine; then I bought earthen pots, broke them into small bits, numbered these pieces, and spread over each of them a different combination of materials. Now I had to have a furnace in which to bake my experiments. I had no idea how furnaces were usually made; so I invented one of my own, and set it up. But I had no idea how much heat was required to melt enamels,—perhaps I heated my furnace too much, perhaps not enough; sometimes my ingredients were all burned up, sometimes they melted not at all; or else some were turned to coal, while others remained undisturbed by the action of the fire."

Meanwhile the resources of the unlucky workman were fast diminishing; for he had abandoned his usual work, by which he earned his living, and kept making new furnaces, "with great expense and trouble, and a great consumption of time and firewood."

This state of affairs much displeased his wife, who complained bitterly, and tried to divert her husband from an occupation which earned for him nothing but disappointment. The cheerful little household changed its aspect; the children were no longer well-dressed, and the shabby furniture and empty cupboards betrayed the decay which was falling upon the family. The father saw with profound grief the wants of his household; but success seemed ever so near to him, that he could not bear to give it up. His hope at that time was but a mirage; and for long afterwards, in this struggle between intelligence and the antagonism of material things, ill fortune kept the upper hand.

One day, tired out by his failures, it occurred to him that a man brought up to baking pottery would know how to bake his specimens better than he could.

"I covered three or four hundred bits of broken vase with different compounds, and sent them to a *fabrique* about a mile and a half from my house. The potters consented to put my patterns with their batch for the oven. Full of impatience, I awaited the result of this experiment. I was on hand when my specimens came out. I looked them anxiously all over; not one was successful!

"The heat had not been strong enough, but I did not know this; I saw only one more useless expense of money. One of the workmen came to me and said, 'You will never make anything out of this; you had better go back to your own business.'"

Palissy shook his head; he had still in his possession some few valuable articles, souvenirs of happier days, which he could sell to renew his experiments. In spite of the reproaches of his wife, he bought more ingredients and more earthenware, and made new combinations.

Failure again! However, he would not be beaten.
Some friends lent him a little money; he sat up at night
to make new mixtures of different substances, all prepared
with such care that he felt sure some of them must be
good. Then he carried them again to the potters, whom
he urged to the greatest care. They only shrugged their
shoulders, and called him "crack brain;" and when the
batch was done, they brought the results to Palissy with
jeers. Some of the pieces were dirty white; others green,
red, or smoked by the fire; but all alike in being dull
and worthless.

It was over. Discouragement took possession of Palissy. "I returned home," he says, "full of confusion
and sadness. Others might seek the secret of enamels.
I must set to work and earn money to pay my debts
and get bread for the family."

Most luckily for him at this time, a task was given him
by government, for which he was well suited, and which
brought him good pay. The king, Francis I., having
had, like many another sovereign, some difficulty with his
faithful subjects in the matter of imposts, now found it
necessary to make a new regulation of taxes; and for this,
among other things, an inspection of the salt marshes on
the coasts of France was needed, in order to name the
right sums for taxation, and a knowledge of arithmetic
was required as well. Palissy was appointed; and to the
great delight of his family, who thought that his mind
would now be forever diverted from the search for enamel,
he set forth to explore the islands and the shores of France.
He drew admirable outlines of the forms of the salt marshes,
and wrote with eloquence upon the sublimity of the sea.

Ease and comfort came back. His task was ended;
but debts were paid, and plenty of money remained.

The first thing he saw on returning home, alas ! was the cup, — his joy and despair. " How beautiful it is ! how brilliant !" he exclaimed ; and once more he threw himself into the pursuit of the elusive enamel.

It was easy to see that the so much admired faience of Italy was simply common baked clay, covered with some substance glazed by heat, but so composed as to adhere to the surface after it had cooled. But what substance ? He had tried all sorts of materials ; why had none of them melted ? Palissy at length decided that the fault had been in using the common potter's furnace. Since the materials were to be vitrified by the process, they should be baked like glass. He broke up three dozen pots, pounded up a great quantity of different ingredients, and spread them with a brush on the fragments ; then he carried them to the nearest glass-works. He was allowed to superintend the baking himself ; he put the specimens in the oven, and passed the night attending the fire. In the morning he took them out. " Oh, joy ! Some of the compounds had begun to melt ; there was no perfect glaze, only a sign that I was on the right road."

It was, however, still a long and weary one. After two more years, Palissy was still far from the discovery of enamelling, but during this time he was acquiring much knowledge. From a simple workman he had become a learned chemist. He says himself, " The mistakes I made in combining my enamels taught me more than the things which came right of themselves."

There came a time, which he had once more resolved should be the last, when he repaired to the glass-works, accompanied by a man loaded with more than three hundred different patterns on bits of pottery. For four hours Bernard gloomily watched the progress of baking. Sud-

denly he started in surprise. Did his eyes deceive him?
No! it was no illusion. One of the pieces in the furnace
was covered with a brilliant glazing, white, polished, excellent. Palissy's joy was immense. "I thought I had
become a new creature," he says. "The enamel was
found; France enriched by a new discovery."

Palissy now hastened to undertake a whole vase. For
many and large pieces there was not room enough at his
disposition in the ovens of the glass-works. He did not
worry about that, for he was quite sure he could construct one of his own. He decided, too, at once to
model and fashion his own vases; for those which he
bought of the potters, made of coarse and heavy forms,
no longer suited his ambition. He now designed forms,
turned and modelled them himself. Thus passed seven
or eight months. At last his vases were done, and he
admired with pride the pure forms given to the clay by
his hands. But his money was giving out again, and his
furnace was not yet built. As he had nothing to pay for
the work, he did all the work himself, — went after bricks
and brought them himself on his back, and then built and
plastered with his own hands. The neighbors looked on
in pity and ridicule. "Look," they said, "at Master
Bernard! He might live at his ease, and yet he makes
a beast of burden of himself!"

Palissy minded their sarcasms not at all. His furnace
was finished in good time, and the first baking of the clay
succeeded perfectly. Now the pottery was to be covered
with his new enamel. Time pressed, for in a few days
there would be no more bread in the house for his children. For a long time he had been living on credit, but
now the butcher and baker refused to furnish anything
more. All about him he saw only unfriendly faces; every

one treated him as a fool. "Let him die of hunger," they said, "since he will not listen to reason."

His wife was the worst of all. She failed to see any heroism in the obstinacy or perseverance of her husband, — no wonder, perhaps, with the sight of her suffering children before her eyes. She went about reciting her misfortunes to all the neighborhood, very unwisely, as she thus ruined the credit of her husband, his last and only resource.

Palissy was already worn out by so much manual labor, to which he was little accustomed ; nevertheless, he worked by night, and all night long, to pound up and prepare the materials for his white enamel, and to spread it upon his vases. A report went abroad, caused by the sight of his lamp constantly burning, that he was trying to coin counterfeit money. He was suspected, despised, and avoided, and went about the streets hanging his head because he had no answer to make to his accusers.

The moment which was to decide his life arrived. The vases were placed in the furnace, and for six continuous days and nights he plied the glowing fire with fuel. The heat was intolerable ; but the enamel resisted, nothing would melt, and he was forced to recognize that there was too little of the glazing substance in the combination to vitrify the others. He set to work to mix another compound, but his vases were spoiled ; he borrowed a few common ones from the pottery. During all this delay he did not dare to let the fire go out, it would take so much wood to start it again. Once more the newly covered pots were placed in the intense furnace ; in three or four hours the test would be completed. Palissy perceived with terror that his fuel was giving out. He ran to his garden, tore up fences, and cut down trees which he had planted himself, and threw all these into the two yawning mouths of the furnace. Not enough ! He went into the house, and seized tables, chairs, and bureaus ; but the house was but poorly furnished, and contained but little to feed the flames. Palissy returned. The rooms were empty, there was absolutely nothing more to take ; then he fell to pulling up the planks of the floor. His wife, frightened to death, stood still and let him go on. The neighbors ran in, at the sound of the axe, and said, " He must be a fool ! "

But soon pity changed to admiration. When Palissy took the vases from the furnace, the common pots which all had seen before dull and coarse, were of a clear pearly white, covered with brilliant polish.

So much emotion and fatigue had told upon the robust constitution of Palissy. " I was," he says, " all used up and dried up on account of such toil, and the heat of the furnace. It was more than a month since I had had a dry shirt on my body, and I felt as if I had reached the door of the sepulchre."

In spite of the success which he had now attained, our potter had by no means reached the end of his misfortunes. He sold his vases, but could not get much for them, as there were but a few, of poor shapes ; for those which he had modelled himself had all failed to take the enamel, and the successful ones were only common things, bought on credit. The small sum which he got by selling them was not enough by any means to cover his expenses, pay his debts, and restore order to the house from which pretty much everything was burned up for firewood in his furnace.

However, he was supported and happy in the thought of his success. He said to himself : " Why be sad, when you have found what you were seeking for? Go on working, and you will put your enemies to shame."

Once more he succeeded in borrowing a little money. He hired a man to help him; and for want of funds, he paid this man by giving him all his own good clothes, while he went himself in rags. The furnace he had made was coming to pieces on account of the intense heat he had maintained in it for six days and nights during his last experiment. He pulled it to pieces with his own hands, working with fingers bleeding and bound up in bandages. Then he fetched water, sand, lime, and stone, and built by himself a new furnace, " without any help or any repose. A feverish resolution doubled my strength, and made me capable of doing things which I should have imagined impossible."

This time the oven heats admirably, the enamels appear to be melting. Palissy goes to rest, and dreams of his new vases, which must bring enough to pay all his debts; his impatient creditors come in the morning to see the things taken from the furnace. Palissy receives them joyfully; he would like to invite the whole town.

When the pieces came out of the oven, they were shining and beautiful; but — always but! — an accident had deprived them of all value. Little stones, which formed a part of the mortar with which the furnace was built, had burst with the heat, and spattered the enamel all over with sharp fragments cutting like a razor, entirely spoiling it of course. Still, the vases were so lovely in form, and the glaze was so beautiful, that several people offered to buy them if they could have them cheap. This the proud potter would not bear. Seizing the vases, he dashed them to the ground; then utterly worn out, he went into the house and threw himself on the bed. His wife followed him, and covered him with reproaches for thus wasting the chance of making a few francs for the family. Soon he recovered his elasticity, reflecting "that a man who has tumbled into a ditch has but one duty, and that is to try to get out of it."

He now set to work at his old business of painting upon glass, and after several months had earned enough to start another batch of vases. Of these, two or three were successful and sold to advantage; the rest were spoiled by ashes which fell upon the enamel in the furnace while it was soft. He therefore invented what he called a "lantern" of baked clay, to put over the vases to protect them in baking. This expedient proved so good that it is still used.

The enamel once discovered, it would be supposed that all trouble was over; but it is not enough to invent a process, — to carry it out, all sorts of little things have to be considered, the least of which, if not attended to, may spoil all the rest. These multiplied accidents, with all the privations and sufferings he had undergone, were attacking the health of Palissy. He says in his simple style, —

"I was so used up in my person, that there was no shape or appearance of curve on my arms or legs; my so-called legs, indeed, were but a straight line, so that when I had gartered my stockings, as soon as I began to walk, they were down on my heels."

His enamelled pottery now began to make a living for its inventor, but so poor a living that many things were wanting, — for instance, a suitable workshop. For five or six years he carried on the work in the open air; either heat, rain, or cold spoiled many of his vases, while he himself, exposed to the weather, "passed whole nights at the mercy of rain and cold, without any aid, comfort, or companionship except that of owls screeching on one side and dogs howling on the other. Sometimes," he continues, " winds and tempests blew with such violence inside and outside of my ovens, that I was obliged to leave, with a total loss of all they contained. Several times when I had thus left everything, without a dry rag upon me, on account of the rain, I came in at midnight or daybreak without any light, staggering like a drunken man, all broken down at the thought of my wasted toil ; and then, all wet and dirty as I was, I found in my bedroom the worst affliction of all, which makes me wonder now why I was not consumed by grief." He means the scolding and reproaches of his wife.

But the time came when his perseverance was rewarded, and his pottery brought him the fame and money he deserved. He was able to make new experiments, and add to the value of his discovery. Having obtained the white enamel, he had the idea of tinting it with all sorts of colors, which he did successfully. He then began to decorate his faience with objects modelled from nature, such as animals, shells, leaves, and branches. Lizards of a bright emerald color, with pointed heads and slender tails, and snakes gliding between stones or curled upon a bank of moss, crabs, frogs, and spiders, all of their natural colors, and disposed in the midst of plants equally well imitated, are the characteristic details of the work of Palissy.

These perfect imitations of Nature were taken actually from Nature herself. Palissy prepared a group of real leaves and stones, putting the little insects or animals he wished to represent in natural attitudes amongst them. He fastened these reptiles, fishes, or insects in their places by fine threads, and then made a mould of the whole in plaster of Paris. When it was done, he removed the little animals from the mould so carefully that he could use them over and over again.

Thus, after sixteen years passed in untiring energy, sixteen years of anxiety and privation, the artist triumphed over all the obstacles opposed to his genius. The humble potter, despised of all, became the most important man in his town. His productions were sought for eagerly, and his reputation established forever.

His life henceforth was not free from events, but these were not connected with his invention. His fame came to the knowledge of the queen mother Catherine de Médicis; for Francis I. was no longer living, and Charles IX. had succeeded Francis II. upon the throne. He was summoned to Court, and employed to build grottos, decorated with his designs, by personages of distinction, — one especially for the queen herself, which he describes in his Discourse of the " Jardin Delectable."

He was in Paris at the time of the terrible massacre of St. Bartholomew, where, as he was a Huguenot, he would doubtless have perished but for the protection of the queen, who helped him to escape with his family.

Later, however, in the midst of the troubles and terrors of the time, he was thrown into the Bastille; and there he died, an old man of eighty years.

VI.

BENJAMIN FRANKLIN.

"WE call the Americans a nation of inventors," said Fergus. "How long has this been true?"

"That is a very curious question," said Uncle Fritz. "You remember we were talking of it before. When I go back to think of the hundred and fifty years before Bunker Hill, I think there must have been a great many inglorious Miltons hidden away in the New England towns. Really, the arts advanced very little between 1630 and 1775. Flint-locks had come in, instead of match-locks. But, actually, the men at Bunker Hill rested over the rail-fence old muskets which had been used in Queen Anne's time; and to this day a 'Queen's arm' is a provincial phrase, in New England, for one of these old weapons, not yet forgotten. That inability to improve its own condition comes to a people which lets another nation do its manufacturing for it. You see much the same thing in Turkey and French Canada. Just as soon as they were thrown on their own resources here, they began to invent."

"But," said Fergus, "there was certainly one great American inventor before that time."

"You mean Franklin,—the greatest American yet, I suppose, if you mean to measure greatness by intellectual power and intellectual achievement. Yes; Franklin's great discovery, and the inventions which followed on it, were made twenty-five years and more before Bunker Hill."

"What is the association between Franklin and Robinson Crusoe?" asked Alice. "I never read of one but I think of the other."

Uncle Fritz's whole face beamed with approbation.

"You have started me upon one of my hobbies," said he; "but I must not ride it too far. Franklin says himself that De Foe's 'Essay on Projects' and Cotton Mather's 'Essay to do Good' were two books which perhaps gave him a turn of thinking which had an influence on some of the events in his after life. And you may notice how an 'Essay on Projects' might start his passion for having things done better than in the ways he saw. The books that he was brought up on and with were books of De Foe's own time, — none of them more popular among reading people of Boston than De Foe's own books, for De Foe was a great light among their friends in England.

"If Robinson Crusoe, on his second voyage, which was in the year 1718, had run into Boston for supplies, as he thought of doing; and if old Judge Sewall had asked him to dinner, — as he would have been likely to do, for Robinson was a godly old gentleman then, of intelligence and fortune, — if there had been by accident a vacant place at the table at the last moment, Judge Sewall might have sent round to Franklin's father to ask him to come in. For the elder Franklin, though only a tallow-chandler, — and only Goodman Franklin, not *Mr.* Franklin, — was a member of the church, well esteemed. He led the singing at the Old South after Judge Sewall's voice broke down.

"Nay, when one remembers how much Sewall had to do with printing, one might imagine that the boy Ben

Franklin should wait at the door with a proof-sheet, and even take off his boy's hat as Robinson Crusoe came in."

Here Bedford Long put in a remark : —

"There are things in Robinson Crusoe's accounts of his experiments in making his pipkins, which ought to bring him into any book of American inventors."

"I never thought before," said Fergus, "that De Foe's experiences in making tiles and tobacco-pipes and drain-pipes fitted him for all that learned discussion of glazing, when Robinson Crusoe makes his pots and pans."

"Good !" said Uncle Fritz ; "that must be so. — Well, as you say, Alice, there are whole sentences in that narrative which you could suppose Franklin wrote, and in his works whole sentences which would fit in closely with De Foe's writing. The style of the younger man very closely resembles that of the older."

"And Franklin would have been very much pleased to hear you say so."

"He was forever inventing," said Uncle Fritz. "As I said, he was worried unless things could be better done. If he was in a storm, he wanted to still the waves. If the chimney smoked, he wanted to make a better fireplace. If he heard a girl play the musical-glasses, he must have and make a better set."

"And if the house was struck by lightning, he went out and put up a lightning-rod."

"He had a little book by which people should make themselves better ; for he rightly considered that unless a man could do this, he could make no other improvement of much account."

And when Uncle Fritz had said this, he found the passage, which he bade John read to them.

FRANKLIN'S METHOD OF GROWING BETTER.

" I made a little book in which I allotted a page for each of the virtues. [He had classified the virtues and made a list of thirteen, which will be named below.]   I ruled each page with red ink, so as to have seven columns, one for each day of the week, marking each column with a letter for the day.   I crossed these columns with thirteen red lines, marking the beginning of each line with the first letter of one of the virtues, on which line and in its proper column I might mark, by a little black spot, every fault I found upon examination to have been committed respecting that virtue upon that day.   The thirteen virtues were: 1. TEMPERANCE ; 2. SILENCE ; 3. ORDER ; 4. RESOLUTION ; 5. FRUGALITY ; 6. INDUSTRY ; 7. SINCERITY ; 8. JUSTICE ; 9. MODERATION ; 10. CLEANLINESS ; 11. TRANQUILLITY ; 12. CHASTITY ; 13. HUMILITY.   Each of these appears, by its full name or its initial, on every page of the book.   But the full name of one only appears on each page.

" My intention being to acquire the habitude of these virtues, I judged it would be well not to distract my attention by attempting the whole at once, but to fix it on one of them at a time, and when I should be master of that, then to proceed to another, — and so on, till I should have gone through the thirteen ; and as the previous acquisition might facilitate the acquisition of certain others, I arranged them with that view. Temperance first, as it tends to procure that coolness and clearness of head which is so necessary where constant vigilance has to be kept up, and a guard maintained against the unremitting attraction of ancient habits, and the force of perpetual temptations."[1] And so he goes on to show how Temperance would prepare for Silence, Silence for Order, Order for Resolution, and thus to the end.

Here is the first page of the book, with the marks for the first six of the virtues.

TEMPERANCE.						
EAT NOT TO DULNESS. DRINK NOT TO ELEVATION.						
	S.	M.	T.	W.	Th.	F.	S.
T.							
S.	*	*		*		*	
O.	*	*	*		*	*	*
R.			*			*	
F.		*			*		
I.			*				
S.							
J.							
M.							
C.							
T.							
C.							
H.							

" I determined to give a week's strict attention to each of the virtues successively. Thus, in the first week my great guard was to avoid every the least offence against *Temperance*, leaving the other virtues to their ordinary chance, only marking every evening the faults of the day.

[1] As St. James says, " The wisdom from above is *first* pure."

Thus, if in the first week I could keep my first line, marked T, clear of spots, I supposed the habit of that virtue so much strengthened, and its opposite weakened, that I might venture extending my attention to include the next, and for the following week keep both lines clear of spots. Proceeding thus to the last, I could go through a course complete in thirteen weeks, and four courses in a year. And like him who having a garden to weed does not attempt to eradicate all the bad herbs at once, which would exceed his reach and his strength, but works on one of the beds at a time, and, having accomplished the first, proceeds to the second, so I should have, I hoped, the encouraging pleasure of seeing on my pages the progress I made in virtue, by clearing successively my lines of their spots, till in the end, by a number of courses, I should be happy in viewing a clean book, after a thirteen weeks' daily examination."

Uncle Fritz said that this plan of Franklin's had been quite a favorite plan of different people at the end of the last century. Richard Lovell Edgeworth, and Mr. Day, and a good many of the other reformers in England, and many in France, really thought that if people only knew what was right they would all begin and do it. They had to learn, by their own experience or somebody's, that the difficulty was generally deeper down.

There was a man, named Droz, who published a little book called "The Art of being Happy," with tables on which every night you were to mark yourself, as a schoolmistress marks scholars at school, 10 for truth, 3 for temper, 5 for industry, 9 for frugality, and so on.[1]

[1] Joseph Droz, born in 1773. His essay was published in 1806, and had come to its fourth edition in 1825.

"But in the long run," said Uncle Fritz, "there may be too much self-examination. If you really look up and not down, and look forward and not back, and loyally lend a hand, why, you can afford to look out and not in, in general."

Fergus brought the talk back to the lightning-rod, and asked where was the earliest hint of it.

The history seems to be this. In the year 1747 a gentleman named Collinson sent to Franklin, from England or Scotland, one of the glass tubes with which people were then trying electrical experiments. Franklin was very much interested. He went on repeating the experiments which had been made in England and on the Continent of Europe. With his general love of society in such things, he had other glass tubes made, and gave them to his friends.

He had one immense advantage over the wise men of England and France, in the superior dryness of our air, which greatly favors such experiments. Almost any one of the young Americans who will read this book has tried the experiment of exciting electricity by shuffling across a Brussels carpet on a dry floor, and then lighting the gas from a gas-jet by the spark. But when you tell an Englishman in London that you have done this, he thinks at first that you are making fun of him. For it is very seldom that the air and the carpet and the floor are all dry enough for the experiment to succeed in England. This difference of climate accounts for the difficulty which the philosophers in England sometimes found in repeating Dr. Franklin's experiments.

When it came to lightning and experiments about that, he had another very great advantage; for we have many more thunder-storms than they have. In the year 1752, when Mr. Watson was very eager to try the lightning experiments in England, he seems to have had, in all the summer, but two storms of thunder and lightning.

Franklin made his apparatus on a scale which now seems almost gigantic. The "conductor" of an electrical machine such as you will generally see in a college laboratory is seldom more than two feet long. Franklin's conductor, which was hung by silk from the top of his room, was a cylinder ten feet long and one foot in diameter, covered with gilt paper. In his "Leyden battery" he used five glass jars, as big as large water-pails, — they held nine gallons each. One night he had arranged to kill a turkey by a shock from two of these. He received the shock himself, by accident, and it almost killed him. He had a theory that if turkeys were killed by electricity, the meat would perhaps be more tender.

He acknowledges Mr. Collinson's present of the glass tube as early as March 28, 1747. On the 11th of July he writes to Collinson that they ("we") had discovered the power of points to withdraw electricity silently and continuously. On this discovery the lightning-rod is based. He describes this quality, first observed by Mr. Hopkinson, in the following letter: —

"The first is the wonderful effect of pointed bodies, both in *drawing off* and *throwing off* the electrical fire.

"For example, place an iron shot, of three or four inches diameter, on the mouth of a clean, dry glass bottle. By a fine silken thread from the ceiling, right over the mouth of the bottle, suspend a small cork ball about the bigness of a marble; the thread of such a length, as that the cork ball may rest against the side of the shot. Electrify the shot, and the ball will be repelled to the distance of four or five inches, more or less, according to the quantity of electricity. When in this state, if you present to the shot the point of a long, slender, sharp bodkin, at six or eight inches distance, the repellency is instantly destroyed, and the cork flies to the shot. A blunt body must be brought within an inch and draw a spark, to produce the same effect. To prove that the electrical fire is *drawn off* by the point, if you take the blade of the bodkin out of the wooden handle, and fix it in a stick of sealing-wax, and then present it at the distance aforesaid, or if you bring it very near, no such effect follows ; but sliding one finger along the wax till you touch the blade, the ball flies to the shot immediately. If you present the point in the dark, you will see, sometimes at a foot distance and more, a light gather upon it, like that of a firefly or glow-worm ; the less sharp the point, the nearer you must bring it to observe the light ; and at whatever distance you see the light, you may draw off the electrical fire, and destroy the repellency. If a cork ball so suspended be repelled by the tube, and a point be presented quick to it, though at a considerable distance, it is surprising to see how suddenly it flies back to the tube. Points of wood will do near as well as those of iron, provided the wood is not dry ; for perfectly dry wood will no more conduct electricity than sealing-wax.

" To show that points will *throw off* as well as *draw off* the electrical fire, lay a long, sharp needle upon the shot, and you cannot electrize the shot so as to make it repel the cork ball. Or fix a needle to the end of a suspended gun-barrel or iron rod, so as to point beyond it like a little bayonet ; and while it remains there, the gun-barrel or rod cannot, by applying the tube to the other end, be electrized so as to give a spark, the fire continually running out silently at the point. In the dark you may see it make the same appearance as it does in the case before mentioned."

The next summer, that of 1748, the experiments went so far, that in a letter of Franklin's to Collinson he proposed the electrical dinner-party, which was such a delight to Harry and Lucy : —

" Chagrined a little that we have been hitherto able to produce nothing in this way of use to mankind, and the hot weather coming on when electrical experiments are not so agreeable, it is proposed to put an end to them for this season, somewhat humorously, in a party of pleasure on the banks of the *Skuylkill*. Spirits, at the same time, are to be fired by a spark sent from side to side through the river, without any other conductor than the water ; an experiment which we some time since performed, to the amazement of many. A turkey is to be killed for our dinner by the *electrical shock*, and roasted by the *electrical jack*, before a fire kindled by the *electrified bottle ;* when the healths of all the famous electricians in England, Holland, France, and Germany are to be drank in *electrified bumpers*, under the discharge of guns from the *electrical battery*."

It was in a letter to Collinson of the next year, 1749, — as I suppose, though it is not dated, — that the project of the lightning-rod first appears. It is too long to copy. The paragraphs most important in this view are the following : —

" 42. An electrical spark, drawn from an irregular body at some distance, is scarcely ever straight, but shows crooked and waving in the air. So do the flashes of lightning, the clouds being very irregular bodies.

" 43. As electrified clouds pass over a country, high hills and high trees, lofty towers, spires, masts of ships, chimneys, &c., as so many prominences and points, draw the electrical fire, and the whole cloud discharges there.

"44. Dangerous, therefore, is it to take shelter under a tree during a thunder-gust. It has been fatal to many, both men and beasts.

"45. It is safer to be in the open field for another reason. When the clothes are wet, if a flash in its way to the ground should strike your head, it may run in the water over the surface of your body; whereas, if your clothes were dry, it would go through the body, because the blood and other humors, containing so much water, are more ready conductors.

"Hence a wet rat cannot be killed by the exploding electrical bottle, when a dry rat may."

In a letter of 1750, based upon observations made in 1749, Franklin said distinctly, after describing some artificial lightning which he had made : —

"If these things are so, may not the knowledge of this power of points be of use to mankind, in preserving houses, churches, ships, &c., from the stroke of lightning, by directing us to fix, on the highest parts of these edifices, upright rods of iron made sharp as a needle, and gilded to prevent rusting, and from the foot of those rods a wire down the outside of the building into the ground, or down round one of the shrouds of a ship, and down her side till it reaches the water? Would not these pointed rods probably draw the electrical fire silently out of a cloud before it came nigh enough to strike, and thereby secure us from that most sudden and terrible mischief?

"To determine the question whether the clouds that contain lightning are electrified or not, I would propose an experiment to be tried where it may be done conveniently. On the top of some high tower or steeple, place a kind of sentry-box, big enough to contain a man and an electrical stand.   From the middle of the stand let an iron rod rise and pass bending out of the door and then upright twenty or thirty feet, pointed very sharp at the end.   If the electrical stand be kept clean and dry, a man standing on it, when such clouds are passing low, might be electrified and afford sparks, the rod drawing fire to him from a cloud. If any danger to the man should be apprehended (though I think there would be none), let him stand on the floor of his box, and now and then bring near to the rod the loop of a wire that has one end fastened to the leads, he holding it by a wax handle ; so the sparks, if the rod is electrified, will strike from the rod to the wire, and not affect him."

The Royal Society " did not think these papers worth printing " !

But, happily, Collinson printed them, and they went all over Europe.   The demonstration of the lightning theory, which he had wrought out by his own experiments, was made in France, May 10, 1752 ; and in Philadelphia by Franklin with the kite in the next month, before he had heard of the success in France.   Franklin's friend Dalibard tried the French experiment.   Here is his account of it, as he sent it to the French Academy, as Roxana translated it for the young people : —

I have had perfect success in following out the course indicated by Mr. Franklin.

I had set up at Marly-la-ville, situated six leagues from Paris, in a fine plain at a very elevated level, a round rod of iron, about an inch in diameter, forty feet long, and sharply pointed at its upper extremity.   To secure greater fineness at the point, I had it armed with tempered steel, and then burnished, for want of gilding, so as to keep it from rusting; beside that, this iron rod is bent near its lower end into two acute but rounded angles; the first angle is two feet from the lower end, and the second takes a contrary direction at three feet from the first.

.   .   .   .

Wednesday, the 10th of May, 1752, between two and three in the afternoon, a man named Coiffier, an old dragoon, whom I had intrusted with making the observations in my absence, having heard rather a loud clap of thunder, hastened at once to the machine, took the phial with the wire, presented the loop of the wire to the rod, saw a small bright spark come from it, and heard it crackle. He then drew a second spark, brighter than the first and with a louder sound! He called his neighbors, and sent for the Prior. This gentleman hastened to the spot as fast as he could : the parishioners, seeing the haste of their priest, imagined that poor Coiffier had been killed by the thunder; the alarm was spread in the village; the hailstorm which began did not prevent the flock from following its shepherd. This honest priest approached the machine, and, seeing 'that there was no danger, went to work himself and drew strong sparks. The cloud from which the storm and hail came was no more than a quarter of an hour in passing directly over our machine, and only this one thunder-clap was heard. As soon as the cloud had passed, and no more sparks were drawn from the iron rod, the Prior of Marly sent off Monsieur Coiffier himself, to bring me the following letter, which he wrote in haste : —

I can now inform you, Sir, of what you are looking for. The experiment is completely successful. To-day, at twenty minutes past two, P. M., the thunder rolled

directly over Marly; the clap was rather loud.   The desire
to oblige you, and my own curiosity, made me leave my
arm-chair, where I was occupied in reading.   I went to
Coiffier's, who had already sent a child to me, whom I met
on the way, to beg me to come.   I redoubled my speed
through a torrent of hail.   When I arrived at the place
where the bent rod was set up, I presented the wire, approaching it several times toward the rod.   At the distance
of an inch and a half, or about that, there came out of the
rod a little column of bluish fire smelling of sulphur, which
struck the loop of the wire with an extreme and rapid energy, and occasioned a sound like that which might be
made by striking on the rod with a key.   I repeated the
experiment at least six times, in the space of about four
minutes, in the presence of several persons; and each experiment which I made lasted the space of a *Pater* and an
Ave.   I tried to go on; the action of the fire slackened
little by little.   I went nearer, and drew nothing more but
a few sparks, and at last nothing appeared.

The thunder-clap which caused this event was followed by no other; it all ended in a great quantity of hail.
I was so occupied with what I saw at the moment of the
experiment, that, having been struck on the arm a little
above my elbow, I cannot say whether it was in touching
the wire or the rod, I was not even aware of the injury
which the blow had given me at the moment when I received it; but as the pain continued, on my return home
I uncovered my arm before Coiffier, and we perceived a
bruised mark winding round the arm, like what a wire
would have made if my bare flesh had been struck by it.
As I was going back from Coiffier's house, I met Monsieur
le Vicaire, Monsieur de Milly, and the schoolmaster, to
whom I related what had just happened.   They all three

declared that they smelt an odor of sulphur, which struck them more as they approached me. I carried the same odor home with me, and my servants noticed it without my having said anything to them about it.

This, Monsieur, is an account given in haste, but simple and true, which I attest, and you may depend on my being ready to give evidence of this event on every opportunity. Coiffier was the first who made the experiment, and repeated it several times; it was only on account of what he had seen that he sent to ask me to come. If other witnesses than he and I are necessary, you will find them. Coiffier is in haste to set out.

I am, with respectful consideration, Monsieur,

Yours, &c.,

[Signed]   RAULET, *Prior of Marly.*

MAY 10, 1752.

"I do not understand," said Uncle Fritz, "how it happened that no one attempted the experiment before. Franklin had proposed it, very distinctly, in 1750. His friend Dr. Stuber says that he was waiting for the erection of a steeple in Philadelphia. You see, the Quakers, who had founded this city, would have none; they derided what they called 'steeple-houses,' little foreseeing what advantage could be drawn from a steeple.

"Meanwhile, in 1750, in October, he did take a view of New York from the 'Dutch Church steeple,' which had been struck by lightning in the spring of that year. And here he was able to confirm his theory, by seeing that 'wire is a good conductor of lightning, as it is of electricity.'"

MUSICAL GLASSES.

While some of the children were reading these electrical passages, others were turning over the next volume ; and to their great delight, they found a picture of the " Musical Glasses."

" I never had the slightest idea what musical glasses were," said Jack ; and he spouted from Goldsmith the passage from " The Vicar of Wakefield," where the fashionable ladies from London talked about " Shakspeare and the musical glasses."

" Were they Dr. Franklin's musical glasses ? "

" I never thought of that," said Uncle Fritz, well pleased ; " but I think it is so. John, look and see what year 'The Vicar of Wakefield' was written in."

John turned to the Cyclopædia, and it proved that Goldsmith wrote that book in 1766.

" And you see," said Uncle Fritz, " that it was in 1762 that Franklin made his improvement, and that Mr. Puckeridge, the Irish gentleman, had arranged his glasses before. I think you would find that the instrument gradually worked its way into fashion, — slowly, as such things then did in England, — and that Goldsmith knew about Dr. Franklin's modification.

" I do not now remember any other place where Goldsmith's life and his touched. But they must have known a great many of the same people. Franklin was all mixed up with the Grub Street people."

Meanwhile John was following up the matter in the Cyclopædia. But he did not find " Armonica." Uncle Fritz bade him try in the " H " volume ; and there, sure enough, was " Harmonica," with quite a little history of the invention. Mr. Puckeridge's fascinating name is there tamed down to Pochrich, probably by some German translator. Dr. Franklin's instrument is described, and the Cyclopædia man adds : —

" From the effect which it was supposed to have upon the nervous system, it has been suggested that the fingers should not be allowed to come in immediate contact with the glasses, but that the tones should be produced by means of keys, as with a harpsichord. Such an instrument has been made, and called the ' *harpsichord harmonica.*' But these experiments have not produced anything of much value. It is impossible that the delicacy, the swell, and the continuation of the tone should be carried to such perfection as in the simpler method. The harmonica, however much it excels all other instruments in the delicacy and duration of its tones, yet is confined to those of a soft and melancholy character and to slow, solemn movements, and can hardly be combined to advantage with other instruments. In accompanying the human voice it throws it into the shade ; and in concerts the other instruments lose in effect, because so far inferior to it in tone. It is therefore best enjoyed by itself, and may produce a charming effect in certain romantic situations."

" ' Romantic situations ' ! I should think so," said Mabel, laughing. " Is not that like the dear German man that wrote this? I see myself lugging my harmonica to the edge of the Kauterskill Falls."

" How do you know he was a German ? " said Alice.

" Because, where John read ' the simpler method,' it says ' the before-mentioned method.' No Englishman or American in his senses ever said ' before-mentioned ' if he could help himself."

"Do let us see how dear Dr. Franklin made his machine."

And the girls unfolded the old-fashioned picture, which is in the sixth volume of Sparks's Franklin, and read his description of it as he wrote it to Beccaria.

" Is it the Beccaria who did about capital punishment? " asked Fergus.

"No," Uncle Fritz said, " though they lived at the same time. They were not brothers. The capital-punishment man was the Marquis *of* Beccaria, and that *of* makes a great difference in Europe. This man 'did' electricity, as you would say; and his name is plain Beccaria without any *of*."

Then Mabel, commanding silence, at last read the letter to Beccaria. And when she had done, Uncle Fritz said that he should think there might be many a boy or girl who could not buy a piano or what he profanely called a Yang-Yang, — by which he meant a reed organ, — who would like to make a harmonica. The letter, in a part not·copied here, tells how to tune the glasses. And any one who·lived near a glass-factory, and was on the good-natured side of a good workman, could have the glasses made without much expense.

Letter of Franklin to J. B. Beccaria.

LONDON, July 13, 1762.

REVEREND SIR, — . . . Perhaps, however, it may be agreeable to you, as you live in a musical country, to have an account of the new instrument lately added here to the great number that charming science was already possessed of. As it is an instrument that seems peculiarly adapted to Italian music, especially that of the soft and plaintive kind, I will endeavor to give you such a description of it, and of the manner of constructing it, that you or any of your friends may be enabled to imitate it, if you incline so to do, without being at the expense and trouble I have been to bring it to its present perfection.

You have doubtless heard of the sweet tone that is drawn from a drinking-glass by passing a wet finger round its brim. One Mr. Puckeridge, a gentleman from Ireland, was the first who thought of playing tunes formed of these tones. He collected a number of glasses of different sizes, fixed them near each other on a table, tuned them by putting into them water more or less, as each note required. The tones were brought out by passing his finger round their brims. He was unfortunately burned here, with his instrument, in a fire which consumed the house he lived in. Mr. E. Delaval, a most ingenious member of our Royal Society, made one in imitation of it, with a better form and choice of glasses, which was the first I saw or heard. Being charmed by the sweetness of its tones, and the music he produced from it, I wished only to see the glasses disposed in a more convenient form, and brought together in a narrower compass, so as to admit of a greater number of tones, and all within reach of hand to a person sitting before the instrument, which I accomplished, after various intermediate trials, and less commodious forms, both of glasses and construction, in the following manner.

The glasses are blown as nearly as possible in the form of hemispheres, having each an open neck or socket in the middle. The thickness of the glass near the brim about a tenth of an inch, or hardly quite so much, but thicker as it comes nearer the neck, which in the largest glasses is about an inch deep, and an inch and a half wide within, these dimensions lessening as the glasses themselves diminish in size, except that the neck of the smallest ought not to be shorter than half an inch. The largest glass is nine inches diameter, and the smallest three inches. Between these two are twenty-three different sizes, differing from each other a quarter of an inch in diameter. To make a single instrument there should be at least six glasses blown of each size ; and out of this number one may probably pick thirty-seven glasses (which are sufficient for three octaves with all the semitones) that will be each either the note one wants or a little sharper than that note, and all fitting so well into each other as to taper pretty regularly from the largest to the smallest. It is true there are not thirty-seven sizes, but it often happens that two of the same size differ a note or half-note in tone, by reason of a difference in thickness, and these may be placed one in the other without sensibly hurting the regularity of the taper form.

The glasses being thus turned, you are to be provided with a case for them, and a spindle on which they are to be fixed. My case is about three feet long, eleven inches every way wide at the biggest end ; for it tapers all the way, to adapt it better to the conical figure of the set of glasses. This case opens in the middle of its height, and the upper part turns up by hinges fixed behind. The spindle, which is of hard iron, lies horizontally from end to end of the box within, exactly in the middle, and is made to turn on brass gudgeons at each end. It is round, an inch in diameter at the thickest end, and tapering to a quarter of an inch at the smallest. A square shank comes from its thickest end through the box, on which shank a wheel is fixed by a screw. This wheel serves as a fly to make the motion equable, when the spindle with the glasses is turned by the foot like a spinning-wheel. My wheel is of mahogany, eighteen inches diameter, and pretty thick, so as to conceal near its circumference about twenty-five pounds of lead. An ivory pin is fixed in the face of this wheel, and about four inches from the axis. Over the neck of this pin is put the loop of the string that comes up from the movable step to give it motion. The case stands on a neat frame with four legs.

To fix the glasses on the spindle, a cork is first to be fitted in each neck pretty tight, and projecting a little without the neck, that the neck of one may not touch the inside of another when put together, for that would make a jarring. These corks are to be perforated with holes of different diameters, so as to suit that part of the spindle on which they are to be fixed. When a glass is put on, by holding it stiffly between both hands, while another turns the spindle, it may be gradually brought to its place. But care must be taken that the hole be not too small, lest, in forcing it up, the neck should split; nor too large, lest the glass, not being firmly fixed, should turn or move on the spindle, so as to touch or jar against its neighboring glass. The glasses are thus placed one in another, the largest on the biggest end of the spindle, which is to the left hand; the neck of this glass is towards the wheel, and the next goes into it in the same position, only about an inch of its brim appearing beyond the brim of the first; thus proceeding, every glass when fixed shows about an inch of its brim (or three quarters of an inch, or half an inch, as they grow smaller) beyond the brim of the glass that contains it; and it is from these exposed parts of each glass that the tone is drawn, by laying a finger upon one of them as the spindle and glasses turn round.

My largest glass is G, a little below the reach of a common voice, and my highest G, including three complete octaves. To distinguish the glasses the more readily to the eye, I have painted the apparent parts of the glasses withinside, every semitone white, and the other notes of the octave with the seven prismatic colors, — viz., C, red; D, orange; E, yellow; F, green; G, blue; A, indigo; B, purple; and C, red again, — so that glasses of the same color (the white excepted) are always octaves to each other.

This instrument is played upon by sitting before the middle of the set of glasses, as before the keys of a harpsichord, turning them with the foot, and wetting them now and then with a sponge and clean water. The fingers should be first a little soaked in water, and quite free from all greasiness; a little fine chalk upon them is sometimes useful, to make them catch the glass and bring out the tone more readily. Both hands are used, by which means different parts are played together. Observe that the tones are best brought out when the glasses turn *from* the ends of the fingers, not when they turn *to* them.

The advantages of this instrument are, that its tones are incomparably sweet, beyond those of any other; that they may be swelled and softened at pleasure by stronger or weaker pressure of the finger, and continued to any length; and that the instrument, being once well tuned, never again wants tuning.

In honor of your musical language, I have borrowed from it the name of this instrument, calling it the Armonica.

With great respect and esteem, I am, &c.,

B. Franklin.

VII.

THEORISTS OF THE EIGHTEENTH CENTURY.

RICHARD LOVELL EDGEWORTH.

AT the next meeting there was a slight deviation from the absolutely expected. Bedford and Mabel desired to dispense with the regular order of the day, and moved for permission to bring in a new inventor, "invented by myself," said Mabel, — "entirely by myself, assisted by Bedford. Nobody that I know of ever heard of him before. He is a new discovery."

"Who is he?" asked Horace, somewhat piqued that there should be any one interesting of whom he had not heard even the name.

"What did he invent?" asked Emma.

"Did he write memoirs?" asked Fergus.

"Did you ever read 'Frank'?" asked Mabel, in what is known as the Socratic method.

There was a slight stir at the mention of this little classic. Few seemed to be able to answer in the affirmative.

"I have read 'Rollo,'" said Horace.

"I have read 'Frank,'" said Will Withers, "and 'Harry and Lucy,' and the 'Parents' Assistant,' and 'Sandford and Merton,' and 'Henry Milner.' In fact, there are few of those books, all kindred volumes, which I have not read. They have had an important effect upon my later life."

"Hinc illae lachrymae," in a low tone from Clem Waters.

For Colonel Ingham, the turn taken by the conversation had a peculiar charm. He was of the generation before the rest, and what were to them but ghostly ideals were to him glad memories of a happy past.

"Good !" said he. "'Frank' was, in a sense, the greatest book ever written. Do you remember that part where Frank lifted up the skirts of his coat when passing through the greenhouse?" he asked of Mabel.

"I should think I did," said Mabel and Will. As for Bedford, he had only a vague recollection of it. The others considered the conversation to be trembling upon the verge of insanity.

"Perhaps," said Florence, gently, "I might be allowed to suggest that although you have heard of ' Frank ' and those other persons mentioned, we have not. I do not think that I ever heard of an inventor named Frank, — did he have any other name? — and I am usually considered," she went on modestly, " tolerably well informed. Therefore the present conversation, though probably edifying in a high degree to those who have read ' Frank,' or who have some interest in horticulture and greenhouses, can hardly fail to be very stupid to those of us who have not."

"My dear child," said the Colonel, "you are right. Mabel and I, and Will and Bedford here, are of the generation that is passing off the stage. We look back to the things of our youth, hardly considering that there are those to whom that period suggests Noah and his ark."

"But who is the inventor?" asked some one who thought that the conversation was gradually leaving the trodden path.

"Oh, we had almost forgotten him," said Bedford.

"The inventor," said Mabel, producing two volumes from under her arm, "is Mr. Richard Lovell Edgeworth, the father of Maria Edgeworth."

"What did he invent?" asked many of the company.

"He invented the telegraph."

"Well, I never knew that before."

"I thought Morse invented the telegraph."

"Did n't Dr. Franklin invent the telegraph?"

"I thought Edison — "

Other remarks were also made, showing a certain amount of incredulity.

"You mistake," said Bedford, placidly; "you are all of you under a misapprehension. I think that you all of you allude to the electric telegraph, — an invention of a later date than that of Mr. Edgeworth, and one of more value, as far as practical affairs are concerned. No ; Mr. Edgeworth invented, or thinks he invented, the telegraph as it was used in the eighteenth century and the early part of the nineteenth, sometimes named the Semaphore. It was n't a difficult invention, and I don't believe it ever came to any very practical use as constructed by Edgeworth, though French telegraphs were very useful."

"What kind of a telegraph was it?"

"Well, it was just the kind of a telegraph that the conductor of a railroad train is when he waves his arms to the engineer to go ahead. There 's an account of it by Edgeworth in one of these books, with pictures to it."

"But my chief interest about Edgeworth," said Mabel, "is in his memoirs, which are written partly by himself and partly by his daughter. They are really very amusing. He was married five times, — once with a door-key when he was only fourteen."

This startling intelligence roused even Colonel Ingham to demand particulars. Was he married to all five at once? to all of them when he was only fourteen?

"No," admitted Mabel, with some regret; "he was married to them all at different times, and he was divorced from the one he married at fourteen with the door-key."

"They were only married for fun," said Bedford. "It was all a joke. They were at a wedding, and they thought it would be funny after the real marriage to have a mock one. So they did, and married Edgeworth to a girl who was there. It was a real marriage, for they were afterwards divorced."

"Well," said Sam Edmeston, "I shall be glad to hear about this gentleman, I'm sure, though I never did hear of him before. But may I ask why it was necessary to introduce him by means of an allusion to 'Frank' and other works which we have few of us ever read, though it is very possible that we may some of us have heard of them?"

"I see why Mabel spoke first of 'Frank,'" said Colonel Ingham. "And I think that she did very well to bring Edgeworth in as she has done. And Edgeworth, though I had not thought of him before, is very fit to be one of our inventors, not so much for his individual accomplishments, which were little more than curious, — telegraph and all, — as for being a good representative of his age. Those of you who know a little of the century between 1750 and 1850 know that it was an age to which many of the secrets of physical science were being opened for the first time. Everybody was going back to Nature to see what he could learn from her. This movement swept all over France and England. Every gentleman dabbled in the sciences, and made his experiments and inventions. Voltaire in France had a great laboratory made for him in which he passed some years in chemical experiments. It was the age, too, of great inventions, — of the application of physical forces to the life of man. The invention of the steam-engine by Watt, and the applications of it to the locomotive and the steamboat, came along toward the end of this period, and marked the work of the greatest men. But every one could not invent a steam-engine. So, by the hundreds of country gentlemen who studied science, chemistry, and astronomy, and the rest, there were constructed hundreds of orreries, globes, carriages; model-telegraphs, and such things ; and it is of these men that Edgeworth is the best, or at least the most available, representative, on account of his very interesting memoirs.

"Such books as 'Harry and Lucy' and 'Frank' are the mirror of this movement. But to this is joined something more, which John Morley speaks of in saying, ' An age touched by the spirit of hope turns naturally to the education of the young.' Then people knew that their own times were about as worthless as times could well be ; but as they learned more, they began to hope that things were improving, and that the children might see better times than those in which the fathers lived. And as physical science was to them an all-important factor in this approaching millennium, they took pains to teach these things to the young. Any of you who have read ' Frank ' or 'Sandford and Merton ' will see what I mean. It was the hope that the children might be able to take the work where the fathers left it, and carry it on. And the children did. But I do not believe that any one of these eighteenth-century theorists had the first or vaguest idea of the point to which his children and grandchildren would carry his work.

"So much for Mr. Edgeworth from my point of view," concluded the Colonel. "You will hear what he thought of himself from Bedford."

EDGEWORTH'S TELEGRAPH.

[DESCRIBED BY HIMSELF.]

Bets of a rash or ingenious sort were in fashion in those days, and one proposal of what was difficult and uncommon led to another. A famous match was at that time pending at Newmarket between two horses that were in every respect as nearly equal as possible. Lord March, one evening at Ranelagh, expressed his regret to Sir Francis Delaval that he was not able to attend Newmarket at the next meeting. "I am obliged," said he, "to stay in London. I shall, however, be at the Turf Coffee House. I shall station fleet horses on the road to bring me the earliest intelligence of the event of the race, and shall manage my bets accordingly."

I asked at what time in the evening he expected to know who was winner. He said about nine in the evening. I asserted that I should be able to name the winning horse at four o'clock in the afternoon. Lord March heard my assertion with so much incredulity as to urge me to defend myself; and at length I offered to lay five hundred pounds, that I would in London name the winning horse at Newmarket at five o'clock in the evening of the day when the great match in question was to be run. Sir Francis, having looked at me for encouragement, offered to lay five hundred pounds on my side; Lord

Eglintoun did the same; Shaftoe and somebody else took up their bets; and the next day we were to meet at the Turf Coffee House, to put our bets in writing. After we went home, I explained to Sir Francis Delaval the means that I proposed to use. I had early been acquainted with Wilkins's " Secret and Swift Messenger; " I had also read in Hooke's Works of a scheme of this sort, and I had determined to employ a telegraph nearly resembling that which I have since published. The machinery I knew could be prepared in a few days.

Sir Francis immediately perceived the feasibility of my scheme, and indeed its certainty of success. It was summer-time; and by employing a sufficient number of persons, we could place our machines so near as to be almost out of the power of the weather. When we all met at the Turf Coffee House, I offered to double my bet; so did Sir Francis. The gentlemen on the opposite side were willing to accept my offer; but before I would conclude my wager, I thought it fair to state to Lord March that I did not depend upon the fleetness or strength of horses to carry the desired intelligence, but upon other means, which I had, of being informed in London which horse had actually won at Newmarket, between the time when the race should be concluded and five o 'clock in the evening. My opponents thanked me for my candor and declined the bet. My friends blamed me extremely for giving up such an advantageous speculation. None of them, except Sir Francis, knew the means which I had intended to employ; and he kept them a profound secret, with a view to use them afterwards for his own purposes. With that energy which characterized everything in which he engaged, he immediately erected, under my directions, an apparatus between his house and part of Piccadilly, —

an apparatus which was never suspected to be telegraphic. I also set up a night telegraph between a house which Sir F. Delaval occupied at Hampstead, and one to which I had access in Great Russell Street, Bloomsbury. This nocturnal telegraph answered well, but was too expensive for common use.

Upon my return home to Hare Hatch, I tried many experiments on different modes of telegraphic communication. My object was to combine secrecy with expedition. For this purpose I intended to employ windmills, which might be erected for common economical uses, and which might at the same time afford easy means of communication from place to place upon extraordinary occasions. There is a windwill at Nettlebed, which can be distinctly seen with a good glass from Assy Hill, between Maidenhead and Henly, the highest ground in England south of the Trent. With the assistance of Mr. Perrot, of Hare Hatch, I ascertained the practicability of my scheme between these places, which are nearly sixteen miles asunder.

I have had occasion to show my claim to the revival of this invention in modern times, and in particular to prove that I had practised telegraphic communication in the year 1767, long before it was ever attempted in France. To establish these truths, I obtained from Mr. Perrot, a Berkshire gentleman, who resided in the neighborhood of Hare-Hatch, and who was witness to my experiments, his testimony to the facts which I have just related. I have his letter; and before its contents were published in the Memoirs of the Irish Academy for the year 1796, I showed it to Lord Charlemont, President of the Royal Irish Academy.

MR. EDGEWORTH'S TELEGRAPH IN IRELAND.

[DESCRIBED BY HIS DAUGHTER.]

In August, 1794, my father made a trial of his telegraph between Pakenham Hall and Edgeworth Town, a distance of twelve miles. He found it to succeed beyond his expectations; and in November following he made another trial of it at Collon, at Mr. Foster's, in the county of Louth. The telegraphs were on two hills, at fifteen miles' distance from each other. A communication of intelligence was made, and an answer received, in the space of five minutes. Mr. Foster — my father's friend, and the friend of everything useful to Ireland — was well convinced of the advantage and security this country would derive from a system of quick and certain communication; and, being satisfied of the sufficiency of this telegraph, advised that a memorial on the subject should be drawn up for Government. Accordingly, under his auspices, a memorial was presented, in 1795, to Lord Camden, then Lord Lieutenant. His Excellency glanced his eye over the paper, and said that he did not think such an establishment necessary, but desired to reserve the matter for further consideration. My father waited in Dublin for some time. The suspense and doubt in which courtiers are obliged to live is very different from that state of philosophical doubt which the wise recommend, and to which they are willing to submit. My father's patience was soon exhausted. The county in which he resided was then in a disturbed state; and he was eager to return to his family, who required his protection. Besides, to state things exactly as they were, his was not the sort of temper suited to attendance upon the great.

The disturbances in the County of Longford were quieted for a time by the military; but again, in the autumn of the ensuing year (September, 1796), rumors of an invasion prevailed, and spread with redoubled force through Ireland, disturbing commerce, and alarming all ranks of well-disposed subjects. My father wrote to Lord Carhampton, then Commander-in-Chief, and to Mr. Pelham (now Lord Chichester), who was then Secretary in Ireland, offering his services. The Secretary requested Mr. Edgeworth would furnish him with a memorial. Aware of the natural antipathy that public men feel at the sight of long memorials, this was made short enough to give it a chance of being read.

(Presented, Oct. 6, 1796.)

Mr. Edgeworth will undertake to convey intelligence from Dublin to Cork, and back to Dublin, by means of fourteen or fifteen different stations, at the rate of one hundred pounds per annum for each station, as long as Government shall think proper; and from Dublin to any other place, at the same rate, in proportion to the distance: provided that when Government chooses to discontinue the business, they shall pay one year's contract over and above the current expense, as some compensation for the prime cost of the apparatus, and the trouble of the first establishment.

In a letter of a single page, accompanying this memorial, it was stated, that to establish a telegraphic corps of men sufficient to convey intelligence to every part of the kingdom where it should be necessary, stations tenable against a mob and against musketry might be effected for the sum of *six or seven thousand pounds*. It was further observed, that of course there must be a considerable difference between a partial and a general plan of telegraphic communication; that Mr. Edgeworth was perfectly willing to pursue either, or to adopt without reserve any better plan that Government should approve. Thanks were returned, and approbation expressed.

Nothing now appeared in suspense except the *mode* of the establishment, whether it should be civil or military. Meantime Mr. Pelham spoke of the Duke of York's wish to have a reconnoitring telegraph, and observed that Mr. Edgeworth's would be exactly what his Royal Highness wanted. Mr. Edgeworth in a few days constructed a portable telegraph, and offered it to Mr. Pelham. He accepted it, and at his request my brother Lovell carried it to England, and presented it to the Duke from Mr. Pelham.

During the interval of my brother's absence in England, my father had no doubt that arrangements were making for a telegraphic establishment in Ireland. But the next time he went to the castle, he saw signs of a change in the Secretary's countenance, who seemed much hurried, — promised he would write, — wrote, and conveyed, in diplomatic form, a final refusal. Mr. Pelham indeed endeavored to make it as civil as he could, concluding his letter with these words : —

The utility of a telegraph may hereafter be considered greater; but I trust that at all events those talents which have been directed to this pursuit will be turned to some other object, and that the public will have the benefit of that extraordinary activity and zeal which I have witnessed on this occasion in some other institution which I am

sure that the ingenuity of the author will not require much
time to suggest.

    I have the honor to be, with great respect, &c.,

T. PELHAM.

DUBLIN CASTLE, Nov. 17, 1796.

    Of his offer to establish a communication from the coast
of Cork to Dublin, at *his own expense*, no notice was
taken. "He had, as was known to Government, expended £500 of his own money; as much more would
have erected a temporary establishment for a year to
Cork. Thus the utility of this invention might have been
tried, and the most prudent government upon earth
could not have accused itself of extravagance in being
partner with a private gentleman in an experiment which
had, with inferior apparatus, and at four times the expense, been tried in France and England, and approved."
The most favorable supposition by which we can account
for the conduct of the Irish Government in this business
is that a superior influence in England forbade them to
proceed. "It must," said my father, "be mortifying to
a viceroy who comes over to Ireland with enlarged views
and benevolent intentions, to discover, when he attempts
to act for himself, that he is peremptorily checked; that
a circle is chalked round him, beyond which he cannot
move."

No personal feelings of pique or disgust prevented my
father from renewing his efforts to be of service to his
country. Two months after the rejection of his telegraph,
on Friday the 30th of December, 1796, the French were
on the Irish coasts. Of this he received intelligence late
at night. Immediately he sent a servant express to the
Secretary, with a letter offering to erect telegraphs, which

he had in Dublin, on any line that Government should direct, and proposing to bring his own men with him; or to join the army with his portable telegraphs, to re-connoitre. His servant was sent back with a note from the Secretary, containing compliments and the promise of a speedy answer; no further answer ever reached him. Upon this emergency he could, with the assistance of his friends, have established an immediate communication between Dublin and the coast, which should not have cost the country one shilling. My father showed no mortification at the neglect with which he was treated, but acknowledged that he felt much "concern in losing an opportunity of saving an enormous expense to the public, and of alleviating the anxiety and distress of thousands." A telegraph was most earnestly wished for at this time by the best-informed people in Ireland, as well as by those whose perceptions had suddenly quickened at the view of immediate danger. Great distress, bankruptcies, and ruin to many families, were the consequences of this attempted invasion. The troops were harassed with contrary orders and forced marches, for want of intelligence, and from that indecision which must always be the consequence of insufficient information. Many days were spent in terror and in fruitless wishes for the English fleet. One fact may mark the hurry and confusion of the time; the cannon and the ball sent to Bantry Bay were of different calibre. At last Ireland was providentially saved by the change of wind, which prevented the enemy from effecting a landing on her coast.

That the public will feel little interest in the danger of an invasion of Ireland which might have happened in the last century; that it can be of little consequence to the public to hear how or why, twenty years ago, this or that man's telegraph was not established, — I am aware; and I am sensible that few will care how cheaply it might have been obtained, or will be greatly interested in hearing of generous offers which were not accepted, and patriotic exertions which were not permitted to be of any national utility. I know that as a biographer I am expected to put private feelings out of the question; and this duty, as far as human nature will permit, I hope I have performed.

The facts are stated from my own knowledge, and from a more detailed account in his own "Letter to Lord Charlemont on the Telegraph," — a political pamphlet, uncommon at least for its temperate and good-humored tone.

Though all his exertions to establish a telegraph in Ireland were at this time unsuccessful, yet he persevered in the belief that in future modes of telegraphic communication would be generally adopted; and instead of his hopes being depressed, they were raised and expanded by new consideration of the subject in a scientific light. In the sixth volume of the "Transactions of the Royal Irish Academy," he published an "Essay on the Art of Conveying Swift and Secret Intelligence," in which he gives a comprehensive view of the uses to which the system may be applied, and a description, with plates, of his own machinery. Accounts of his apparatus and specimens of his vocabulary have been copied into various popular publications, therefore it is sufficient here to refer to them. The peculiar advantages of his machinery consist, in the first place, in being as free from friction as possible, consequently in its being easily moved, and not easily destroyed by use; in the next place, on its being simple, consequently easy to make and to repair. The superior advantage of his vocabulary arises from its being undecipherable. This depends on his employing the numerical figures instead of the alphabet. With a power of almost infinite change, and consequently with defiance of detection, he applies the combination of numerical figures to the words of a common dictionary, or to any length of phrase in any given vocabulary. He was the first who made this application of figures to telegraphic communication.

Much has been urged by various modern claimants for the honor of the invention of the telegraph. In England the claims of Dr. Hooke and of the Marquis of Worcester to the original idea are incontestable. But the invention long lay dormant, till wakened into active service by the French. Long before the French telegraph appeared, my father had tried his first telegraphic experiments. As he mentions in his own narrative, he tried the use of windmill sails in 1767 in Berkshire ; and also a nocturnal telegraph with lamps and illuminated letters, between London and Hampstead. He refers for the confirmation of the facts to a letter of Mr. Perrot's, a Berkshire gentleman who was with him at the time. The original of this letter is now in my possession. It was shown in 1795 to the President of the Royal Irish Academy. The following is a copy of it : —

DEAR SIR, — I perfectly recollect having several conversations with you in 1767 on the subject of a speedy and secret conveyance of intelligence. I recollect your going up the hills to see how far and how distinctly the arms (and the position of them) of Nettlebed Windmill sails were to be discovered with ease.

As to the experiments from Highgate to London by

means of lamps, I was not present at the time, but I remember your mentioning the circumstance to me in the same year.　All these particulars were brought very strongly to my memory when the French, some years ago, conveyed intelligence by signals; and I then thought and declared that the merit of the invention undoubtedly belonged to you.　I am very glad that I have it in my power to send you this confirmation, because I imagine there is no other person now living who can bear witness to your observations in Berkshire.

I remain, dear Sir,

Your affectionate friend,

JAMES L. PERROT.

BATH, Dec. 9, 1795.

Claims of priority of invention are always listened to with doubt, or, at best, with impatience.　To those who bring the invention to perfection, who actually adapt it to use, mankind are justly most grateful, and to these, rather than to the original inventors, grant the honors of a triumph.　Sensible of this, the matter is urged no farther, but left to the justice of posterity.

I am happy to state, however, one plain fact, which stands independent of all controversy, that my father's was the *first*, and I believe the only, telegraph which ever spoke across the Channel from Ireland to Scotland.　He was, as he says in his essay on this subject, "ambitious of being the first person who should connect the islands more closely by facilitating their mutual intercourse;" and on the 24th of August, 1794, my brothers had the satisfaction of sending by my father's telegraph four messages across the Channel, and of receiving immediate answers, before a vast concourse of spectators.

Edgeworth to Dr. Darwin.

EDGEWORTHTOWN, Dec. 11, 1794.

I have been employed for two months in experiments upon a telegraph of my own invention. I tried it partially twenty-six years ago. It differs from the French in distinctness and expedition, as the intelligence is not conveyed alphabetically. . . .

I intended to detail my telegraphs (in the plural), but I find that I have not room at present. If you think it worth while, you shall have the whole scheme before you, which I know you will improve for me. Suffice it, that by day, at eighteen or twenty miles' distance, I show, by four pointers, isosceles triangles, twenty feet high, on four imaginary circles, eight imaginary points, which correspond with the figures

0, 1, 2, 3, 4, 5, 6, 7.

So that seven thousand different combinations are formed, of four figures each, which refer to a dictionary of words that are referred to, — of lists of the navy, army, militia, lords, commons, geographical and technical terms, &c., besides an alphabet. So that everything one wishes may be transmitted with expedition.

By night, white lights are used.

Dr. Darwin to Mr. Edgeworth.

DERBY, March 15, 1795.

DEAR SIR, — I beg your pardon for not immediately answering your last favor, which was owing to the great influence the evil demon has at present in all affairs on this earth. That is, I lost your letter, and have in vain looked over some scores of papers, and cannot find it. Secondly, having lost your letter, I daily hoped to find it again — without success.

The telegraph you described I dare say would answer the purpose. It would be like a giant wielding his long arms and talking with his fingers; and those long arms might be covered with lamps in the night. You would place four or six such gigantic figures in a line, so that they should spell a whole word at once; and other such figures in sight of each other, all round the coast of Ireland; and thus fortify yourselves, instead of Friar Bacon's wall of brass round England, with the brazen head, which spoke, " Time is ! Time was ! Time is past ! "

MR. EDGEWORTH'S MACHINE.

Having slightly mentioned the contrivances made use of by the ancients for conveying intelligence swiftly, and having pointed out some of the various important uses to which this art may be applied, I shall endeavor to give a clear view of my attempts on this subject.

Models of the French telegraph have been so often exhibited, and the machine itself is so well known, that it is not necessary to describe it minutely in this place. It is sufficient to say that it consists of a tall pole, with three movable arms, which may be seen at a considerable distance through telescopes; these arms may be set in as many different positions as are requisite to express all the different letters of the alphabet. By a successive combination of letters shown in this manner, words and sentences are formed and intelligence communicated. No doubt can be made of the utility of this machine, as it has been applied to the most important purposes. It is obviously liable to mistakes, from the number of changes requisite for each word, and from the velocity with which it must be moved to convey intelligence with any tolerable expedition.

The name, however, which is well chosen, has become so familiar, that I shall, with a slight alteration, adopt it for the apparatus which I am going to describe. *Telegraph* is a proper name for a machine which describes at a distance. *Telelograph*, or contractedly *Tellograph*, is a proper name for a machine that describes *words* at a distance.

Dr. Hooke, to whom every mechanic philosopher must recur, has written an essay upon the subject of conveying swift intelligence, in which he proposes to use large wooden letters in succession. The siege of Vienna turned his attention to the business. His method is more cumbrous than the French telegraph, but far less liable to error.

I tried it before I had seen Hooke's work, in the year 1767 in London, and I could distinctly read letters illuminated with lamps in Hampstead Churchyard, from the house of Mr. Elers in Great Russell Street, Bloomsbury, to whom I refer for date and circumstance. To him and to Mr. E. Delaval, F.R.S., to Mr. Perrot, of Hare Hatch, and to Mr Woulfe the chemist, I refer for the precedency which I claim in this invention. In that year I invented the idea of my present tellograph, proposing to make use of windmill sails instead of the hands or pointers which I now employ. Mr. Perrot was so good as to accompany me more than once to a hill near his house to observe with a telescope the windmill at Nettlebed, which places are, I think, sixteen miles asunder. My intention at that time was to convey not only a swift but an unsuspected mode of intelligence. By means of common windmills this might have been effected, before an account of the French telegraph was made public.

My machinery consists of four triangular pointers or hands [each upon a separate pedestal, ranged along in a row], each of which points like the hand of a clock to different situations in the circles which they describe. It is easy to distinguish whether a hand moving vertically points perpendicularly downwards or upwards, horizontally to the right or left, or to any of the four intermediate positions.

The eye can readily perceive the eight different positions in which one of the pointers is represented [on the plate attached to the article in the " Transactions," but here omitted]. Of these eight positions seven only are employed to denote figures, the upright position of the hand or pointer being reserved to represent o, or zero. The figures thus denoted refer to a vocabulary in which all the words are numbered. Of the four pointers, that which appears to the left hand of the observer represents thousands ; the others hundreds, tens, and units, in succession, as in common numeration.

[By these means, as Mr. Edgeworth showed, numbers from 1 up to 7,777, omitting those having a digit above 7, could be displayed to the distant observer, who on referring to his vocabulary discovered that they meant such expressions as it might seem convenient to transmit by this excellent invention.]

Although the electric telegraphs have long since superseded telegraphs of this class in public use, the young people of Colonel Ingham's class took great pleasure in the next summer in using Mr. Edgeworth's telegraph to communicate with each other, by plans easily made in their different country homes.

It may interest the casual reader to know that the first words in the first message transmitted on the telegraph between Scotland and Ireland, alluded to above, were represented by the numbers 2,645, 2,331, 573, 1,113, 244, 2,411, 6,336, which being interpreted are, —

" Hark from basaltic rocks and giant walls,"

and so on with the other lines, seven in number. This is Mr. Edgeworth's concise history of telegraphy before his time.

The art of conveying intelligence by sounds and signals is of the highest antiquity. It was practised by Theseus in the Argonautic expedition, by Agamemnon at the siege of Troy, and by Mardonius in the time of Xerxes. It is mentioned frequently in Thucydides. It was used by Tamerlane, who had probably never heard of the black sails of Theseus ; by the Moors in Spain ; by the Welsh in Britain ; by the Irish ; and by the Chinese on that famous wall by which they separated themselves from Tartary.

All this detail about Mr. Edgeworth's telegraph resulted in much search in the older encyclopædias. Quite full accounts were found, by the young people, of his system, and of the French system afterwards employed, and worked in France until the electric telegraph made all such inventions unnecessary.

Before the next meeting, Bedford Long, who lived on Highland Street in Roxbury, and Hugh, who lived on the side of Corey Hill, were able to communicate with each other by semaphore ; and at the next meeting they arranged two farther stations, so that John, at Cambridge, and Jane Fortescue, at Lexington, were in the series.

There being some half an hour left that afternoon, the children amused themselves by looking up some other of Mr. Edgeworth's curious experiments and vagaries.

MORE OF MR. EDGEWORTH'S FANCIES.

During my residence at Hare Hatch another wager was proposed by me among our acquaintance, the purport of which was that I undertook to find a man who should, with the assistance of machinery, walk faster than any other person that could be produced. The machinery which I intended to employ was a huge hollow wheel, made very light, withinside of which, in a barrel of six feet diameter, a man should walk. Whilst he stepped thirty inches, the circumference of the large wheel, or rather wheels, would revolve five feet on the ground ; and as the machinery was to roll on planks and on a plane somewhat inclined, when once the *vis inertiæ* of the machine should be overcome, it would carry on the man within it as fast as he could possibly walk. I had provided means of regulating the motion, so that the wheel should not run away with its master. I had the wheel made ; and when it was so nearly completed as to require but a few hours' work to finish it, I went to London for Lord Effingham, to whom I had promised that he should be present at the first experiment made with it. But the bulk and extraordinary appearance of my machine had attracted the notice of the country neighborhood ; and, taking advantage of my absence, some idle curious persons went to the carpenter I employed, who lived on Hare Hatch Common. From him they obtained the great wheel which had been left by me in his care. It was not finished. I had not yet furnished it with the means of stopping or moderating its motion. A young lad got into it; his companions launched it on a path which led gently down hill towards a very steep chalk-pit. This pit was at such a distance as to be out of their thoughts when they set the wheel in motion. On it ran. The lad withinside plied his legs with all his might. The spectators, who at first stood still to behold the operation, were soon alarmed by the shouts of their companion, who perceived his danger. The vehicle became quite ungovernable; the velocity increased as it ran down hill. Fortunately the boy contrived to jump from his rolling prison before it reached the chalk-pit; but the wheel went on with such velocity as to outstrip its pursuers, and, rolling over the edge of the precipice, it was dashed to pieces.

The next day, when I came to look for my machine, intending to try it on some planks which had been laid for it, I found, to my no small disappointment, that the object of all my labors and my hopes was lying at the bottom of a chalk-pit, broken into a thousand pieces. I could not at that time afford to construct another wheel of this sort, and I cannot therefore determine what might have been the success of my scheme.

As I am on the subject of carriages, I shall mention a sailing-carriage that I tried on this common. The carriage was light, steady, and ran with amazing velocity. One day, when I was preparing for a sail in it with my friend and schoolfellow Mr. William Foster, my wheel-boat escaped from its moorings just as we were going to step on board. With the utmost difficulty I overtook it; and as I saw three or four stage-coaches on the road, and feared that this sailing-chariot might frighten their horses, I, at the hazard of my life, got into my carriage while it was under full sail, and then, at a favorable part of the road, I used the means I had of guiding it easily out of the way. But the sense of the mischief which must have ensued if I had not succeeded in getting into the machine at the proper place and stopping it at the right moment was so strong as to deter me from trying any more experiments on this carriage in such a dangerous place.

Such should never be attempted except on a large common, *at a distance from a high* road. It may not, however, be amiss to suggest that upon a long extent of iron railway in an open country carriages properly constructed might make profitable voyages, from time to time, with sails instead of horses; for though a constant or regular intercourse could not be thus carried on, yet goods of a certain sort, that are salable at any time, might be stored till wind and weather were favorable.

When Bedford had read this passage, John Fordyce said he had travelled hundreds of miles on the Western railways where Mr. Edgeworth's sails could have been applied without a "stage-coach" to be afraid of them.

JACK THE DARTER.

In one of my journeys from Hare Hatch to Birmingham, I accidentally met with a person whom I, as a mechanic, had a curiosity to see. This was a sailor, who had amused London with a singular exhibition of dexterity. He was called *Jack the Darter*. He threw his darts, which consisted of thin rods of deal of about half an inch in diameter and of a yard long, to an amazing height and distance ; for instance, he threw them over what was then called the New Church in the Strand. Of this feat I had heard, but I entertained some doubts upon the subject. I had inquired from my friends where this man could be found, but had not been able to discover him. As I was driving towards Birmingham in an open carriage of a singular construction, I overtook a man who walked remarkably fast, but who stopped as I passed him, and eyed my equipage with uncommon curiosity. There was something in his manner that made me speak to him ; and from the sort of questions he asked about my carriage, I found that he was a clever fellow. ·I soon learned that he had walked over the greatest part of England, and that he was perfectly acquainted with London. It came into my head to inquire whether he had ever seen the exhibition about which I was so desirous to be informed.

" Lord ! sir," said he, " I am myself Jack the Darter." He had a roll of brown paper in his hand, which he unfolded, and soon produced a bundle of the light deal sticks which he had the power of darting to such a distance. He readily consented to gratify my curiosity ; and after he had thrown some of them to a prodigious height, I asked him to throw some of them horizontally. At the first trial he threw one of them eighty yards with great ease. I observed that he coiled a small string round the stick, by which he gave it a rotary motion that preserved it from altering its course ; and at the same time it allowed the arm which threw it time to exercise its whole force.

If anything be simply thrown from the hand, it is clear that it can acquire no greater velocity than that of the hand that throws it ; but if the body that is thrown passes through a greater space than the hand, whilst the hand continues to communicate motion to the body to be impelled, the body will acquire a velocity nearly double to that of the hand which throws it. The ancients were aware of this ; and they wrapped a thong of leather round their javelins, by which they could throw them with additional violence. This invention did not, I believe, belong to the Greeks ; nor do I remember its being mentioned by Homer or Xenophon. It was in use among the Romans, but at what time it was introduced or laid aside I know not. Whoever is acquainted with the science of projectiles will perceive that this invention is well worthy of their attention.

A ONE-WHEELED CHAISE.

After having satisfied my curiosity about Jack the Darter, I proceeded to Birmingham. I mentioned that I travelled in a carriage of a singular construction. It was a one-wheeled chaise, which I had had made for the purpose of going conveniently in narrow roads. It was made fast by shafts to the horse's sides, and was furnished with two weights or counterpoises, that hung below the shafts. The seat was not more than eight and twenty or thirty inches from the ground, in order to bring the centre of gravity of the whole as low as possible. The footboard turned upon hinges fastened to the shafts, so that when it met with any obstacle it gave way, and my legs were warned to lift themselves up. In going through water my legs were secured by leathers, which folded up like the sides of bellows ; by this means I was pretty safe from wet. On my road to Birmingham I passed through Long Compton, in Warwickshire, on a Sunday. The people were returning from church, and numbers stopped to gaze at me. There is, or was, a shallow ford near the town, over which there was a very narrow bridge for horse and foot passengers, but not sufficiently wide for wagons or chaises. Towards this bridge I drove. The people, not perceiving the structure of my one-wheeled vehicle, called to me with great eagerness to warn me that the bridge was too narrow for carriages. I had an excellent horse, which went so fast as to give but little time for examination. The louder they called, the faster I drove; and when I had passed the bridge, they shouted after me with surprise. I got on to Shipstone upon Stone; but before I had dined there I found that my fame had overtaken me. My carriage was put into a coach-house, so that those who came from Long Compton, not seeing it, did not recognize me. I therefore had an opportunity of hearing all the exaggerations and strange conjectures which were made by those who related my passage over the narrow bridge. There were posts on the bridge, to prevent, as I suppose, more than one horseman from passing at once. Some of the spectators asserted that my carriage had gone over these posts; others said that it had not wheels, which was indeed literally true; but they meant to say that it was without any wheel. Some were sure that no carriage ever went so fast; and all agreed that at the end of the bridge, where the floods had laid the road for some way under water, my carriage swam on the surface of the water.

VIII.

JAMES WATT.

"UNCLE FRITZ," said Mabel Liddell, the next afternoon that our friends had gathered together for a reading, "would it not be well for us all to go down into the kitchen this afternoon, and watch the steam come out of the kettle as Ellen makes tea for us?"

"Why should it be well, Mabel?" said Colonel Ingham. "For my part, I should prefer to remain in my own room, more especially as I consider my armchair to be more suited to the comfort of one already on the downward path in life than is the kitchen table, where we should have to sit should we invade the premises of our friends below."

"I was thinking," said Mabel, "of the manner in which James Watt when a child invented the steam-engine, from observing the motion of the top of the teakettle; and as we are to read about Watt this afternoon I thought we might be in a more fit condition to understand his invention, and might more fully comprehend his frame of mind while perfecting his great work, should we also fix our eyes and minds on the top of the teakettle in Ellen's kitchen."

"Mabel, my child," said Uncle Fritz, "you talk like a book, and a very interesting one at that; but I think, as the youngest of us would say, that you are just a little off in your remarks. And as I observe that Clem, who is going to read this afternoon, desires to deliver a sermon of which your conversation seems to be the text, I will request all to listen to him before we consider seriously vacating this apartment, however poor it may be," — and he glanced fondly around at the comfortable arrangements that everywhere pervaded the study, — "and seek the regions below."

"I only wanted to say," began Clem, "that although Watt did on one occasion (in his extreme youth) look at a teakettle with some interest, he was not in the habit, at the time when he devoted most thought to the steam-engine, of having a teakettle continually before him that he might gain inspiration from observing the steam issue from its nose. And, as Watt dispensed with this aid, I have no doubt that we may do so as well, contenting ourselves with the results of the experiments in the vaporization of water, which Ellen is now conducting in the form of tea. Besides all this, however, I do want to say some things, before we read aloud this afternoon (I hope this is n't really too much like a sermon), about the steam-engine and the part that Watt had in perfecting it."

At this point the irrepressible Mabel was heard to whisper to Bedford, who sat next her : "Was n't it curious that the same mind which grasped the immense capabilities of the steam-engine should have been able also to construct such a delicate lyric as

> 'How doth the little busy bee
> Improve each shining hour' ? "

"Mabel," said Colonel Ingham, "you are absolutely unbearable. If you do not keep in better order I shall be sorry that I dissuaded you from descending to the kitchen.

I see nothing incongruous myself in indulging in mechanical experiments, and in throwing one's thoughts into the form of verse," — here the old gentleman colored slightly, as though he recollected something of the sort, — " but it may be well to counteract the impression your conversation may have made by stating that Isaac Watts did not invent the steam-engine, nor did James Watt write the beautiful words you have just quoted. — Now, Clem, I believe you have the floor."

" Well," said Clem, " I only want the floor for a short time in order to explain about Watt and the steam-engine, and how much he was the inventor of it, before we begin to read.

" There are various points about the steam-engine which are really Watt's invention, — the separate condenser, for instance, — but the idea of the steam-engine was not original with him ; that is, when he saw the steam in the teakettle raise the lid and drop it again, he was not the first to speculate on the power of steam."

" Are you going to read us that part in the book, Clem ?" asked Bedford, with some interest.

" Yes, if you like," said Clem. " I guess it tells about it in Mr. Smiles's ' Life of Watt.' " So he began to overhaul the book he had brought, and shortly discovered the anecdote referred to by Mabel with such interest, and read it.

" On one occasion he [James Watt] was reproved by Mrs. Muirhead, his aunt, for his indolence at the tea-table. ' James Watt,' said the worthy lady, ' I never saw such an idle boy as you are. Take a book, or employ yourself usefully ; for the last hour you have not spoken one word, but taken off the lid of that kettle and put it on again, holding now a cup and now a silver spoon over the steam, watching how it rises from the spout, catching and counting the drops it falls into.' In the view of M. Arago, the little James before the teakettle, becomes the great engineer, preparing the discoveries which were soon to immortalize him. In our opinion, the judgment of the aunt was the truest. There is no reason to suppose that the mind of the boy was occupied with philosophical theories on the condensation of steam, which he compassed with so much difficulty in his maturer years. This is more probably an afterthought borrowed from his subsequent discoveries. Nothing is commoner than for children to be amused with such phenomena in the same way that they will form air-bubbles in a cup of tea, and watch them sailing over the surface till they burst. The probability is that little James was quite as idle as he seemed."

" That is very interesting," remarked Mabel. " Don't you think now, Uncle Fritz, we had better go into the kitchen?" And she looked appealingly at the old gentleman, who merely held up his finger for silence as Clem continued his lecture.

"What I meant to say," Clem went on, " was that other people before Watt had found out the power of steam, and had used it too. There was one Hero of Alexandria, who lived about two thousand years ago, who used steam for many interesting purposes, notably for animating various figures that took part in the idolatrous worship of his time, and thus in deceiving the common people. But his contrivances, though engines which went by steam, would hardly be called steam-engines. Between Hero of Alexandria, of 160 B. C., and the Marquis of Worcester, of 1650 A. D., there does not seem to have been much doing in the way of inventing the steam-engine. But the Marquis of Worcester in Charles II.'s time was a great philosopher, and did nobody knows exactly what with steam. But though he did great things, he did not produce a particularly capable engine, though he seems to have known more about steam than anybody else did at his time. After the Marquis of Worcester and before Watt, there were three men who did much towards inventing and improving the steam-engine. Their names were Savery, Papin, and Newcomen. I don't propose to tell you about the inventions of each one; but it's well enough to remember that each one did important service in getting the steam-engine to the point where Watt took hold of it. As it was on Newcomen's engine that Watt made his first serious experiments, I think we should all like to know something about it."

THE NEWCOMEN ENGINE.

Newcomen's engine may be thus briefly described: The steam was generated in a separate boiler, as in Savery's engine, from which it was conveyed into a vertical cylinder underneath a piston fitting it closely, but movable upwards and downwards through its whole length. The piston was fixed to a rod, which was attached by a joint or chain to the end of a lever vibrating upon an axis, the other end being attached to a rod working a pump. When the piston in the cylinder was raised, steam was let into the vacated space through a tube fitted into the top of the boiler, and mounted with a stopcock. The pump-rod at the further end of the lever being thus depressed, cold water was applied to the sides of the cylinder, on which the steam within it was condensed, a vacuum was produced, and the external air, pressing upon the top of the piston, forced it down into the empty cylinder. The pump-rod was thereby raised; and, the operation of depressing it being repeated, a power was thus produced which kept the pump continuously at work. Such, in a few words, was the construction and action of Newcomen's first engine.[1]

While the engine was still in its trial state, a curious accident occurred which led to a change in the mode of condensation, and proved of essential importance in establishing Newcomen's engine as a practical working power. The accident was this: in order to keep the cylinder as free from air as possible, great pains were taken to prevent it passing down by the side of the piston, which was carefully wrapped with cloth or leather; and, still further to keep the cylinder air-tight, a quantity of water was kept constantly on the upper side of the piston. At one of the early trials the inventors were surprised to see the engine make several strokes in unusually quick succession; and on searching for the cause, they found it to consist in *a hole in the piston*, which had let the cold water in a jet into the inside of the cylinder, and thereby produced a rapid vacuum by the condensation of the continued steam. A new light suddenly broke upon Newcomen. The idea of condensing by injection of cold water directly into the cylinder, instead of applying it on the outside, at once occurred to him; and he proceeded to embody the expedient which had thus been accidentally suggested as part of his machine. The result was

---

[1] The first steam-engines were devised in order to supply some motor for the pumps which were necessary, all over England, to keep the mines free from water. The locomotive engine, as will be seen later, owes its birth to the efforts of colliery engineers to find some means of drawing coal better than the horse-power generally in use.

the addition of the injection pipe, through which, when the piston was raised and the cylinder full of steam, a jet of cold water was thrown in, and, the steam being suddenly condensed, the piston was at once driven down by the pressure of the atmosphere.

An accident of a different kind shortly after led to the improvement of Newcomen's engine in another respect. To keep it at work, one man was required to attend the fire, and another to turn alternately the two cocks, one admitting the steam into the cylinder, the other admitting the jet of cold water to condense it. The turning of these cocks was easy work, usually performed by a boy. It was, however, a very monotonous duty, though requiring constant attention. To escape the drudgery and obtain an interval for rest or perhaps for play, a boy named Humphrey Potter, who turned the cocks, set himself to discover some method of evading his task. He must have been an ingenious boy, as is clear from the arrangement he contrived with this object. Observing the alternate ascent and descent of the beam above his head, he bethought him of applying the movement to the alternate raising and lowering of the levers which governed the cocks. The result was the contrivance of what he called the *scoggan* (meaning presumably the loafer or lazy boy), consisting of a catch worked by strings from the beam of the engine. This arrangement, when tried, was found to answer the purpose intended. The action of the engine was thus made automatic; and the arrangement, though rude, not only enabled Potter to enjoy his play, but it had the effect of improving the working power of the engine itself; the number of strokes which it made being increased from six or eight to fifteen or sixteen in the minute. This invention was afterward greatly improved by

Mr. Henry Beighton, of Newcastle-on-Tyne, who added the plug-rod and hand-gear. He did away with the catches and strings of the boy Potter's rude apparatus, and substituted a rod suspended from the beam, which alternately opened and shut the tappets. attached to the steam and injection cocks.

Thus, step by step, Newcomen's engine grew in power and efficiency, and became more and more complete as a self-acting machine. It will be observed that, like all other inventions, it was not the product of any one man's ingenuity, but of many. One contributed one improvement, and another another. The essential features of the atmospheric engine were not new. The piston and cylinder had been known as long ago as the time of Hero. The expansive force of steam and the creation of a vacuum by its condensation had been known to the Marquis of Worcester, Savery, Papin, and many more. Newcomen merely combined in his machine the result of their varied experience ; and, assisted by the persons who worked with him, down to the engine-boy Potter, he advanced the invention several important stages ; so that the steam-engine was no longer a toy or a scientific curiosity, but had become a powerful machine capable of doing useful work.

JAMES WATT AND THE STEAM-ENGINE.

It was in the year 1759 that Robison[1] first called the attention of his friend Watt to the subject of the steam-engine. Robison was then only in his twentieth, and

---

[1] John Robison, at this time a student at Glasgow College, and afterwards Professor of Natural Philosophy at Edinburgh. He was at one time Master of the Marine Cadet Academy at Cronstadt.

Watt in his twenty-third year. Robison's idea was that the power of steam might be advantageously applied to the driving of wheel-carriages; and he suggested that it would be the most convenient for the purpose to place the cylinder with its open end downwards to avoid the necessity of using a working-beam. Watt admits that he was very ignorant of the steam-engine at the time; nevertheless, he began making a model with two cylinders of tin plate, intending that the pistons and their connecting-rods should act alternately on two pinions attached to the axles of the carriage-wheels. But the model, being slightly and inaccurately made, did not answer his expectations. Other difficulties presented themselves, and the scheme was laid aside because Robison left Glasgow to go to sea. Indeed, mechanical science was not yet ripe for the loco-motive. Robison's idea had, however, dropped silently into the mind of his friend, where it grew from day to day, slowly and at length fruitfully.

At his intervals of leisure and in the quiet of his even-ings, Watt continued to prosecute his various studies. He was shortly attracted by the science of chemistry, then in its infancy. Dr. Black was at that time occupied with the investigations which led to his discovery of the theory of latent heat, and it is probable that his familiar conversations with Watt on the subject induced the latter to enter upon a series of experiments with the view of giving the theory some practical direction. His attention again and again reverted to the steam-engine, though he had not yet seen even a model of one. Steam was as yet almost unknown in Scotland as a working power. The first engine was erected at Elphinstone Colliery, in Stirlingshire, about the year 1750; and the second more than ten years later, at Govan Colliery, near Glasgow, where it was known by the

startling name of " The Firework." This had not, however, been set up at the time Watt had begun to inquire
into the subject. But he found that the college possessed
the model of a Newcomen engine for the use of the Natural Philosophy class, which had been sent to London for
repair. On hearing of its existence, he suggested to his
friend Dr. Anderson, Professor of Natural Philosophy, the
propriety of getting back the model; and a sum of money
was placed by the Senatus at the professor's disposal, " to
recover the steam-engine from Mr. Sisson, instrument-
maker in London."

In the mean time Watt sought to learn all that had been
written on the subject of the steam-engine. He ascertained from Desaguliers, Switzer, and other writers, what
had been accomplished by Savery, Newcomen, Beighton,
and others; and he went on with his own independent
experiments. His first apparatus was of the simplest possible kind. He used common apothecaries' phials for his
steam reservoirs, and canes hollowed out for his steam-
pipes. In 1761 he proceeded to experiment on the force
of steam by means of a small Papin's digester and a syringe.
The syringe was only the third of an inch in diameter, fitted
with a solid piston; and it was connected with the digester
by a pipe furnished with a stopcock, by which the steam
was admitted or shut off at will. It was also itself provided
with a stopcock, enabling a communication to be opened
between the syringe and the outer air to permit the steam
in the syringe to escape. The apparatus, though rude,
enabled the experimenter to ascertain some important
facts. When the steam in the digester was raised and the
cock turned, enabling it to rush against the lower side of
the piston, he found that the expansive force of the steam
raised a weight of fifteen pounds, with which the piston

was loaded. Then on turning on the cock and shutting off the connection with the digester at the same time that a passage was opened to the air, the steam was allowed to escape, when the weight upon the piston, being no longer counteracted, immediately forced it to descend.

Watt saw that it would be easy to contrive that the cocks should be turned by the machinery itself with perfect regularity. But there was an objection to this method. Water is converted into vapor as soon as its elasticity is sufficient to overcome the weight of the air which keeps it down. Under the ordinary pressure of the atmosphere water acquires this necessary elasticity at 212°; but as the steam in the digester was prevented from escaping, it acquired increased heat, and by consequence increased elasticity. Hence it was that the steam which issued from the digester was not only able to support the piston and the air which pressed upon its upper surface, but the additional load with which the piston was weighted. With the imperfect mechanical construction, however, of those days, there was a risk lest the boiler should be burst by the steam, which was apt to force its way through the ill-made joints of the machine. This, conjoined with the great expenditure of steam on the high-pressure system, led Watt to abandon the plan; and the exigencies of his business for a time prevented him from pursuing his experiments.

At length the Newcomen model arrived from London; and in 1763 the little engine, which was destined to become so famous, was put into the hands of Watt. The boiler was somewhat smaller than an ordinary teakettle. The cylinder of the engine was only of two inches diameter and six inches stroke. Watt at first regarded it as merely "a fine plaything." It was, however, enough to set him upon a track of thinking which led to the most important results. When he had repaired the model and set it to work, he found that the boiler, though apparently large enough, could not supply steam in sufficient quantity, and only a few strokes of the piston could be obtained, when the engine stopped. The fire was urged by blowing, and more steam was produced; but still it would not work properly. Exactly at the point at which another man would have abandoned the task in despair, the mind of Watt became thoroughly roused. "Everything," says Professor Robison, "was to him the beginning of a new and serious study; and I knew that he would not quit it till he had either discovered its insignificance or had made something of it." Thus it happened with the phenomena presented by the model of the steam-engine. Watt referred to his books, and endeavored to ascertain from them by what means he might remedy the defects which he found in the model; but they could tell him nothing. He then proceeded with an independent course of experiments, resolved to work out the problem for himself. In the course of his inquiries he came upon a fact which, more than any other, led his mind into the train of thought which at last conducted him to the invention of which the results were destined to prove so stupendous. This fact was the existence of latent heat.

In order to follow the track of investigation pursued by Watt, it is necessary for a moment to revert to the action of the Newcomen pumping-engine. A beam, moving upon a centre, had affixed to one end of it a chain attached to the piston of the pump, and at the other a chain attached to a piston that fitted into the steam-cylinder. It was by driving this latter piston up and down the cylinder that the pump was worked. To communicate the necessary movement to the piston, the steam generated in a boiler was admitted to the bottom of the cylinder, forcing out the air through a valve, where its pressure on the under side of the piston counterbalanced the pressure of the atmosphere on its upper side. The piston, thus placed between two equal forces, was drawn up to the top of the cylinder by the greater weight of the pump-gear at the opposite extremity of the beam. The steam, so far, only discharged the office of the air it displaced; but if the air had been allowed to remain, the piston once at the top of the cylinder could not have returned, being pressed as much by the atmosphere underneath as by the atmosphere above it. The steam, on the contrary, which was admitted by the exclusion of air, *could be condensed*, and a vacuum created, by injecting cold water through the bottom of the cylinder. The piston, being now unsupported, was forced down by the pressure of the atmosphere on its upper surface. When the piston reached the bottom, the steam was again let in, and the process was repeated. Such was the engine in ordinary use for pumping water at the time that Watt began his investigations.

Among his other experiments, he constructed a boiler which showed by inspection the quantity of water evaporated in any given time, and the quantity of steam used in every stroke of the engine. He was astonished to discover that a *small* quantity of water in the form of steam heated a large quantity of cold water injected into the cylinder for the purpose of cooling it; and upon further examination he ascertained that steam heated six times its weight of cold water to 212°, which was the temperature of the steam itself. " Being struck with this remarkable fact," says Watt, " and not understanding the reason of it, I mentioned it to my friend Dr. Black, who then explained to me his doctrine of latent heat, which he had

taught for some time before this period (the summer of
1764) ; but having myself been occupied by the pursuits
of business, if I had heard of it I had not attended to it,
when I thus stumbled upon one of the material facts by
which that beautiful theory is supported."

When Watt found that water in its conversion into
vapor became such a reservoir of heat, he was more
than ever bent on economizing it ; for the great waste of
heat involving so heavy a consumption of fuel was felt to
be the principal obstacle to the extended employment of
steam as a motive power. He accordingly endeavored,
with the same quantity of fuel, at once to increase the
production of steam and to diminish its waste. He
increased the heating surface of the boiler by making
flues through it ; he even made his boiler of wood, as
being a worse conductor of heat than the brickwork
which surrounds common furnaces ; and he cased the
cylinders and all the conducting pipes in materials which
conducted heat very slowly. But none of these contrivances were effectual ; for it turned out that the chief
expenditure of steam, and consequently of fuel, in the
Newcomen engine, was occasioned by the reheating of
the cylinder after the steam had been condensed, and
the cylinder was consequently cooled by the injection
into it of the cold water. Nearly four fifths of the whole ·
steam employed was condensed on its first admission,
before the surplus could act upon the piston. Watt
therefore came to the conclusion that to make a perfect
steam-engine it was necessary that *the cylinder should be
always as hot as the steam that entered it ;* but it was
equally necessary that the steam should be condensed
when the piston descended, nay, that it should be
cooled down below 100°, or a considerable amount of

vapor would be given off, which would resist the descent of the piston, and diminish the power of the engine. Thus the cylinder was never to be at a less temperature than 212°, and yet at each descent of the piston it was to be less than 100°, — conditions which, on the very face of them, seemed to be wholly incompatible.

Though still occupied with his inquiries and experiments as to steam, Watt did not neglect his proper business, but was constantly on the look-out for improvements in instrument-making. A machine which he invented for drawing in perspective proved a success; and he made a considerable number of them to order, for customers in London as well as abroad. He was also an indefatigable reader, and continued to extend his knowledge of chemistry and mechanics by perusal of the best books on these sciences.

Above all subjects, however, the improvement of the steam-engine continued to keep the fastest hold upon his mind. He still brooded over his experiments with the Newcomen model, but did not seem to make much way in introducing any practical improvement in its mode of working. His friend Robison says he struggled long to condense with sufficient rapidity without injection, trying one experiment after another, finding out what would *not* do, and exhibiting many beautiful specimens of ingenuity and fertility of resource. He continued, to use his own words, "to grope in the dark, misled by many an *ignis fatuus.*" It was a favorite saying of his that "Nature has a weak side, if we can only find it out;" and he went on groping and feeling for it, but as yet in vain. At length light burst upon him, and all at once the problem over which he had been brooding was solved.

THE SEPARATE CONDENSER.

One Sunday afternoon, in the spring of 1765, he went to take an afternoon walk on the Green, then a quiet grassy meadow used as a bleaching and grazing ground. On week days the Glasgow lasses came thither with their largest kail-pots to boil their clothes in; and sturdy queans might be seen, with coats kilted, trampling blankets in their tubs. On Sundays the place was comparatively deserted; and hence Watt, who lived close at hand, went there to take a quiet afternoon stroll. His thoughts were as usual running on the subject of his unsatisfactory experiments with the Newcomen engine, when the first idea of the separate condenser suddenly flashed upon his mind. But the notable discovery is best told in his own words, as related to Mr. Robert Hart, many years after : —

"I had gone to take a walk on a fine Sabbath afternoon. I had entered the Green by the gate at the foot of Charlotte Street, and had passed the old washing-house. I was thinking upon the engine at the time, and had gone as far as the herd's house, when the idea came into my mind that as the steam was an elastic body, it would rush into a vacuum, and if a communication were made between the cylinder and an exhausted vessel, it would rush into it and might be then condensed without cooling the cylinder. I then saw that I must get rid of the condensed steam and the injection water if I used a jet, as in Newcomen's engine. Two ways of doing this occurred to me. First, the water might be run off by a descending pipe, if an off-let could be got at the depth of 35 or 36 feet, and any air might be extracted by a small pump. The second was to make the pump large enough to extract both water and air." He continued: "I had not walked farther than the Golf-house when the whole thing was arranged in my mind."

Great and prolific ideas are almost always simple. What seems impossible at the outset appears so obvious when it is effected, that we are prone to marvel that it did not force itself at once upon the mind. Late in life Watt, with his accustomed modesty, declared his belief that if he had excelled, it had been by chance, and the neglect of others. To Professor Jardine he said that when it was analyzed the invention would not appear so great as it seemed to be. "In the state," said he, "in which I found the steam-engine, it was no great effort of mind to observe that the quantity of fuel necessary to make it work would forever prevent its extensive utility. The next step in my progress was equally easy, — to inquire what was the cause of the great consumption of fuel : this, too, was readily suggested, viz., the waste of fuel which was necessary to bring the whole cylinder, piston, and adjacent parts from the coldness of water to the heat of steam, no fewer than from fifteen to twenty times in a minute." The question then occurred, How was this to be avoided or remedied? It was at this stage that the idea of carrying on the condensation in a separate vessel flashed upon his mind, and solved the difficulty.

Mankind has been more just to Watt than he was to himself. There was no accident in the discovery. It had been the result of close and continuous study; and the idea of the separate condenser was merely the last step of a long journey, a step which could not have been taken unless the road which led to it had been traversed. Dr. Black says, "This capital improvement flashed upon his mind at once, and filled him with rapture," — a state-ment which, in spite of the unimpassioned nature of Watt, we can readily believe.

On the morning following his Sunday afternoon's walk on Glasgow Green, Watt was up betimes, making arrange-ments for a speedy trial of his new plan. He borrowed from a college friend a large brass syringe, an inch and a third in diameter, and ten inches long, of the kind used by anatomists for injecting arteries with wax previous to dissection. The body of the syringe served for a cylinder, the piston-rod passing through a collar of leather in its cover. A pipe connected with the boiler was inserted at both ends for the admission of steam, and at the upper end was another pipe to convey the steam to the conden-ser. The axis of the stem of the piston was drilled with a hole, fitted with a valve at its lower end, to permit the water produced by the condensed steam on first filling the cylinder to escape. The first condenser made use of was an improvised cistern of tinned plate, provided with a pump to get rid of the water formed by the condensation of the steam, both the condensing-pipes and the air-pump being placed in a reservoir of cold water.

"The steam-pipe," says Watt, "was adjusted to a small boiler. When the steam was produced, it was admitted into the cylinder, and soon issued through the perforation of the rod and at the valve of the condenser; when it was judged that the air was expelled, the steam-cock was shut, and the air-pump piston-rod was drawn up, which leaving the small pipes of the condenser in a state of vacuum, the steam entered them, and was condensed. The piston of the cylinder immediately rose, and lifted a weight of about eighteen pounds, which was hung to the lower end of the piston-rod. The exhaustion-cock was shut, the steam was re-admitted into the cylinder, and the operation was re-peated. The quantity of steam consumed and the weights it could raise were observed, and, excepting the non-application of the steam-case and external covering, the invention was complete in so far as regarded the savings of steam and fuel."

COMPLETING THE INVENTION.

But although the invention was complete ˈin Watt's mind, it took him many long and laborious years to work out the details of the engine. His friend Robison, with whom his intimacy was maintained during these interesting experiments, has given a graphic account of the difficulties which he successively encountered and overcame. He relates that on his return from the country, after the college vacation in 1765, he went to have a chat with Watt and communicate to him some observations he had made on Desaguliers' and Belidor's account of the steam-engine. He went straight into the parlor, without ceremony, and found Watt sitting before the fire looking at a little tin cistern which he had on his knee. Robison immediately started the conversation about steam ; his mind, like Watt's, being occupied with the means of avoiding the excessive waste of heat in the Newcomen engine. Watt all the while kept looking into the fire, and after a time laid down the cistern at the foot of his chair, saying nothing. It seems that Watt felt rather nettled that Robison had communicated to a mechanic of the town a contrivance which he had hit upon for turning the cocks of his engine. When Robison therefore pressed his inquiry, Watt at length looked at him and said briskly, " You need not fash yourself any more about that, man. I have now made an engine that shall not waste a particle of steam. It shall all be boiling hot, — ay, and hot water injected, if I please." He then pushed the little tin cistern with his foot under the table.

Robison could learn no more of the new contrivance from Watt at that time ; but on the same evening he accidentally met a mutual acquaintance, who, supposing he knew as usual the progress of Watt's experiments, observed to him, " Well, have you seen Jamie Watt ? " " Yes." " He 'll be in fine spirits now with his engine ? " " Yes," said Robison, " very fine spirits." " Gad ! " said the other, " the separate condenser 's the thing ; keep it but cold enough, and you may have a perfect vacuum, whatever be the heat of the cylinder." This was Watt's secret, and the nature of the contrivance was clear to Robison at once.

It will be observed that Watt had not made a secret of it to his other friends. Indeed, Robison himself admitted that one of Watt's greatest delights was to communicate the results of his experiments to others, and set them upon the same road to knowledge with himself; and that no one could display less of the small jealousy of the tradesman than he did. To his intimate friend Dr. Black he communicated the progress made by him at every stage. The Doctor kindly encouraged him in his struggles, cheered him in his encounter with difficulty, and, what was of still more practical value at the time, helped him with money to enable him to prosecute his invention. Communicative though Watt was disposed to be, he learnt reticence when he found himself exposed to the depredations of the smaller fry of inventors. Robison says that had he lived in Birmingham or London at the time, the probability is that some one or other of the numerous harpies who live by sucking other people's brains would have secured patents for his more important inventions, and thereby deprived him of the benefits of his skill, science, and labor. As yet, however, there were but few mechanics in Glasgow capable of understanding or appreciating the steam-engine ; and the intimate friends to whom he freely spoke of his discovery were too honorable to take advantage of his confidence. Shortly after Watt communicated to Robison the different stages of his invention, and the results at which he had arrived, much to the delight of his friend.

It will be remembered that in the Newcomen engine the steam was only employed for the purpose of producing a vacuum, and that its working power was in the down stroke, which was effected by the pressure of the air upon the piston ; hence it is now usual to call it the atmospheric engine. Watt perceived that the air which followed the piston down the cylinder would cool the latter, and that steam would be wasted by reheating it. In order, therefore, to avoid this loss of heat, he resolved to put an air-tight cover upon the cylinder, with a hole and stuffing-box for the piston-rod to slide through, and to admit steam above the piston, to act upon it instead of the atmosphere. When the steam had done its duty in driving down the piston, a communication was opened between the upper and lower part of the cylinder ; and the same steam, distributing itself equally in both compartments, sufficed to restore equilibrium. The piston was now drawn up by the weight of the pump-gear ; the steam beneath it was then condensed in the separate vessel so as to produce a vacuum, and a fresh jet of steam from the boiler was let in above the piston, which forced it again to the bottom of the cylinder. From an atmospheric engine it had thus become a true steam-engine, and with much greater economy of steam than when the air did half the duty. But it was not only important to keep the air from flowing down the inside of the cylinder; the air which circulated within cooled the metal and condensed a portion of the steam within; and this Watt proposed to remedy by a second cylinder, surrounding the first, with an interval between the two which was to be kept full of steam.

One by one these various contrivances were struck out, modified, settled, and reduced to definite plans, — the separate condenser, the air and water pumps, the use of fat and oil (instead of water, as in the Newcomen engine) to keep the piston working in the cylinder air-tight, and the enclosing of the cylinder itself within another to prevent the loss of heat. These were all emanations from the first idea of inventing an engine working by a piston, in which the cylinder should be continually hot and perfectly dry. "When once," says Watt, "the idea of separate condensation was started, all these improvements followed as corollaries in quick succession, so that in the course of one or two days the invention was thus far complete in my mind."

WATT MAKES HIS MODEL.

The next step was to construct a model engine for the purpose of embodying the invention in a working form. With this object, Watt hired an old cellar, situated in the first wide entry to the north of the beef-market in King Street, and then proceeded with his model. He found it much easier, however, to prepare his plan than to execute it. Like most ingenious and inventive men, Watt was extremely fastidious; and this occasioned considerable delay in the execution of the work. His very inventiveness to some extent proved a hindrance; for new expedients were perpetually occurring to him, which he thought would be improvements, and which he, by turns, endeavored to introduce. Some of these expedients he admits proved fruitless, and all of them occasioned delay. Another of his chief difficulties was in finding competent workmen to execute his plans. He himself had been accustomed only to small metal work, with comparatively delicate tools, and had very little experience " in the practice of mechanics *in great*," as he termed it. He was therefore under the necessity of depending, in a great measure, upon the handiwork of others. But mechanics capable of working out Watt's designs in metal were then with difficulty to be found. The beautiful self-action and workmanship which have since been called into being, principally by his own invention, did not then exist. The only available hands in Glasgow were the blacksmiths and tinners, little capable of constructing articles out of their ordinary walks; and even in these they were often found clumsy, blundering, and incompetent. The result was, that in consequence of the malconstruction of the larger parts, Watt's first model was only partially successful. The experiments made with it, however, served to verify the expectations he had formed, and to place the advantages of the invention beyond the reach of doubt. On the exhausting-cock being turned, the piston, when loaded with eighteen pounds, ascended as quickly as the blow of a hammer; and the moment the steam-cock was opened, it descended with like rapidity, though the steam was weak, and the machine snifted at many openings.

Satisfied that he had laid hold of the right principle of a working steam-engine, Watt felt impelled to follow it to an issue. He could give his mind to no other business in peace until this was done. He wrote to a friend that he was quite barren on every other subject. "My whole thoughts," said he, "are bent on this machine. I can think of nothing else." He proceeded to make another and bigger, and, he hoped, a more satisfactory engine in the following August; and with that object he removed from the old cellar in King Street to a larger apartment in the then disused pottery, or delftwork, near the Broomielaw. There he shut himself up with his assistant, John Gardiner, for the purpose of erecting his engine. The cylinder was five or six inches in diameter, with a two-feet stroke. The inner cylinder was enclosed in a wooden steam-case, and placed inverted, the piston working through a hole in the bottom of the steam-case. After two months continuous application and labor it was finished and set to work; but it leaked in all directions, and the piston was far from air-tight. The condenser also was in a bad way, and needed many alterations. Nevertheless, the engine readily worked with ten and a half pounds pressure on the inch, and the piston lifted a weight of fourteen pounds. The improvement of the cylinder and piston continued Watt's chief difficulty, and taxed his ingenuity to the utmost. At so low an ebb was the art of making cylinders that the one he used was not bored, but hammered, the collective mechanical skill of Glasgow being then unequal to the boring of a cylinder of the simplest kind; nor, indeed, did the necessary appliances for the purpose then exist anywhere else. In the Newcomen engine a little water was found upon the upper surface of the piston, and sufficiently filled up the interstices between the piston and the cylinder. But when Watt employed steam to drive down the piston, he was deprived of this resource, for the water and steam could not coexist. Even if he had retained the agency of the air above, the drip of water from the crevices into the lower part of the cylinder would have been incompatible with keeping the cylinder hot and dry, and, by turning into vapor as it fell upon the heated metal, it would have impaired the vacuum during the descent of the piston.

While he was occupied with this difficulty, and striving to overcome it by the adoption of new expedients, such as leather collars and improved workmanship, he wrote to a friend, " My old white-iron man is dead ; " the old white-iron man, or tinner, being his leading mechanic. Unhappily, also, just as he seemed to have got the engine into working order, the beam broke, and, having great difficulty in replacing the damaged part, the accident threatened, together with the loss of his best workman, to bring the experiment to an end. Though discouraged by these misadventures, he was far from defeated. But he went on as before, battling down difficulty inch by inch, and holding good the ground he had won, becoming every day more strongly convinced that he was in the right track, and that the important uses of the invention, could he but find time and means to perfect it, were beyond the reach of doubt. But how to find the means ! Watt himself was a comparatively poor man ; having no money but what he earned by his business of mechanical-instrument making, which he had for some time been neglecting through his devotion to the construction of his engine. What he wanted was capital, or the help of a capitalist willing to advance him the necessary funds to perfect his invention. To give a fair trial to the new apparatus would involve an expenditure of several thousand pounds; and who on the spot could be expected to invest so large a sum in trying a machine so entirely new, depending for its success on physical principles very imperfectly understood?

There was no such help to be found in Glasgow. The tobacco lords,[1] though rich, took no interest in steam power; and the manufacturing class, though growing in importance, had full employment for their little capital in their own concerns.

"How Watt succeeded in interesting Dr. Roebuck in his project, and thus obtained funds to continue his experiments; how he finally joined with Matthew Boulton in the great firm of Boulton and Watt, manufacturers of steam-engines; how they pumped out all the water in the Cornish mines; and how Watt finally attained prosperity as well as success, — is an interesting story, but rather too long for these winter afternoons; and as the story of the *invention* of the steam-engine is substantially told in the foregoing pages, we must stop our reading here, more especially as it seems to be tea-time, and I hear Ellen ringing the bell for supper."

[1] The principal men of Glasgow were the importers of tobacco from Virginia.

IX.

ROBERT FULTON.

THEY were to continue their talk and reading by following along the developments in the use of steam.

"Uncle Fritz," said Fanchon, "these agnostics make so much fun of our dear Harry and Lucy, that they will not let me quote from 'The Botanic Garden.'"

Emma promised that they would laugh as little as they could.

" 'The Botanic Garden,' " said Fanchon, "was a stately, and I am afraid some of you would say very pompous, poem, written by Dr. Darwin."

"Dr. Darwin write poetry!"

"It is not the Dr. Charles Darwin whom you have heard of; it was his grandfather," said Uncle Fritz.

And Fanchon went on: "All I ever knew of 'The Botanic Garden' was in the quotations of our dear Harry and Lucy and Frank. But dear Uncle Fritz has taken down the book for me, and here it is, with its funny old pictures of Ladies' Slippers and such things."

"I do not see what Ladies' Slippers have to do with steam-engines," said Bedford Long, scornfully.

"No!" said Fanchon, laughing; "but I do, and that is the difference between you and me. Because, you see, I have read 'Harry and Lucy,' and you have not." And

she opened "The Botanic Garden" at the place where
she had put in a mark, and read : —

> " Pressed by the ponderous air, the piston falls
> Resistless, sliding through its iron walls ;
> Quick moves the balance beam of giant birth,
> Wields its large limbs, and nodding shakes the earth.
> The giant power, from earth's remotest caves
> Lifts, with strong arm, her dark reluctant waves,
> Each caverned rock and hidden depth explores,
> Drags her dark coals, and digs her shining ores."

"That is rather stilted poetry," said Uncle Fritz, "but a
hundred years ago people were used to stilted poetry.   It
describes sufficiently well the original pumping-engine of
Watt, and the lifting of coal from the shafts of the deep
English mines.   Now, it was not till Watt had made his
improvements on the pumping-engine, — say in 1788, —
that it was possible to go any farther in the use of steam
than its application to such absolutely stationary purposes.
It is therefore, I think, a good deal to the credit of Dr.
Darwin, that within three years after Watt's great improvement in the condensing-engine the Doctor should have
written this : —

> 'Soon shall thy arm, unconquered steam, afar
> Drag the slow barge or drive the rapid car.'

It was twelve years after he wrote this, that Fulton had
an experimental steamboat on the river Seine in France.
It was sixteen years after, that, with one of Watt's own
engines, Fulton drove the 'Clermont' from New York to
Albany in thirty-six hours, and revolutionized the world in
doing it.

"Poor James Mackintosh was in virtual exile in Calcutta
at that time, and he wrote this in his journal: 'A boat

propelled by steam has gone a hundred and fifty miles upon the Hudson in thirty-six hours. Four miles an hour would bring Calcutta within a hundred days of London. Oh that we had lived a hundred years later!' In less than fifty years after Mackintosh wrote those words, Calcutta was within thirty days of London.

"When Harry and Lucy read these verses in 1825, the 'rapid car' was still in the future."

"Yes," said Fanchon; "but Harry says, 'The rapid car is to come, and I dare say that will be accomplished soon, papa; do not you think it will?'"

"I have sometimes wondered," said Uncle Fritz, "whether our American word 'car' where the English say 'wagon' did not come from the 'rapid car' of Dr. Darwin. Read on, Fanchon." And he put his finger on the lines which Fanchon read : —

> "Or on wide waving wings, expanded, bear
> The flying chariot through the fields of air."

"Monsieur ——, the French gentleman, tried a light steam-engine for the propulsion of a balloon in 1872 ; but it does not seem to have had power enough. Messrs. Renard and Krebs, in their successful flight of August last, used an electric battery.

"But we are getting away from Fulton, who is really the first who drove the 'slow barge,' and indeed made it a very fast one."

"Did you know him?" asked Emma Fortinbras, whose ideas of chronology are very vague.

"Oh, no!" said Uncle Fritz; "he died young and before my time. But I did know a personal companion and friend, nay, a bedfellow of his, Benjamin Church, who was with him in Paris at one of the crises of his life. Fulton had a little steamboat on the river Seine, as I said just now; and he had made interest with Napoleon to have it examined by a scientific committee. Steam power was exactly what Napoleon wanted, to take his great army across from Boulogne to England. The day came for the great experiment. Church and Fulton slept, the night before, in the same bed in their humble lodgings in Paris. At daybreak a messenger waked them. He had come from the river to say that the weight of boiler and machinery had been too much for the little boat, that her timbers had given way, and that the whole had sunk to the bottom of the river. But for this misfortune, the successful steamboat would have sailed upon the Seine, and, for aught I know, Napoleon's grandchildren would now be emperors of England."

Until Watt had completed the structure of the double-acting condensing-engine, the application of steam to any but the single object of pumping water had been almost impracticable. It was not enough, in order to render it applicable to general purposes, that the condensation of the water should take place in a separate vessel, and that steam itself should be used, instead of atmospheric pressure, as the moving power; but it was also necessary that the steam should act as well during the ascent as during the descent of the piston. Before steam could be used in moving paddle-wheels, it was in addition necessary that a ready and convenient mode of making the motion of the piston continuous and rotary, should be discovered. All these improvements upon the original form of the steam-engine are due to Watt, and he did not complete their perfect combination before the year 1786.

Evans, who, in this country, saw the possibility of constructing a double-acting engine, even before Watt, and had made a model of his machine, did not succeed in obtaining funds to make an experiment upon a large scale before 1801. We conceive, therefore, that all those who projected the application of steam to vessels before 1786, may be excluded, without ceremony, from the list of those entitled to compete with Fulton for the honors of invention. No one, indeed, could have seen the powerful action of a pumping-engine without being convinced that the energy which was applied so successfully to that single purpose, might be made applicable to many others ; but those who entertained a belief that the original atmospheric engine, or even the single-acting engine of Watt, could be applied to propel boats by paddle-wheels, showed a total ignorance of mechanical principles. This is more particularly the case with all those whose projects bore the strongest resemblance to the plan which Fulton afterwards carried successfully into effect. Those who approached most nearly to the attainment of success, were they who were farthest removed from the plan of Fulton. His application was founded on the properties of Watt's double-acting engine, and could not have been used at all, until that instrument of universal application had received the last finish of its inventor.

In this list of failures, from proposing to do what the instrument they employed was incapable of performing, we do not hesitate to include Savery, Papin, Jonathan Hulls, Périer, the Marquis de Jouffroy, and all the other names of earlier date than 1786, whom the jealousy of the French and English nations have drawn from oblivion for the purpose of contesting the priority of Fulton's claims. The only competitor, whom they might have brought forward with some shadow of plausibility, is Watt himself. No sooner had that illustrious inventor completed his double-acting engine, than he saw at a glance the vast field of its application. Navigation and locomotion were not omitted; but living in an inland town, and in a country possessing no rivers of importance, his views were limited to canals alone. In this direction he saw an immediate objection to the use of any apparatus, of which so powerful an agent as his engine should be the mover; for it was clear, that the injury which would be done to the banks of the canal, would prevent the possibility of its introduction. Watt, therefore, after having conceived the idea of a steamboat, laid it aside, as unlikely to be of any practical value.

The idea of applying steam to navigation was not confined to Europe. Numerous Americans entertained hopes of attaining the same object, but, before 1786, with the same want of any reasonable hopes of success. Their fruitless projects were, however, rebuked by Franklin, who, reasoning upon the capabilities of the engine in its original form, did not hesitate to declare all their schemes impracticable; and the correctness of his judgment is at present unquestionable.

Among those who, before the completion of Watt's invention, attempted the structure of steamboats, must be named with praise Fitch and Rumsey. They, unlike those whose names have been cited, were well aware of the real difficulties which they were to overcome; and both were the authors of plans which, if the engine had been incapable of further improvement, might have had a partial and limited success. Fitch's trial was made in 1783, and Rumsey's in 1787. The latter date is subsequent to Watt's double-acting engine; but as the project consisted merely in pumping in water, to be afterwards forced out at the stern, the single-acting engine was probably employed. Evans, whose engine might have answered the purpose, was employed in the daily business of millwright; and although he might, at any time, have driven these competitors from the field, he took no steps to apply his dormant invention.

Fitch, who had watched the graceful and rapid way of the Indian canoe, saw in the oscillating motion of the old pumping-engine the means of impelling paddles in a manner similar to that given them by the human arm. This idea is extremely ingenious, and was applied in a simple and beautiful manner. But the engine was yet too feeble and cumbrous to yield an adequate force; and when it received its great improvement from Watt, a more efficient mode of propulsion had become practicable, and must have superseded Fitch's paddles had they even come into general use.

The experiments of Fitch and Rumsey in the United States, although generally considered unsuccessful, did not deter others from similar attempts. The great rivers and arms of the sea which intersect the Atlantic coast, and, still more, the innumerable navigable arms of the Father of Waters, appeared to call upon the ingenious machinist to contrive means for their more convenient navigation.

The improvement of the engine by Watt was now familiarly known; and it was evident that it possessed sufficient powers for the purpose. The only difficulty which existed, was in the mode of applying it. The first person who entered into the inquiry was John Stevens, of Hokoken, who commenced his researches in 1791. In these he was steadily engaged for nine years, when he became the associate of Chancellor Livingston and Nicholas Roosevelt. Among the persons employed by this association was Brunel, who has since become distinguished in Europe as the inventor of the block machinery used in the British navy-yards, and as the engineer of the tunnel beneath the Thames.

Even with the aid of such talent, the efforts of this association were unsuccessful, — as we now know, from no error in principle, but from defects in the boat to which it was applied. The appointment of Livingston as ambassador to France broke up this joint effort; and, like all previous schemes, it was considered abortive, and contributed to throw discredit upon all undertakings of the kind. A grant of exclusive privileges on the waters of the State of New York was made to this association without any difficulty, it being believed that the scheme was little short of madness.

Livingston, on his arrival in France, found Fulton domiciliated with Joel Barlow. The conformity in their pursuits led to intimacy, and Fulton speedily communicated to Livingston the scheme[1] which he had laid before Earl Stanhope in 1793. Livingston was so well pleased with it that he at once offered to provide the funds necessary for an experiment, and to enter into a contract for Fulton's aid in introducing the method into the United States, provided the experiment were successful.

Fulton had, in his early discussion with Lord Stanhope, repudiated the idea of an apparatus acting on the principle of the foot of an aquatic bird, and had proposed paddle-wheels in its stead. On resuming his inquiries after his arrangements with Livingston, it occurred to him to compose wheels with a set of paddles revolving upon an

---

[1] Earl Stanhope, among other projects, had conceived "the hope of being able to apply the steam-engine to navigation by the aid of a peculiar apparatus modelled after the foot of an aquatic fowl." Fulton, on being consulted by the Earl, doubted the feasibility, and suggested the very means which he afterward made successful upon the Hudson.

endless chain extending from the stem to the stern of the boat. It is probable that the apparent want of success which had attended the experiments of Symington [1] led him to doubt the correctness of his original views.

That such doubt should be entirely removed, he had recourse to a series of experiments upon a small scale. These were performed at Plombières, a French watering-place, where he spent the summer of 1802. In these experiments the superiority of the paddle-wheel over every other method of propulsion that had yet been proposed, was fully established. His original impressions being thus confirmed, he proceeded, late in the year 1803, to construct a working model of his intended boat, which model was deposited with a commission of French *savans*. He at the same time began building a vessel sixty-six feet in length and eight feet in width. To this an engine was adapted; and the experiment made with it was so satisfactory, as to leave little doubt of final success.

Measures were therefore immediately taken, preparatory to constructing a steamboat on a larger scale in the United States. For this purpose, as the workshops of neither France nor America could at that time furnish an engine of good quality, it became necessary to resort to England for that purpose. Fulton had already experienced the difficulty of being compelled to employ artists unacquainted with the subject. It is, indeed, more than probable, that, had he not, during his residence in Birmingham, made himself familiar, not only with the general features, but with the most minute details of the engine of Watt, the experiment on the Seine could not have been

---

1 Symington was an engineer who had been carrying out some experiments of Miller of Dalswinton in regard to the practicability of steam navigation.

made.   In this experiment, and in the previous investigations, it became obvious that the engine of Watt required
important modifications in order to adapt it to navigation.
These modifications had been planned by Fulton ; but it
now became important, that they should be more fully
tested.   An engine was therefore ordered from Watt and
Boulton, without any specification of the object to which it
was to be applied ; and its form was directed to be varied
from their usual models, in conformity to sketches furnished
by Fulton.

The order for an engine intended to propel a vessel of
large size, was transmitted to Watt and Boulton in 1803.
At about the same time, Chancellor Livingston, having
full confidence in the success of the enterprise, caused an
application to be made to the legislature of New York for
an exclusive privilege of navigating the waters of that
State by steam, that which was granted on a former occasion having expired.

This privilege was granted with little opposition.   Indeed, those who might have been inclined to object, saw
so much of the impracticable and even of the ridiculous in
the project, that they conceived the application unworthy
of serious debate.   The condition attached to the grant
was, that a vessel should be propelled by steam at the rate
of four miles an hour, within a prescribed space of time.
This reliance upon the reserved rights of the States proved
a fruitful source of vexation to Livingston and Fulton, and
imbittered the close of the life of the latter, and reduced
his family to penury.   It can hardly be doubted that, had
an expectation been entertained, that the grant of a State
was ineffectual, and that the jurisdiction was vested in the
general government, a similar grant might have been obtained from Congress.   The influence of Livingston with

the administration was deservedly high, and that administration was supported by a powerful majority ; nor would it have been consistent with the principles of the opposition to vote against any act of liberality to the introducer of a valuable application of science. Livingston, however, confiding in his skill as a lawyer, preferred the application to the State, and was thus, by his own act, restricted to a limited field.

Before the engine ordered from Watt and Boulton was completed, Fulton visited England, and thus had an opportunity of visiting Birmingham, and directing, in person, its construction. It could only have been at this time, if ever, that he saw the boat of Symington ; [1] but a view of it could have produced no effect upon his own plans, which had been matured in France, and carried, so far as the engine was concerned, to such an extent as to admit of no alteration.

The engine was at last completed, and reached New York in 1806. Fulton, who returned to his native country about the same period, immediately undertook the construction of a boat in which to place it. In ordering his engine and in planning the boat, Fulton exhibited plainly how far his scientific researches and practical experiments had placed him before all his competitors. He had evidently ascertained, what each successive year's experience proves more fully, the great advantages possessed by large steamboats over those of smaller size ; and thus, while all previous attempts had been made in smaller vessels, he alone resolved to make his final experiment in one of great dimensions. That a vessel,

---

[1] Who subsequently made charge that Fulton, having seen his steamboat and made copious notes thereon, had thus been able to make his boat upon the Hudson.

intended to be propelled by steam, ought to have very different proportions, and lines of a character wholly distinct from those of vessels intended to be navigated by sails, was evident to him. No other theory, however, of the resistance of fluids was admitted at the time than that of Bossut, and there were no published experiments except those of the British Society of Arts. Judged in reference to these, the model chosen by Fulton was faultless, although it will not stand the test of an examination founded upon a better theory and more accurate experiments.

The vessel was finished and fitted with her machinery in August, 1807. An experimental excursion was forthwith made, at which a number of gentlemen of science and intelligence were present. Many of these were either sceptical or absolute unbelievers. But a few minutes served to convert the whole party, and satisfy the most obstinate doubters, that the long-desired object was at last accomplished. Only a few weeks before, the cost of constructing and finishing the vessel threatening to exceed the funds with which he had been provided by Livingston, Fulton had attempted to obtain a supply by the sale of one third of the exclusive right granted by the State of New York. No person was found possessed of the faith requisite to induce him to embark in the project. Those who had rejected this opportunity of investment, were now the witnesses of the completion of the scheme, which they had considered as an inadequate security for the desired funds.

Within a few days from the time of the first experiment with the steamboat, a voyage was undertaken in it to Albany. This city, situated at the natural head of the navigation of the Hudson, is distant, by the line of the channel of the river, rather less than one hundred and fifty miles from New York. By the old post-road, the distance is one hundred and sixty miles, at which that by water is usually estimated. Although the greater part of the channel of the Hudson is both deep and wide, yet for about fourteen miles below Albany this character is not preserved, and the stream, confined within comparatively small limits, is obstructed by bars of sand or spreads itself over shallows. In a few remarkable instances, the sloops, which then exclusively navigated the Hudson, had effected a passage in about sixteen hours; but a whole week was not unfrequently employed in the voyage, and the average time of passage was not less than four entire days. In Fulton's first attempt to navigate this stream, the passage to Albany was performed in thirty-two hours, and the return in thirty.

Up to this time, although the exclusive grant had been sought and obtained from the State of New York, it does not appear that either he or his associate had been fully aware of the vast opening which the navigation of the Hudson presented for the use of steam. They looked to the rapid Mississippi and its branches, as the place where their triumph was to be achieved; and the original boat, modelled for shallow waters, was announced as intended for the navigation of that river. But even in the very first attempt, numbers, called by business or pleasure to the northern or western parts of the State of New York, crowded into the yet untried vessel; and when the success of the attempt was beyond question, no little anxiety was manifested, that the steamboat should be established as a regular packet between New York and Albany.

With these indications of public feeling Fulton immediately complied, and regular voyages were made at stated times until the end of the season. These voyages were not, however, unattended with inconvenience. The boat, designed for a mere experiment, was incommodious; and many of the minor arrangements by which facility of working and safety from accident to the machinery were to be insured, were yet wanting. Fulton continued a close and attentive observer of the performance of the vessel; every difficulty, as it manifested itself, was met and removed by the most masterly as well as simple contrivances. Some of these were at once adopted, while others remained to be applied while the boat should be laid up for the winter. He thus gradually formed in his mind the idea of a complete and perfect vessel; and in his plan, no one part which has since been found to be essential to the ease of manœuvre or security, was omitted. But the eyes of the whole community were now fixed upon the steamboat; and as all those of competent mechanical knowledge were, like Fulton himself, alive to the defects of the original vessel, his right to priority of invention of various important accessories has been disputed.

The winter of 1807–8 was occupied in remodelling and rebuilding the vessel, to which the name "Clermont" was now given. The guards and housings for the wheels, which had been but temporary structures, applied as their value was pointed out by experience, became solid and essential parts of the boat. For a rudder of the ordinary form, one of surface much more extended in its horizontal dimensions was substituted. This, instead of being moved by a tiller, was acted upon by ropes applied to its extremity; and these ropes were adapted to a steering-wheel, which was raised aloft towards the bow of the vessel.

It had been shown by the numbers who were transported during the first summer, that at the same price for passage, many were willing to undergo all the inconveniences of the original rude accommodations, in preference to encountering the delays and uncertainty to which the passage in sloops was exposed. Fulton did not, however, take advantage of his monopoly, but with the most liberal spirit, provided such accommodations for passengers, as in convenience and even splendor, had not before been approached in vessels intended for the transportation of travellers. This was, on his part, an exercise of almost improvident liberality. By his contract with Chancellor Livingston, the latter undertook to defray the whole cost of the engine and vessel, until the experiment should result in success; but from that hour each was to furnish an equal share of all investments. Fulton had no patrimonial fortune, and what little he had saved from the product of his ingenuity was now exhausted. But the success of the experiment had inspired the banks and capitalists with confidence, and he now found no difficulty in obtaining, in the way of loan, all that was needed. Still, however, a debt was thus contracted which the continued demands made upon him for new investments never permitted him to discharge. The "Clermont," thus converted into a floating palace, gay with ornamental painting, gilding, and polished woods, began her course of passages for the second year in the month of April.

The first voyage of this year was of the most discouraging character. Chancellor Livingston, who had, by his own experiments, approached as near to success as any other person who, before Fulton, had endeavored to navigate by steam, and who had furnished all the capital necessary for the experiment, had plans and projects of his own. These he urged into execution in spite of the opposition of Fulton. The boiler furnished by Watt and Boulton was not adapted to the object. Copied from those used on the land, it required that its fireplace and flues should be constructed of masonry. These added so much weight to the apparatus, that the rebuilt boat would hardly have floated had they been retained. In order to replace this boiler, Livingston had planned a compound structure of wood and copper, which he insisted should be tried.

It is only necessary for us to say, that this boiler proved a complete failure. Steam began to issue from its joints a few hours after the " Clermont " left New York. It then became impossible to keep up a proper degree of tension, and the passage was thus prolonged to forty-eight hours. These defects increased after leaving Albany on the return, and the boiler finally gave way altogether within a few miles of New York. The time of the downward passage was thus extended to fifty-six hours. Fulton was, however, thus relieved from all further interference ; this fruitless experiment was decisive as to his superiority over his colleague in mechanical skill. He therefore immediately planned and directed the execution of a new boiler, which answered the purpose perfectly ; and although there are many reasons why boilers of a totally different form and of subsequent invention should be preferred, it is, for its many good properties, extensively used, with little alteration, up to the present day. But a few weeks sufficed to build and set this boiler, and in the month of June the regular passages of the " Clermont " were renewed.

In observing the hour appointed for departure, both from New York and Albany, Fulton determined to insist upon the utmost regularity. It required no little perseverance and resolution to carry this system of punctuality into effect.   Persons accustomed to be waited for by packet-boats and stages, assented with great reluctance to what they conceived to be a useless adherence to precision of time.   The benefits of this punctuality were speedily perceptible ; the whole system of internal communication of the State of New York was soon regulated by the hours of arrival and departure of Fulton's steamboats ; and the same system of precision was copied in all other steamboat lines.   The certainty of conveyance at stated times being thus secured, the number of travellers was instantly augmented ; and before the end of the second summer, the boat became far too small for the passengers, who crowded to avail themselves of this novel, punctual, and unprecedentedly rapid method of transport.

Such success, however, was not without its alloy.   The citizens of Albany and the river towns saw, as they thought, in the steamboat, the means of enticing their customers from their ancient marts to the more extensive market of the chief city ; the skippers of the river mourned the inevitable loss of a valuable part of their business ; and innumerable projectors beheld with envy the successful enterprise of Fulton.

Among the latter class was one who, misled by false notions of mechanical principles, fancied that in the mere oscillations of a pendulum lay a power sufficient for any purpose whatever.   Availing himself of a well-constructed model, he exhibited to the inhabitants of Albany a pendulum which continued its motions for a considerable time, without requiring any new impulse, and at the same time propelled a pair of wheels.   These wheels, however, did not work in water.   Those persons who felt themselves aggrieved by the introduction of steamboats, quickly embraced this project, prompted by an enmity to Fulton, and determined, if they could not defeat his object, at least to share in the profits of its success.

It soon appeared, from preliminary experiments, made in a sloop purchased for the purpose, that a steam-engine would be required to give motion to the pendulum ; and it was observed that the water-wheels, when in connection with the pendulum, had a very irregular motion. A fly-wheel was therefore added, and the pendulum was now found to be a useless incumbrance. Enlightened by these experiments, the association proceeded to build two boats ; and these were exact copies, not only of the hull and all the accessories of the " Clermont," but the engine turned out to be identical in form and structure with one which Fulton was at the very time engaged in fitting to his second boat, " The Car of Neptune."

The pretence of bringing into use a new description of prime mover was of course necessarily abandoned, and the owners of the new steamboats determined boldly to test the constitutionality of the exclusive grant to Fulton. Fulton and Livingston, in consequence, applied to the Court of Chancery of the State of New York for an injunction, which was refused. On an appeal to the Court of Errors this decision of the Chancellor was reversed ; but the whole of the profits which might have been derived from the business of the year were prevented from accruing to Livingston and Fulton, who, compelled to contend in price with an opposition supported by popular feeling in Albany, were losers rather than gainers by the operations of the season.

As no appeal was taken from this last decision, the waters of the State of New York remained in the exclusive possession of Fulton and his partner, until the death of the former. This exclusive possession was not, however, attended with all the advantages that might have been anticipated. The immense increase of travel which the facilities of communication created, rendered it imperative upon the holders of the monopoly to provide new facilities by the construction of new vessels. The cost of these could not be defrayed out of the profits. Hence new and heavy debts were necessarily contracted by Fulton, while Livingston, possessed of an ample fortune, required no pecuniary aid beyond what he was able to meet from his own resources.

The most formidable opposition which was made to the privileges of Fulton, was founded upon the discoveries of Fitch. We have seen, that he constructed a boat which made some passages between Trenton and Philadelphia ; but the method which he used, was that of paddles, which are far inferior to the paddle-wheel. Of the inferiority of the method of paddles, had any doubt remained, positive evidence was afforded in the progress of this dispute ; for in order to bring the question to the test of a legal decision, a boat propelled by them was brought into the waters of the State of New York. The result of the experiment was so decisive, that when the parties engaged in the enterprise had succeeded in their designs, they made no attempt to propel their boats by any other method than that of wheels.

Fulton, assailed in his exclusive privileges derived from State grants, took, for his further protection, a patent from the general government. This is dated in 1809, and was followed by another, for improvements upon it, in 1811. It now appeared, that the very circumstance in which the greatest merit of his method consists, was to be the obstacle to his maintaining an exclusive privilege. Discarding all complexity, he had limited himself to the simple means of adapting paddle-wheels to the crank of Watt's engine ; and, under the patent laws, it seems hardly possible that such a simple yet effectual method could be guarded by a specification. As has been the case with many other important discoveries, the most ignorant conceived that they might themselves have discovered it ; and those unacquainted with the history of the attempts at navigation by steam, were compelled to wonder that it had been left for Fulton to bring it into successful operation.

Before the death of Fulton, the steamboats on the Hudson River were increased in number to five. A sixth was built under his direction for the navigation of the Sound ; and, this water being rendered unsafe by the presence of an enemy's[1] squadron, the boat plied for a time upon the Hudson. In the construction of this boat he had, in his own opinion, exhausted the power of steam in navigation, having given it a speed of nine miles an hour ; and it is a remarkable fact, which manifests his acquaintance with theory and skill in calculation, that he in all cases predicted with almost absolute accuracy, the velocity of the vessels he caused to be constructed. The engineers of Great Britain came, long after, to a similar conclusion in respect to the maximum of speed.

It is now, however, well known, that, with a proper construction of prows, the resistance to vessels moving at higher velocities than nine miles an hour, increases in a much less ratio than had been inferred from experiments made upon wedge-shaped bodies ; and that the velocity of the pistons of steam-engines may be conveniently increased beyond the limit fixed by the practice of Watt.

For these important discoveries the world is indebted

---

[1] This was in the course of the War of 1812.

principally to Robert L. Stevens.   That Fulton must have reached them in the course of his own practice can hardly be doubted, had his valuable life been spared to watch the performance of the vessels he was engaged in building at the time of his premature death.[1]   These were, a large boat intended for the navigation of the Hudson, to which the name of his partner, Chancellor Livingston, was given, and one planned for the navigation of the ocean.   The latter was constructed with the intention of making a passage to St. Petersburg ; but this scheme was interrupted by his death, which took place at the moment he was about to add to his glory, as the first constructor of a successful steamboat, that of being the first navigator of the ocean by this new and mighty agent.

[1] Fulton died Feb. 24, 1815 ; he was born in 1765.

X.

GEORGE STEPHENSON AND THE LOCO-MOTIVE.

"WHAT I say is this," said Nahum, "that all your Vesuvius dividends, and all your pickers and slobbers, and shirtings at four cents, and all the rest of your great cotton victory, depend on railroads. If your father could not go to Lewiston and see his foreman and people, and come back before you can say Jack Robinson, there would be no mills at Lewiston such as there are. There might be a poor little sawmill making shingles, as you free-traders want." This with scorn at Fergus, perhaps, or some one else suspected of views unfavorable to protection.

Then Nahum shook hands with Uncle Fritz, and apologized for his zeal, adding: "I am telling the boys why I want to go to Altoona, and to become a railroad man. I say that the new plant in India might knock cotton higher than a kite, and that people might learn to live without novels or magazines, but that they must have transportation all the same. And I am going into the railroad business. I am going to hew down the mountains and fill up the valleys." The boy was fairly eloquent in his enthusiasm.

"It is in your blood, my brave fellow," said Uncle Fritz. "People thought your grandfather was crazy when he said it, sixty years ago. But it proved he was the seer and the prophet, and they were the fools."

"And who invented railroads?" asked Blanche.

"As to that, the man invented a railroad who first put two boards down over two ruts to make a cart run easier. Almost as soon as there were mines, there must have been some sort of rail for the use of the wagons which brought out the ore. These rails became so useful that they were continued from the mine to the high-road, whatever it was. But it was not till the first quarter of this century, that rails were laid for general use. The earliest railroad in the United States was laid at the quarries in Quincy, in Massachusetts, in 1825."

Uncle Fritz was so well pleased at their eagerness that he brought out for them some of the old books, and some of the new. In especial he bade them all read Smiles's "Life of Stephenson" before they came to him again. For to George Stephenson, as they soon learned, more than to any one man, the world owes the step forward which it made when locomotives were generally used on railroads. Since that time the improvements in both have gone on together.

Before they met again, at Uncle Fritz's suggestion, Fergus and Hester prepared this sketch of the details of Stephenson's earlier invention, purposely that Uncle Fritz might use it when these papers should be printed together.

GEORGE STEPHENSON.

An efficient and economical working locomotive engine still remained to be invented, and to accomplish this object Stephenson now applied himself. Profiting by what his predecessors had done, — warned by their failures and encouraged by their partial successes, — he began his labors. There was still wanting the man who should accomplish for the locomotive what James Watt had done for the steam-engine, and combine in a complete form the best points in the separate plans of others, embodying with them such original inventions and adaptations of his own, as to entitle him to the merit of inventing the working locomotive, as James Watt is to be regarded as the inventor of the working condensing-engine.. This was the great work upon which George Stephenson now entered, though probably without any adequate idea of the ultimate importance of his work to society and civilization.

He proceeded to bring the subject of constructing a "Travelling Engine," as he denominated the locomotive, under the notice of the lessees of the Killingworth Colliery,[1] in the year 1813. Lord Ravensworth, the principal partner, had already formed a very favorable opinion of the new colliery engine-wright from the improvements which he had effected in the colliery engines, both above and below ground; and after considering the matter, and hearing Stephenson's explanations, he authorized him to proceed with the construction of a locomotive, though his lordship was by some called a fool for advancing money for such a purpose. " The first locomotive that I made," said Stephenson, many years after, when speaking of his early career at a public meeting in Newcastle, "was at Kil-

---

[1] Killingworth is a town some seven or eight miles north of Newcastle, in Northumberland. George Stephenson was at this time the engine-wright of the colliery. It may be said here that the principal use for which the early locomotive engines and railroads were designed was to convey coal from the pit to a market. It was not till the success of the mining and quarrying railways led to the building of the Liverpool and Manchester Road, between two great cities, that the value of the railroad for the transfer of passengers was recognized.

lingworth Colliery, and with Lord Ravensworth's money. Yes, Lord Ravensworth and partners were the first to intrust me, thirty-two years since, with money to make a locomotive engine. I said to my friends, there was no limit to the speed of such an engine, if the works could be made to stand."

Our engine-wright had, however, many obstacles to encounter before he could get fairly to work upon the erection of his locomotive. His chief difficulty was in finding workmen sufficiently skilled in mechanics and in the use of tools to follow his instructions, and embody his designs in a practical shape. The tools then in use about the colliery were rude and clumsy, and there were no such facilities, as now exist, for turning out machinery of any entirely new character. Stephenson was under the necessity of working with such men and tools as were at his command, and he had in a great measure to train and instruct the workmen himself. The new engine was built in the workshops at the West Morr, the leading mechanic being John Thirlwall, the colliery blacksmith, — an excellent mechanic in his way, though quite new to the work now intrusted to him.

In this first locomotive, constructed at Killingworth, Stephenson to some extent followed the plan of Blenkinsop's engine. The wrought-iron boiler was cylindrical, eight feet in length and thirty-four inches in diameter, with an internal flue-tube twenty inches wide passing through it. The engine had two vertical cylinders, of eight inches diameter and two feet stroke, let into the boiler, which worked the propelling gear with cross-heads and connecting-rods. The power of the two cylinders was combined by means of spur-wheels, which communicated the motive power to the wheels supporting the engine on the rail. The engine thus worked upon what is termed the second motion. The chimney was of wrought-iron, round which was a chamber extending back to the feed-pumps, for the purpose of heating the water previous to its injection into the boiler. The engine had no springs, and was mounted on a wooden frame supported on four wheels. In order to neutralize as much as possible the jolts and shocks which such an engine would necessarily encounter, from the obstacles and inequalities of the then very imperfect plate-way, the water-barrel, which served for a tender, was fixed to the end of a lever and weighted; the other end of the lever being connected with the frame of the locomotive carriage. By this means the weight of the two was more equally distributed, though the contrivance did not by any means compensate for the total absence of springs.

The wheels of the locomotive were all smooth, Stephenson having satisfied himself by experiment that the adhesion between the wheels of a loaded engine and the rail would be sufficient for the purposes of traction.[1]

The engine was, after much labor and anxiety, and frequent alterations of parts, at length brought to completion, having been about ten months in hand. It was placed upon the Killingworth Railway on the 25th of July, 1814, and its powers were tried on the same day. On an ascending gradient of ·1 in 450, the engine succeeded in drawing after it eight loaded carriages, of thirty tons weight, at about four miles an hour; and for some time after it continued regularly at work.

Although a considerable advance upon previous loco-

---

[1] It had been generally the opinion that cog-wheels must be used which should fit into cogs in the rail. Otherwise it was imagined the wheels would revolve without proceeding.

motives, "Blucher" (as the engine was popularly called) was nevertheless a somewhat cumbrous and clumsy machine. The parts were huddled together. The boiler constituted the principal feature ; and, being the foundation of the other parts, it was made to do duty not only as a generator of steam, but also as a basis for the fixings of the machinery and for the bearings of the wheels and axles. The want of springs was seriously felt ; and the progress of the engine was a succession of jolts, causing considerable derangement to the working. The mode of communicating the motive power to the wheels by means of the spur-gear also caused frequent jerks, each cylinder alternately propelling or becoming propelled by the other, as the pressure of the one upon the wheels became greater or less than the pressure of the other ; and when the teeth of the cog-wheels became at all worn, a rattling noise was produced during the travelling of the engine.

As the principal test of the success of the locomotive was its economy as compared with horse-power, careful calculations were made with the view of ascertaining this important point. The result was, that it was found the working of the engine was at first barely economical ; and at the end of the year the steam-power and the horse-power were ascertained to be as nearly as possible upon a par in point of cost.

We give the remainder of the history of George Stephenson's efforts to produce an economical working locomotive in the words of his son Robert, as communicated to Mr. Smiles in 1856, for the purposes of his father's "Life."

"A few months of experience and careful observation upon the operation of this (his first) engine convinced my father that the complication arising out of the action of the two cylinders being combined by spur-wheels would prevent their coming into practical application. He then directed his attention to an entire change in the construction and mechanical arrangements, and in the following year took out a patent, dated Feb. 28, 1815, for an engine which combined in a remarkable degree the essential requisites of an economical locomotive, — that is to say, few parts, simplicity in their action, and great simplicity in the mode by which power was communicated to the wheels supporting the engine.

" This second engine consisted, as before, of two vertical cylinders; which communicated directly with each pair of the four wheels that supported the engine by a cross-head and a pair of connecting-rods. But in attempting to establish a direct communication between the cylinders and the wheels that rolled upon the rails, considerable difficulties presented themselves. The ordinary joints could not be employed to unite the engine, which was a rigid mass, with the wheels rolling upon the irregular surface of the rails ; for it was evident that the two rails of the line of railway could not always be maintained at the same level with respect to each other, — that one wheel at the end of the axle might be depressed into a part of the line which had subsided, while the other would be elevated. In such a position of the axle and wheels it was clear that a rigid communication between the cross-head and the wheels was impracticable. Hence it became necessary to form a joint at the top of the piston-rod where it united with the cross-head, so as to permit the cross-head always to preserve complete parallelism with the axle of the wheels with which it was in communication.

" In order to obtain the flexibility combined with direct action, which was essential for insuring power and avoiding needless friction and jars from irregularities in the rail, my father employed the 'ball and socket joint' for effecting a union between the ends of the cross-heads, where they were united with the crank-pins attached to each driving-wheel. By this arrangement the parallelism between the cross-head and the axle was at all times maintained, it being permitted to take place without producing jar or friction upon any part of the machine.

"The next important point was to combine each pair of wheels by some simple mechanism, instead of the cog-wheels which had formerly been used. My father began by inserting each axle into two cranks, at right angles to each other, with rods communicating horizontally between them. An engine was made upon this plan, and answered extremely well. But at that period (1815) the mechanical skill of the country was not equal to the task of forging cranked axles of the soundness and strength necessary to stand the jars incident to locomotive work; so my father was compelled to fall back upon a substitute which, though less simple and less efficient, was within the mechanical capabilities of the workmen of that day, either for construction or repair. He adopted a chain, which rolled over indented wheels placed on the centre of each axle, and so arranged that the two pairs of wheels were effectually coupled and made to keep pace with each other. But these chains after a few years' use became stretched, and then the engines were liable to irregularity in their working, especially in changing from working back to forward again. Nevertheless, these engines continued in profitable use upon the Killingworth Colliery Railway for some years. Eventually the chain was laid aside, and the wheels were united by rods on the *outside* instead of rods and crank-axles inside, as specified in the

original patent; and this expedient completely answered
the purpose required, without involving any expensive or
difficult workmanship.

"Another important improvement was introduced in
this engine. The eduction steam had hitherto been
allowed to escape direct into the open atmosphere; but
my father having observed the great velocity with which
the smoke issued from the chimney of the same engine,
thought that by conveying the eduction steam into the
chimney, and there allowing it to escape in a vertical direction, its velocity would be imparted to the smoke from
the engine, or to the ascending current of air in the chimney. The experiment was no sooner made than the
power of the engine became more than doubled; combustion was stimulated, as it were, by a blast; consequently, the power of the boiler for generating steam was
increased, and in the same proportion, the useful duty of
the engine was augmented.

"Thus, in 1815 my father had succeeded in manufacturing an engine which included the following important
improvements on all previous attempts in the same direction: simple and direct communication between the
cylinder and the wheels rolling upon the rails; joint adhesion of all the wheels, attained by the use of horizontal connecting-rods; and, finally, a beautiful method of
exciting the combustion of fuel by employing the waste
steam which had formerly been allowed to escape use-
lessly. It is perhaps not too much to say that this
engine, as a mechanical contrivance, contained the germ
of all that has since been effected. It may be regarded,
in fact, as a type of the present locomotive engine.

"In describing my father's application of the waste
steam for the purpose of increasing the intensity of com-

bustion in the boiler, and thus increasing the power of the engine without adding to its weight, and while claiming for this engine the merit of being a type of all those which have been successfully devised since the commencement of the. Liverpool and Manchester Railway, it is necessary to observe that the next great improvement in the same direction, the 'multitubular boiler,' which took place some years later, could never have been used without the help of that simple expedient, *the steam-blast*, by which power only, the burning of coke was rendered possible.

"I cannot pass over this last-named invention of my father's without remarking how slightly, as an original idea, it has been appreciated; and yet how small would be the comparative value of the locomotive engine of the present day, without the application of that important invention.

"Engines constructed by my father in the year 1818, upon the principles just described, are in use on the Killingworth Colliery Railway to this very day (1856), conveying, at the speed of perhaps five or six miles an hour, heavy coal-trains, probably as economically as any of the more perfect engines now in use."

The invention of the steam-blast by George Stephenson in 1815 was fraught with the most important consequences to railway locomotion; and it is not saying too much to aver that the success of the locomotive has been in a great measure the result of its adoption. Without the steam-blast, by means of which the intensity of combustion is maintained at its highest point, producing a correspondingly rapid evolution of steam, high rates of speed could not have been kept up; the advantages of the multitubular boiler (afterward invented) could never have been fully tested; and locomotives might still have been dragging themselves unwieldily along at a rate of a little more than five or six miles an hour.

As the period drew near for the opening of the line, the question of the tractive power to be employed was anxiously discussed. At the Brusselton decline, fixed engines must necessarily be made use of; but with respect to the mode of working the railway generally, it was decided that horses were to be largely employed, and arrangements were made for their purchase.

Although locomotives had been regularly employed in hauling coal-wagons on the Middleton Colliery Railway, near Leeds, for more than twelve years, and on the Wylam and Killingworth Railways, near Newcastle, for more than ten years, great scepticism still prevailed as to the economy of employing them for the purpose in lieu of horses. In this case, it would appear that seeing was *not* believing. The popular scepticism was as great at Newcastle, where the opportunities for accurate observation were the greatest, as anywhere else. In 1824 the scheme of a canal between that town and Carlisle again came up; and although a few timid voices were raised on behalf of a railway, the general opinion was still in favor of a canal. The example of the Hetton Railway, which had been successfully worked by Stephenson's locomotives for two years past, was pointed to in proof of the practicability of a locomotive line between the two places; but the voice of the press, as well as of the public, was decidedly against the " new-fangled roads."

When such was the state of public opinion as to railway locomotion, some idea may be formed of the clear-sightedness and moral courage of the Stockton and Darlington directors in ordering three of Stephenson's locomotive engines, at a cost of several thousand pounds, against the opening of the railway.

These were constructed after Stephenson's most matured designs, and embodied all the improvements which he had contrived up to that time. No. 1 engine, the "Locomotion," which was first delivered, weighed about eight tons. It had one large flue, or tube, through the boiler, by which the heated air passed direct from the furnace at the one end, lined with fire-bricks, to the chimney at the other. The combustion in the furnace was quickened by the adoption of the steam-blast in the chimney. The heat raised was sometimes so great, and it was so imperfectly abstracted by the surrounding water, that the chimney became almost red-hot. Such engines, when put to their speed, were found capable of running at the rate of from twelve to sixteen miles an hour; but they were better adapted for the heavy work of hauling coal-trains at low speed — for which, indeed, they were specially constructed — than for running at the higher speed afterward adopted. Nor was it contemplated by the directors as possible, at the time when they were ordered, that locomotives could be made available for the purposes of passenger travelling. Besides, the Stockton and Darlington Railway did not run through a district in which passengers were supposed to be likely to constitute any considerable portion of the traffic.

We may easily imagine the anxiety felt by George Stephenson during the progress of the works toward completion, and his mingled hopes and doubts — though the doubts were but few — as to the issue of this great experiment. When the formation of the line near Stockton was well advanced, the engineer one day, accompanied by his son Robert and John Dixon, made a journey of inspection of the works. The party reached Stockton, and proceeded to dine at one of the inns there. After dinner, Stephenson ventured on the very unusual measure of ordering in a bottle of wine, to drink success to the railway. John Dixon relates with pride the utterance of the master on the occasion. "Now, lads," said he to the two young men, "I venture to tell you that I think you will live to see the day when railways will supersede almost all other methods of conveyance in this country, — when mail-coaches will go by railway, and railroads will become the great highways for the king and all his subjects. The time is coming when it will be cheaper for a working man to travel on a railway than to walk on foot. I know there are great and almost insurmountable difficulties to be encountered, but what I have said will come to pass as sure as you now hear me. I only wish I may live to see the day, though that I can scarcely hope for, as I know how slow all human progress is, and with what difficulty I have been able to get the locomotive introduced thus far, notwithstanding my more than ten years' successful experiment at Killingworth." The result, however, outstripped even George Stephenson's most sanguine expectations; and his son Robert, shortly after his return from America in 1827, saw his father's locomotive generally adopted as the tractive power on mining-railways.

Tuesday, the 27th of September, 1825, was a great day for Darlington. The railway, after having been under construction for more than three years, was at length about to be opened. The project had been the talk of the neighborhood for so long that there were few people within a range of twenty miles who did not feel more or less interested about it. Was it to be a failure or a success? Opinions were pretty equally divided as to the railway; but as regarded the locomotive, the general belief was that it would "never answer." However, there was the locomotive "No. 1" delivered upon the line, and ready to draw the first train of wagons on the opening day.

A great concourse of people assembled on the occasion. Some came from Newcastle and Durham, many from the Aucklands, while Darlington held a general holiday and turned out all its population. To give *éclat* to the opening, the directors of the company issued a programme of the proceedings, intimating the times at which the procession of wagons would pass certain points along the line. The proprietors assembled as early as six in the morning at the Brusselton fixed engine, where the working of the inclined planes was successfully rehearsed. A train of wagons laden with coals and merchandise was drawn up the western incline by the fixed engine, a length of nineteen hundred and sixty yards in seven and a half minutes, and then lowered down the incline on the eastern side of the hill, eight hundred and eighty yards, in five minutes.

At the foot of the incline the procession of vehicles was formed, consisting of the locomotive engine No. 1, driven by George Stephenson himself; after it, six wagons loaded with coals and flour; then a covered coach containing directors and proprietors; next, twenty-one coal-wagons fitted up for passengers (with which they were crammed); and lastly, six more wagons loaded with coals.

Strange to say, a man on a horse, carrying a flag with the motto of the company inscribed on it, *Periculum privatum utilitas publica*,[1] headed the procession! A lithographic view of the great event, published shortly after, duly exhibits the horseman and his flag. It was not

---

[1] "The private risk is the public benefit."

thought so dangerous a place, after all. The locomotive was only supposed to be able to go at the rate of from four to six miles an hour, and an ordinary horse could easily keep ahead of that.

Off started the procession, with the horseman at its head. A great concourse of people stood along the line. Many of them tried to accompany it by running, and some gentlemen on horseback galloped across the fields to keep up with the train. The railway descending with a gentle decline toward Darlington, the rate of speed was consequently variable. At a favorable part of the road Stephenson determined to try the speed of the engine, and he called upon the horseman with the flag to get out of his way! Most probably, deeming it unnecessary to carry his *periculum privatum* farther, the horseman turned aside, and Stephenson "put on the steam." The speed was at once raised to twelve miles an hour, and, at a favorable part of the road, to fifteen. The runners on foot, the gentlemen on horseback, and the horseman with the flag were consequently soon left far behind. When the train reached Darlington, it was found that four hundred and fifty passengers occupied the wagons, and that the load of men, coals, and merchandise amounted to about ninety tons.

At Darlington the procession was rearranged. The six loaded coal-wagons were left behind, and other wagons were taken on with a hundred and fifty more passengers, together with a band of music. The train then started for Stockton, — a distance of only twelve miles, — which was reached in about three hours. The day was kept throughout the district as a holiday; and horses, gigs, carts, and other vehicles, filled with people, stood along the railway, as well as crowds of persons on foot, waiting to see the train pass. The whole population of Stockton turned out to receive the procession, and, after a walk through the streets, the inevitable dinner in the Town Hall wound up the day's proceedings.

The principal circumstances connected with the construction of the " Rocket," as described by Robert Stephenson to Mr. Smiles, may be briefly stated. The tubular principle was adopted in a more complete manner than had yet been attempted. Twenty-five copper tubes, each three inches in diameter, extended from one end of the boiler to the other, the heated air passing through them on its way to the chimney; and the tubes being surrounded by the water of the boiler. It will be obvious that a large extension of the heating surface was thus effectually secured. The principal difficulty was in fitting the copper tubes in the boiler ends so as to prevent leakage. They were manufactured by a Newcastle coppersmith, and soldered to brass screws which were screwed into the boiler ends, standing out in great knobs. When the tubes were thus fitted, and the boiler was filled with water, hydraulic pressure was applied; but the water squirted out at every joint, and the factory floor was soon flooded. Robert went home in despair; and in the first moment of grief he wrote to his father that the whole thing was a failure. By return of post came a letter from his father, telling him that despair was not to be thought of, — that he must "try again;" and he suggested a mode of overcoming the difficulty, which his son had already anticipated and proceeded to adopt. It was to bore clean holes in the boiler ends, fit in the smooth copper tubes as tightly as possible, solder up, and then raise the steam. This plan succeeded perfectly; the expansion of the copper completely filling up all interstices, and producing a perfectly water-tight boiler, capable of standing extreme external pressure.

The mode of employing the steam-blast for the purpose of increasing the draught in the chimney, was also the subject of numerous experiments. When the engine was first tried, it was thought that the blast in the chimney was not sufficiently strong for the purpose of keeping up the intensity of the fire in the furnace, so as to produce high-pressure steam with the required velocity. The expedient was therefore adopted of hammering the copper tubes at the point at which they entered the chimney, whereby the blast was considerably sharpened; and on a farther trial it was found that the draught was increased to such an extent as to enable abundance of steam to be raised. The rationale of the blast may be simply explained by referring to the effect of contracting the pipe of a water-hose, by which the force of the jet of water is proportionately increased. Widen the nozzle of the pipe and the jet is, in like manner, diminished. So is it with the steam-blast in the chimney of the locomotive.

Doubts were, however, expressed whether the greater draught obtained by the contraction of the blast-pipe were not counterbalanced in some degree by the pressure upon the piston. Hence a series of experiments was made with pipes of different diameters, and their efficiency was tested by the amount of vacuum that was produced in the smoke-box. The degree of rarefaction was determined by a glass tube fixed to the bottom of the smoke-box, and descending into a bucket of water, the tube being open at both ends. As the rarefaction took place, the water would of course rise in the tube, and the height to which it rose above the surface of the water in the bucket was

made the measure of the amount of rarefaction. These
experiments proved that a considerable increase of draught
was obtained by the contraction of the orifice; accordingly, the two blast-pipes opening from the cylinders into
either side of the " Rocket " chimney, and turned up
within it, were contracted slightly below the area of the
steam-ports; and before the engine left the factory, the
water rose in the glass tube three inches above the water
in the bucket.

The other arrangements of the " Rocket " were briefly
these : The boiler was cylindrical with flat ends, six feet in
length, and three feet four inches in diameter. The upper half of the boiler was used as a reservoir for the steam,
the lower half being filled with water. Through the lower
part the copper tubes extended, being open to the fire-
box at one end, and to the chimney at the other. The
fire-box, or furnace, two feet wide and three feet high,
was attached immediately behind the boiler, and was also
surrounded with water. The cylinders of the engine were
placed on each side of the boiler, in an oblique position,
one end being nearly level with the top of the boiler at its
after end, and the other pointing toward the centre of the
foremost or driving pair of wheels, with which the connection was directly made from the piston-rod to a pin on
the outside of the wheel. The engine, together with its
load of water, weighed only four tons and a quarter; and
it was supported on four wheels, not coupled. The tender was four-wheeled, and similar in shape to a wagon, —
the foremost part holding the fuel, and the hind part a
water-cask.

When the " Rocket " was finished, it was placed upon
the Killingworth Railway for the purpose of experiment.
The new boiler arrangement was found perfectly success-

ful. The steam was raised rapidly and continuously, and in a quantity which then appeared marvellous. The same evening Robert despatched a letter to his father at Liverpool, informing him to his great joy, that the " Rocket " was "all right," and would be in complete working trim by the day of trial. The engine was shortly after sent by wagon to Carlisle, and thence shipped for Liverpool.

The time so much longed for by George Stephenson had now arrived, when the merits of the passenger locomotive were about to be put to the test. He had fought the battle for it until now, almost single-handed. Engrossed by his daily labors and anxieties, and harassed by difficulties and discouragements which would have crushed the spirit of a less resolute man, he had held firmly to his purpose through good and through evil report. The hostility which he had experienced from some of the directors opposed to the adoption of the locomotive, was the circumstance that caused him the greatest grief of all ; for where he had looked for encouragement, he found only carping and opposition. But his pluck never failed him ; and now the " Rocket " was upon the ground to prove, to use his own words, " whether he was a man of his word or not."

Great interest was felt at Liverpool, as well as throughout the country, in the approaching competition. Engineers, scientific men, and mechanics arrived from all quarters to witness the novel display of mechanical ingenuity on which such great results depended. The public generally were no indifferent spectators, either. The populations of Liverpool, Manchester, and the adjacent towns felt that the successful issue of the experiment would confer upon them individual benefits and local advantages almost incalculable, while populations at a distance waited for the result with almost equal interest.

On the day appointed for the great competition of locomotives at Rainhill, the following engines were entered for the prize : —

1. Messrs. Braithwaite and Ericsson's "Novelty."
2. Mr. Timothy Hackworth's "Sanspareil."
3. Messrs. R. Stephenson & Co.'s "Rocket."
4. Mr. Burstall's "Perseverance."

Another engine was entered by Mr. Brandreth, of Liverpool, — the "Cycloped," weighing three tons, worked by a horse in a frame, — but it could not be admitted to the competition. The above were the only four exhibited, out of a considerable number of engines constructed in different parts of the country in anticipation of this contest, many of which could not be satisfactorily completed by the day of trial.

The day fixed for the competition was the 1st of October; but to allow sufficient time to get the locomotives into good working order, the directors extended it to the 6th. On the morning of the 6th the ground at Rainhill presented a lively appearance, and there was as much excitement as if the St. Leger were about to be run. Many thousand spectators looked on, among whom were some of the first engineers and mechanicians of the day. A stand was provided for the ladies; the "beauty and fashion" of the neighborhood were present, and the side of the railroad was lined with carriages of all descriptions.

It was quite characteristic of the Stephensons that although their engine did not stand first on the list for trial, it was the first that was ready; and it was accordingly ordered out by the judges for an experimental trip. Yet the "Rocket" was by no means the "favorite" with either the judges or the spectators. Nicholas Wood has since stated that the majority of the judges were strongly predisposed in favor of the "Novelty," and that nine tenths, if not ten tenths, of the persons present were against the "Rocket" because of its appearance.[1] Nearly every person favored some other engine, so that there was nothing for the "Rocket" but the practical test. The first trip made by it was quite successful. It ran about twelve miles, without interruption,. in about fifty-three minutes.

The "Novelty" was next called out. It was a light engine, very compact in appearance, carrying the water and fuel upon the same wheels as the engine. The weight of the whole was only three tons and one hundred-weight. A peculiarity of this engine was that the air was driven or forced through the fire by means of bellows. The day being now far advanced, and some dispute having arisen as to the method of assigning the proper load for the "Novelty," no particular experiment was made farther than that the engine traversed the line by way of exhibition, occasionally moving at the rate of twenty-four miles an hour. The "Sanspareil," constructed by Mr. Timothy Hackworth, was next exhibited, but no particular experiment was made with it on this day. This engine differed but little in its construction from the locomotive last supplied by the Stephensons to the Stockton and Darlington Railway, of which Mr. Hackworth was the locomotive foreman.

The contest was postponed until the following day ; but before the judges arrived on the ground, the bellows for creating the blast in the "Novelty" gave way, and it was

---

[1] It had a sort of resemblance to a grasshopper, caused by the angle at which the piston and cylinder were placed.

found incapable of going through its performance.   A defect was also detected in the boiler of the "Sanspareil," and some farther time was allowed to get it repaired. The large number of spectators who had assembled to witness the contest were greatly disappointed at this postponement; but to lessen it, Stephenson again brought out the "Rocket," and attaching to it a coach containing thirty-four persons, he ran them along the line at the rate of from twenty-four to thirty miles an hour, much to their gratification and amazement. Before separating, the judges ordered the engine to be in readiness by eight o'clock on the following morning, to go through its definitive trial according to the prescribed conditions.

On the morning of the 8th of October the "Rocket" was again ready for the contest. The engine was taken to the extremity of the stage, the fire-box was filled with coke, the fire lighted, and the steam raised until it lifted the safety-valve loaded to a pressure of fifty pounds to the square inch. This proceeding occupied fifty-seven minutes. The engine then started on its journey, dragging after it about thirteen tons weight in wagons, and made the first ten trips backward and forward along the two miles of road, running the thirty-five miles, including stoppages, in an hour and forty-eight minutes. The second ten trips were in like manner performed in two hours and three minutes. The maximum velocity attained during the trial trip was twenty-nine miles an hour, or about three times the speed that one of the judges of the competition had declared to be the limit of possibility. The average speed at which the whole of the journeys were performed was fifteen miles an hour, or five miles beyond the rate specified in the conditions published by the company. The entire performance excited the greatest astonishment among the assembled spectators; the directors felt confident that their enterprise was now on the eve of success; and George Stephenson rejoiced to think that, in spite of all false prophets and fickle counsellors, the locomotive system was now safe. When the "Rocket," having performed all the conditions of the contest, arrived at the "grand stand" at the close of its day's successful run, Mr. Cropper — one of the directors favorable to the fixed-engine system — lifted up his hands, and exclaimed, "Now has George Stephenson at last delivered himself."

Neither the "Novelty" nor the "Sanspareil" was ready for trial until the 10th, on the morning of which day an advertisement appeared, stating that the former engine was to be tried on that day, when it would perform more work than any engine on the ground. The weight of the carriages attached to it was only seven tons. The engine passed the first post in good style; but in returning, the pipe from the forcing-pump burst and put an end to the trial. The pipe was afterward repaired, and the engine made several trips by itself, in which it was said to have gone at the rate of from twenty-four to twenty-eight miles an hour.

The "Sanspareil" was not ready until the 13th; and when its boiler and tender were filled with water, it was found to weigh four hundred-weight beyond the weight specified in the published conditions as the limit of four-wheeled engines; nevertheless, the judges allowed it to run on the same footing as the other engines, to enable them to ascertain whether its merits entitled it to favorable consideration. It travelled at the average speed of about fourteen miles an hour with its load attached; but at the eighth trip the cold-water pump got wrong, and the engine could proceed no farther.

It was determined to award the premium to the successful engine on the following day, the 14th, on which occasion there was an unusual assemblage of spectators. The owners of the "Novelty" pleaded for another trial, and it was conceded. But again it broke down. Then Mr. Hackworth requested the opportunity for making another trial of his "Sanspareil." But the judges had now had enough of failures, and they declined, on the ground that not only was the engine above the stipulated weight, but that it was constructed on a plan which they could not recommend for adoption by the directors of the company. One of the principal practical objections to this locomotive was the enormous quantity of coke consumed or wasted by it, — about six hundred and ninety-two pounds per hour when travelling, — caused by the sharpness of the steam-blast in the chimney, which blew a large proportion of the burning coke into the air.

The "Perseverance" of Mr. Burstall was found unable to move at more than five or six miles an hour, and it was withdrawn from the contest at an early period. The "Rocket" was thus the only engine that had performed, and more than performed, all the stipulated conditions; and it was declared to be entitled to the prize of £500, which was awarded to the Messrs. Stephenson and Booth[1] accordingly. And farther to show that the engine had been working quite within its powers, George Stephenson ordered it to be brought upon the ground and detached from all incumbrances, when, in making two trips, it was found to travel at the astonishing rate of thirty-five miles an hour.

The "Rocket" had thus eclipsed the performances of

---

[1] Mr. Henry Booth, secretary to the Liverpool and Manchester Railway, suggested to Mr. Stephenson the idea of a multitubular boiler.

all locomotive engines that had yet been constructed, and outstripped even the sanguine expectations of its constructors. It satisfactorily answered the report of Messrs. Walker and Rastrick, and established the efficiency of the locomotive for working the Liverpool and Manchester Railway, and indeed all future railways. The " Rocket " showed that a new power had been born into the world, full of activity and strength, with boundless capability of work. It was the simple but admirable contrivance of the steam-blast, and its combination with the multitubular boiler, that at once gave locomotion a vigorous life, and secured the triumph of the railway system. As has been well observed, this wonderful ability to increase and multiply its powers of performance with the emergency that demands them, has made this giant engine the noblest creation of human wit, the very lion among machines.

The success of the Rainhill experiment, as judged by the public, may be inferred from the fact that the shares of the company immediately rose ten per cent, and nothing farther was heard of the proposed twenty-one fixed engines, engine-houses, ropes, etc. All this cumbersome apparatus was thenceforth effectually disposed of.

When the reading was over, Bedford said : " When I heard you were going to have George Stephenson this afternoon, I wrote to my cousin Prentiss Armstrong, who has been at the locomotive works at Altoona for several years, and asked him about locomotives nowadays, that I might be able to compare them with the locomotives of George Stephenson's time. This is his letter, which I 'll read, if there be no objection : " —

DEAR BEDFORD, — Speaking roughly, a freight-engine of the " Consolidation " type (eight driving-wheels and two truck-wheels) weighs from forty-seven to forty-eight tons of two thousand pounds. On a road with no grades over twenty feet to the mile (1 in 250) it will haul over one thousand tons at fifteen miles an hour. If the train is of merchandise, it will be of say fifty cars, each weighing ten tons and carrying ten tons. If it is of coal or ore, the cars will each carry twenty or twenty-five tons."

["The 'Rocket,'" said Bedford, "which was the successful engine at the Rainhill competition, weighed a little over four tons and had four wheels. Dragging a weight of thirteen tons in wagons, it made thirty-five miles in about two hours."]

Our Engine No. 2 [continued the letter] made a mile on a level in forty-three seconds with no train, but there are very few such records. Two of our fast trains (four cars each, weighing twenty-five tons) make a schedule in one place (level) of nine miles in eight minutes. I have seen a record of a run on the Bound Brook route of four cars, ten miles in eight minutes. I think this must have been down hill.

I hope these facts will answer your views. If there 's anything else that I can get up for you, I shall be glad to do it.

Yours truly,
PRENTISS ARMSTRONG.

XI.

ELI WHITNEY.

THE young people all came in laughing.

"And what is it?" said Uncle Fritz, good-naturedly.

"It is this," said Alice, "that I say that all this is very entertaining about Palissy the Potter and Benvenuto Cellini; and I have been boasting that I know as much of the steam-engine as Lucy did, who was 'sister to Harry.' But I do not see that this is going to profit Blanche when she shall make her celebrated visit to Mr. Bright, and when he asks her what is the last sweet thing in creels or in fly-frames."

"Is it certain that Blanche is to go?" said Uncle Fritz, doubtfully.

"Oh, dear, Uncle Fritz, do you know?" said Blanche, in mock heroics; "are you in the sacred circle which decides? Will the Vesuvius pass its dividend, or will it scatter its blessings right and left, so that we can go to Paris and all the world be happy?"

"I wish I knew," said Colonel Ingham; "for on that same dividend depends the question whether I build four new rooms at Little Crastis for the accommodation of my young friends when they visit me there."

"Could you tell us," said Fergus, "what is the cause of the depression in the cotton-manufacture?"

"Don't tell him, Uncle Fritz," said Fanchon, "for the two best of reasons, — first, that half of us will not understand if you do ; and second, that none of us will remember."

Colonel Ingham laughed. " And third," he said, " that we are to talk about Inventions and Inventors, and we shall not get to Fergus's grand question till we come to the series on ' Political Economy and Political Economists.'

" You are all quite right in all your suggestions and criticisms. It is quite time that you girls should know something of the industry which is important not only to all the Southern States, but to all the manufacturing States. Cotton is the cheapest article for clothing in the world, and the use of it goes farther and farther every year. The manufacture is also improving steadily. Thirty men, women, and children will make as much cotton cloth to-day as a hundred could make the year you were born, Hester. I saw cottons for sale to-day at four cents a yard which would have cost nearly three times that money thirty years ago. So I have laid out for you these sketches of the life of Eli Whitney, on whose simple invention, as you remember, all this wealth of production may be said to depend. You college boys ought to be pleased to know, that within a year after this man graduated from Yale College, he had made an invention and set it a going, which entirely changed the face of things in his own country. At that moment there was so little cotton raised in America, that Whitney himself had never seen cotton wool or cotton seed, when he was first asked if he could make a machine which would separate one from the other. It was so little known, indeed, that when John Jay of New York negotiated a treaty of commerce with England in 1794, the year after Whitney's invention, he did not know that any cotton was produced in the United States. The treaty did not provide for our cotton, and had to be changed after it was brought back to America. With this invention by Whitney, it was possible to clean cotton from the seed. The Southern States, which before had no staple of importance, had in that moment an immense addition to their resources. Alabama, Mississippi, Louisiana, and Tennessee, besides the States in the old thirteen, were settled almost wholly to call into being new lands for raising cotton. To these were afterwards added Arkansas, Florida, and Texas. With this new industry slave labor became vastly more profitable; and the institution of slavery, which would else have died out probably, received an immense stimulus. Fortunately for the country and the world, the Constitution had fixed the year 1808, as the end of the African slave trade. But, up to that date, slaves were pushed in with a constantly increasing rapidity, so that the new States were peopled very largely with absolute barbarians. There is hardly another instance in history where it is so easy to trace in a very few years, results so tremendous following from a single invention by a single man.

"Fortunately for us, Miss Lamb has just published a portrait of Eli Whitney in the 'Magazine of History.' Here it is, in the October number of the 'Magazine of History.'

"As to processes of manufacture, of course we can learn little or nothing about them here. But you had better read carefully this article in Ure's 'Dictionary of Arts,' though it is a little old-fashioned, and then you will be prepared to make up parties to go out to the Hecla, or up to Lowell or Lawrence, where you can see with your own eyes.

"And now I will read you a little sketch of the life of Eli Whitney."

ELI WHITNEY.

Eli Whitney was born at Westborough, Worcester County, Massachusetts, Dec. 8, 1765. His parents belonged to the middle class in society, who, by the labors of husbandry, managed by uniform industry and strict frugality to provide well for a rising family.

The paternal ancestors of Mr. Whitney emigrated from England among the early settlers of Massachusetts, and their descendants were among the most respectable farmers of Worcester County. His maternal ancestors, of the name of Fay, were also English emigrants, and ranked among the substantial yeomanry of Massachusetts. A family tradition respecting the occasion of their coming to this country may serve to illustrate the history of the times. The story is, that about two hundred years ago, the father of the family, who resided in England, a man of large property and great respectability, called together his sons and addressed them thus: " America is to be a great country. I am too old to emigrate myself; but if any one of you will go, I will give him a double share of my property." The youngest son instantly declared his willingness to go, and his brothers gave their consent. He soon set off for the New World, and landed in Boston, in the neighborhood of which place he purchased a large tract of land, where he enjoyed the satisfaction of receiving two visits from his venerable father. His son John Fay, from whom the subject of this memoir is immediately descended, removed from Boston to Westborough, where he became the proprietor of a large tract of land, since known by the name of the Fay Farm.

From the sister of Mr. Whitney, we have derived some particulars respecting his childhood and youth, and we shall present the anecdotes to our readers in the artless style in which they are related by our correspondent, believing that they would be more acceptable in this simple dress than if, according to the modest suggestion of the writer, they should be invested with a more labored diction. The following incident, though trivial in itself, will serve to show at how early a period certain qualities of strong feeling tempered by prudence, for which Mr. Whitney afterward became distinguished, began to display themselves. When he was six or seven years old he had overheard the kitchen maid, in a fit of passion, calling his mother, who was in a delicate state of health, hard names, at which he expressed great displeasure to his sister. "She thought," said he, "that I was not big enough to hear her talk so about my mother. I think she ought to have a flogging; and if I knew how to bring it about, she should have one." His sister advised him to tell their father. "No," he replied, "it will hurt his feelings and mother's too; and besides, it is likely the girl will say she never said so, and that would make a quarrel. It is best to say nothing about it."

Indications of his mechanical genius were likewise developed at a very early age. Of his early passion for such employments, his sister gives the following account: "Our father had a workshop, and sometimes made wheels of different kinds, and chairs. He had a variety of tools, and a lathe for turning chair-posts. This gave my brother an opportunity of learning the use of tools when very young. He lost no time; but as soon as he could handle tools, he was always making something in the shop, and seemed not to like working on the farm. On a time, after the death of our mother, when our father had been absent from home two or three days, on his return he inquired of the housekeeper what the boys had been doing. She told him what B. and J. had been about. 'But what has Eli been doing?' said he. She replied he had been making a fiddle. 'Ah,' said he, despondingly, 'I fear Eli will have to take his portion in fiddles.' He was at this time about twelve years old. His sister adds that this fiddle was finished throughout, like a common violin, and made tolerably good music. It was examined by many persons, and all pronounced it to be a remarkable piece of work for such a boy to perform. From this time he was employed to repair violins, and had many nice jobs, which were always executed to the entire satisfaction, and often to the astonishment, of his customers. His father's watch being the greatest piece of mechanism that had yet presented itself to his observation, he was extremely desirous of examining its interior construction, but was not permitted to do so. One Sunday morning, observing that his father was going to meeting, and would leave at home the wonderful little machine, he immediately feigned illness as an apology for not going to church. As soon as the family were out of sight, he flew to the room where the watch hung, and taking it down he was so delighted with its motions that he took it all to pieces before he thought of the consequences of his rash deed ; for his father was a stern parent, and punishment would have been the reward of his idle curiosity, had the mischief been detected. He, however, put all the work so neatly together that his father never discovered his audacity until he himself told him, many years afterwards.

"Whitney lost his mother at an early age, and when he was thirteen years old his father married a second time. His stepmother, among her articles of furniture, had a handsome set of table knives that she valued very highly.

Whitney could not but see this, and said to her, 'I could make as good ones if I had tools, and I could make the necessary tools if I had a few common tools to make them with.' His stepmother thought he was deriding her, and was much displeased; but it so happened, not long afterwards, that one of the knives got broken, and he made one exactly like it in every respect except the stamp on the blade. This he would likewise have executed, had not the tools required been too expensive for his slender resources."

When Whitney was fifteen or sixteen years of age he suggested to his father an enterprise, which was an earnest of the similar undertakings in which he engaged on a far greater scale in later life. This being the time of the Revolutionary War, nails were in great demand and bore a high price. At that period nails were made chiefly by hand, with little aid from machinery. Young Whitney proposed to his father to procure him a few tools, and to permit him to set up the manufacture. His father consented; and he went steadily to work, and suffered nothing to divert him from his task until his day's work was completed. By extraordinary diligence he gained time to make tools for his own use, and to put in knife-blades, and to perform many other curious little jobs which exceeded the skill of the country artisans. At this laborious occupation the enterprising boy wrought alone, with great success, and with much profit to his father, for two winters, pursuing the ordinary labors of the farm during the summers. At this time he devised a plan for enlarging his business and increasing his profits. He whispered his scheme to his sister, with strong injunctions of secrecy; and requesting leave of his father to go to a neighboring town, without specifying his object, he set out on horseback in quest of a fellow-laborer. Not finding one as easily as he had anticipated, he proceeded from town to town with a perseverance which was always a strong trait of his character, until, at a distance of forty miles from home, he found such a workman as he desired. He also made his journey subservient to his mechanical skill, for he called at every workshop on his way and gleaned all the information he could respecting the mechanical arts.

At the close of the war the business of making nails was no longer profitable; but a fashion prevailing among the ladies of fastening on their bonnets with long pins, he contrived to make those with such skill and dexterity that he nearly monopolized the business, although he devoted to it only such seasons of leisure as he could redeem from the occupations of the farm, to which he now principally betook himself. He added to this article, the manufacture of walking-canes, which he made with peculiar neatness.

In respect to his proficiency in learning while young, we are informed that he early manifested a fondness for figures and an uncommon aptitude for arithmetical calculations, though in the other rudiments of education he was not particularly distinguished. Yet at the age of fourteen he had acquired so much general information, as to be regarded on this account, as well as on account of his mechanical skill, a very remarkable boy.

From the age of nineteen, young Whitney conceived the idea of obtaining a liberal education; but, being warmly opposed by his stepmother, he was unable to procure the decided consent of his father, until he had reached the age of twenty-three years. But, partly by the avails of his manual labor and partly by teaching a village school, he had been so far able to surmount the obstacles thrown in his way, that he had prepared himself for the Freshman Class in Yale College, which he entered in May, 1789.

The propensity of Mr. Whitney to mechanical inventions and occupations, was frequently apparent during his residence at college. On a particular occasion, one of the tutors, happening to mention some interesting philosophical experiment, regretted that he could not exhibit it to his pupils, because the apparatus was out of order and must be sent abroad to be repaired. Mr. Whitney proposed to undertake this task, and performed it greatly to the satisfaction of the faculty of the college.

A carpenter being at work upon one of the buildings of the gentleman with whom Mr. Whitney boarded, the latter begged permission to use his tools, during the intervals of study; but the mechanic, being a man of careful habits, was unwilling to trust them with a student, and it was only after the gentleman of the house had become responsible for all damages, that he would grant the permission. But Mr. Whitney had no sooner commenced his operations than the carpenter was surprised at his dexterity, and exclaimed, " There was one good mechanic spoiled when you went to college."

Soon after Mr. Whitney took his degree, in the autumn of 1792, he entered into an engagement with a Mr. B. of Georgia, to reside in his family as a private teacher. On his way thither, he was so fortunate as to have the company of Mrs. Greene, the widow of General Greene, who, with her family, was returning to Savannah after spending the summer at the North. At that time it was deemed unsafe to travel through our country without having had the small-pox, and accordingly Mr. Whitney prepared himself for the excursion, by procuring inoculation while in New York. As soon as he was sufficiently recovered, the party set sail for Savannah. As his health was not fully re-established, Mrs. Greene kindly invited him to go with the family to her residence at Mulberry Grove, near Savannah, and remain until he was recruited. The invitation was accepted; but lest he should not yet have lost all power of communicating that dreadful disease, Mrs. Greene had white flags (the meaning of which was well understood) hoisted at the landing and at all the avenues leading to the house. As a requital for her hospitality, her guest procured the virus and inoculated all the servants of the household, more than fifty in number, and carried them safely through the disorder.

Mr. Whitney had scarcely set his foot in Georgia, before he was met by a disappointment which was an earnest of that long series of adverse events which, with scarcely an exception, attended all his future negotiations in the same State. On his arrival he was informed that Mr. B. had employed another teacher, leaving Whitney entirely without resources or friends, except those whom he had made in the family of General Greene. In these benevolent people, however, his case excited much interest; and Mrs. Greene kindly said to him, " My young friend, you propose studying the law; make my house your home, your room your castle, and there pursue what studies you please." He accordingly began the study of the law under that hospitable roof.

Mrs. Greene was engaged in a piece of embroidery in which she employed a peculiar kind of frame, called a *tambour*. She complained that it was badly constructed, and that it tore the delicate threads of her work. Mr. Whitney, eager for an opportunity to oblige his hostess, set himself to work and speedily produced a tambour-frame, made on a plan entirely new, which he presented to her. Mrs. Greene and her family were greatly delighted with it, and thought it a wonderful proof of ingenuity.

Not long afterwards a large party of gentlemen, consisting principally of officers who had served under the General in the Revolutionary Army, came from Augusta and the upper country, to visit the family of General Greene. They fell into conversation upon the state of agriculture among them, and expressed great regret that there was no means of cleansing the green seed cotton, or separating it from its seed, since all the lands which were unsuitable for the cultivation of rice, would yield large crops of cotton. But until ingenuity could devise some machine which would greatly facilitate the process of cleaning, it was vain to think of raising cotton for market. Separating one pound of the clean staple from the seed was a day's work for a woman; but the time usually devoted to picking cotton was the evening, after the labor of the field was over. Then the slaves — men, women, and children — were collected in circles, with one whose duty it was to rouse the dozing and quicken the indolent. While the company were engaged in this conversation, " Gentlemen," said Mrs. Greene, " apply to my young friend Mr. Whitney; he can make anything." Upon which she conducted them into a neighboring room, and showed them her tambour-frame and a number of toys which Mr. Whitney had made or repaired for the children. She then introduced the gentlemen to Whitney himself, extolling his genius and commending him to their notice and friendship. He modestly disclaimed all pretensions to mechanical genius; and when they named their object, he replied that he had never seen either cotton or cotton seed in his life. Mrs. Greene said to one of the gentlemen, " I have accomplished my aim. Mr. Whitney is a very deserving young man, and to bring him into notice was my object. The interest which our friends now feel for him will, I hope, lead to his getting some employment to enable him to prosecute the study of the law."

But a new turn, that no one of the company dreamed of, had been given to Mr. Whitney's views. It being out of season for cotton in the seed, he went to Savannah and searched among the warehouses and boats until he found a small parcel of it. This he carried home, and communicated his intentions to Mr. Miller, who warmly encouraged him, and assigned him a room in the basement of the house, where he set himself to work with such rude materials and instruments as a Georgia plantation afforded. With these resources, however, he made tools better suited to his purpose, and drew his own wire (of which the teeth of the earliest gins were made),— an article which was not at that time to be found in the market of Savannah. Mrs. Greene and Mr. Miller were the only persons ever admitted to his workshop, and the only persons who knew in what way he was employing himself. The many hours he spent in his mysterious pursuits, afforded matter of great curiosity and often of raillery to the younger members of the family. Near the close of the winter, the machine was so nearly completed as to leave no doubt of its success.

Mrs. Greene was eager to communicate to her numerous friends the knowledge of this important invention, peculiarly important at that time, because then the market was glutted with all those articles which were suited to the climate and soil of Georgia, and nothing could be found to give occupation to the negroes and support to the white inhabitants. This opened suddenly to the planters boundless resources of wealth, and rendered the occupations of the slaves less unhealthy and laborious than they had been before.

Mrs. Greene, therefore, invited to her house gentlemen

from different parts of the State ; and on the first day after they had assembled, she conducted them to a temporary building which had been erected for the machine, and they saw with astonishment and delight, that more cotton could be separated from the seed in one day, by the labor of a single hand, than could be done in the usual manner in the space of many months.

Mr. Whitney might now have indulged in bright reveries of fortune and of fame ; but we shall have various opportunities of seeing that he tempered his inventive genius with an unusual share of the calm, considerate qualities of the financier. Although urged by his friends to secure a patent and devote himself to the manufacture and introduction of his machines, he coolly replied that, on account of the great expenses and trouble which always attend the introduction of a new invention, and the difficulty of enforcing a law in favor of patentees, in opposition to the individual interests of so large a number of persons as would be concerned in the culture of this article, it was with great reluctance that he should consent to relinquish the hopes of a lucrative profession, for which he had been destined, with an expectation of indemnity either from the justice or the gratitude of his countrymen, even should the invention answer the most sanguine anticipations of his friends.

The individual who contributed most to incite him to persevere in the undertaking, was Phineas Miller. Mr. Miller was a native of Connecticut and a graduate of Yale College. Like Mr. Whitney, soon after he had completed his education at college, he came to Georgia as a private teacher in the family of General Greene, and after the decease of the General, he became the husband of Mrs. Greene. He had qualified himself for the profession of the law, and was a gentleman of cultivated mind and superior talents; but he was of an ardent temperament, and therefore well fitted to enter with zeal into the views which the genius of his friend had laid open to him. He also had considerable funds at command, and proposed to Mr. Whitney to become his joint adventurer, and to be at the whole expense of maturing the invention until it should be patented. If the machine should succeed in its intended operation, the parties agreed, under legal formalities, "that the profits and advantages arising therefrom, as well as all privileges and emoluments to be derived from patenting, making, vending, and working the same, should be mutually and equally shared between them." This instrument bears date May 27, 1793; and immediately afterward they commenced business under the firm of Miller and Whitney.

An invention so important to the agricultural interest (and, as it has proved, to every department of human industry) could not long remain a secret. The knowledge of it soon spread through the State, and so great was the excitement on the subject, that multitudes of persons came from all quarters of the State to see the machine; but it was not deemed safe to gratify their curiosity until the patent right had been secured. But so determined were some of the populace to possess this treasure, that neither law nor justice could restrain them; they broke open the building by night, and carried off the machine. In this way the public became possessed of the invention; and before Mr. Whitney could complete his model and secure his patent, a number of machines were in successful operation, constructed with some slight deviation from the original, with the hope of escaping the penalty for evading the patent right.

As soon as the copartnership of Miller and Whitney was formed, Mr. Whitney repaired to Connecticut, where, as far as possible, he was to perfect the machine, obtain a patent, and manufacture and ship to Georgia such a number of machines as would supply the demand.

Within three days after the conclusion of the copartnership, Mr. Whitney having set out for the North, Mr. Miller commenced his long correspondence relative to the cotton-gin. The first letter announces that encroachments upon their rights had already begun. "It will be necessary," says Mr. Miller, "to have a considerable number of gins made, to be in readiness to send out as soon as the patent is obtained, in order to satisfy the absolute demands, and make people's heads easy on the subject; *for I am informed of two other claimants for the honor of the invention of cotton-gins, in addition to those we knew before.*"

On the 20th of June, 1793, Mr. Whitney presented his patent to Mr. Jefferson, then Secretary of State; but the prevalence of the yellow fever in Philadelphia (which was then the seat of government) prevented his concluding the business relative to the patent until several months afterwards. To prevent being anticipated, he took, however, the precaution to make oath to the invention before the notary public of the city of New Haven, which he did on the 28th of October of the same year.

Mr. Jefferson, who had much curiosity in regard to mechanical inventions, took a peculiar interest in this machine, and addressed to the inventor an obliging letter, desiring farther particulars respecting it, and expressing a wish to procure one for his own use.[1] Mr. Whitney accordingly sketched the history of the invention, and of the

---

[1] This letter is dated Nov. 24, 1793.

construction and performances of the machine. "It is about a year," says he, "since I first turned my attention to constructing this machine, at which time I was in the State of Georgia. Within about ten days after my first conception of the plan, I made a small though imperfect model. Experiments with this encouraged me to make one on a larger scale; but the extreme difficulty of procuring workmen and proper materials in Georgia prevented my completing the larger one until some time in April last. This, though much larger than my first attempt, is not above one third as large as the machines may be made with convenience. The cylinder is only two feet two inches in length, and six inches in diameter. It is turned by hand, and requires the strength of one man to keep it in constant motion. It is the stated task of one negro to clean fifty weight (I mean fifty pounds after it is separated from the seed) of the green cotton seed per day."

In the year 1812 Mr. Whitney made application to Congress for the renewal of his patent for the cotton-gin. In his memorial he presented a history of the struggles he had been forced to encounter in defence of his right, observing that he had been unable to obtain any decision on the merits of his claim until he had been *eleven years* in the law, and *thirteen years* of his patent term had expired. He sets forth that his invention had been a source of opulence to thousands of the citizens of the United States; that, as a labor-saving machine, it would enable one man to perform the work of a thousand men; and that it furnishes to the whole family of mankind, at a very cheap rate, the most essential article of their clothing. Hence he humbly conceived himself entitled to a further remuneration from his country, and thought he ought to be admitted to a more liberal participation with his fellow-citizens in the benefits of his invention. Although so great advantages had been already experienced, and the prospect of future benefits was so promising, still, many of those whose interest had been most enhanced by this invention, had obstinately persisted in refusing to make any compensation to the inventor. The very men whose wealth had been acquired by the use of this machine, and who had grown rich beyond all former example, had combined their exertions to prevent the patentee from deriving any emolument from his invention. From that State in which he had first made and where he had first introduced his machine, and which had derived the most signal benefits from it, he had received nothing ; and from no State had he received the amount of half a cent per pound on the cotton cleaned with his machines in one year. Estimating the value of the labor of one man at twenty cents per day, the whole amount which had been received by him for his invention was not equal to the value of the labor saved in *one hour* by his machines then in use in the United States. "This invention," he proceeds, "now gives to the southern section of the Union, over and above the profits which would be derived from the cultivation of any other crop, an annual emolument of at least *three millions* of dollars."[1] The foregoing statement does not rest on conjecture, it is no visionary speculation, — all these advantages have been realized ; the planters of the Southern States have counted the cash, felt the weight of it in their pockets, and heard the exhilarating sound of its collision. Nor do the advantages stop here. This immense source of wealth is but just beginning to be opened. Cotton is a more cleanly and

[1] This was in 1812, twenty years after the invention of the gin. The saving in 1885 is enormously greater.

healthful article of cultivation than tobacco and indigo, which it has superseded, and does not so much impoverish the soil. This invention has already trebled the value of the land through a large extent of territory; and the degree to which the cultivation of cotton may be still augmented, is altogether incalculable. This species of cotton has been known in all countries where cotton has been raised, from time immemorial, but was never known as an article of commerce until since this method of cleaning it was discovered. In short (to quote the language of Judge Johnson), "if we should assert that the benefits of this invention exceed *one hundred millions of dollars*, we could prove the assertion by correct calculation." It is objected that if the patentee succeeds in procuring the renewal of his patent, he will be too rich. There is no probability that the patentee, if the term of his patent were extended for twenty years, would ever obtain for his invention one half as much as many an individual will gain by use of it. Up to the present time, the whole amount of what he has acquired from this source (after deducting his expenses) does not exceed one half the sum which a single individual has gained by the use of the machine in one year. It is true that considerable sums have been obtained from some of the States where the machine is used; but no small portion of these sums has been expended in prosecuting his claim in a State where nothing has been obtained, and where his machine has been used to the greatest advantage.

There was much more which was curious, laid out in different books; but the call came for supper, and the young people obeyed.

XII.

JAMES NASMYTH.

THE STEAM-HAMMER.

"MY dear Uncle Fritz, I have found something very precious."

" I hope it is a pearl necklace, my dear," was his reply, "though I see no one who needs such ornaments less."

Hester waltzed round the room, and dropped a very low courtesy before Uncle Fritz in acknowledgment of his compliment ; and all the others clapped their hands. They asked her, more clamorously than Uncle Fritz, what she had found.

" I have found a man—"

" That is more than Diogenes could."

" Horace, I shall send you out of the room, or back on first principles. Do you not know that it is not nice to interrupt? "

" I have found a man, Uncle Fritz, who is an inventor, a great inventor ; and he is very nice, and he likes people and people like him, and he always succeeds, — his things turn out well, like Dr. Franklin's ; and he says the world has always been grateful to him. He never sulks or complains ; he knows all about the moon, and makes wonderful pictures of it ; and he 's enormously rich, I believe, too, — but that 's not so much matter. The best of all is, that he began just as we begin. He had a nice father and

a nice mother and a good happy home, and was brought
up like good decent children. Now really, Uncle Fritz,
you must n't laugh ; but do you not think that most of the
people whose lives we read have to begin horridly ? They
have to be beaten when they are apprentices, or their
fathers and mothers have to die, or they have to walk
through Philadelphia with loaves of bread under their arms,
or to be brought up in poor-houses or something. Now,
nothing of that sort happened to my inventor. And I am
very much encouraged. For my father never beat me, and
my mother never scolded me half as much as I deserved,
and I never was in a poor-house, and I never carried a
loaf of bread under my arm, and so I really was afraid I
should come to no good. But now I have found my
new moon-man, I am very much encouraged."

The others laughed heartily at Hester's zeal, and
Blanche asked what Hester's hero had invented, and
what was his name. The others turned to Uncle Fritz
half incredulously. But Uncle Fritz came to Hester's
relief.

"Hester is quite right," he said; "and his name it is
James Nasmyth. He has invented a great many things,
quite necessary in the gigantic system of modern machine-
building. He has chosen the steam-hammer for his device. Here is a picture of it on the outside of his Life.
You see I was ready for you, Hester."

The children looked with interest on the device, and
Fergus said that it was making heraldry do as it should,
and speak in the language of the present time.

Then Uncle Fritz bade Hester find for them a passage in the biography where Mr. Nasmyth tells how he
changed the old motto of the family. Oddly enough,
the legend says that the first Nasmyth took his name

after a romantic escape, when one of his pursuers, finding him disguised as a blacksmith, cried out, "Ye 're *nae smyth*."

It is a little queer that this name should have been given to the family of a man, who, in his time, forged heavier pieces of iron than had ever been forged before, and, indeed, invented the machinery by which this should be done. The old Scotch family had for a motto the words

"Non arte, sed Marte."

With a very just pride, James Nasmyth has changed the motto, and made it

"Non Marte, sed arte."

That is, while they said, "Not by art, but by war," this man, who has done more work for the world, directly or indirectly, than any of Aladdin's genii, says, "Not by war, but by art."

Hester was well pleased that their old friend justified her enthusiasm so entirely. He and she began dipping into her copy and his copy of the biography, which is one of the most interesting books of our time.

JAMES NASMYTH.

My grandfather, Michael Naesmyth, like his father and grandfather, was a builder and architect. The buildings he designed and erected for the Scotch nobility and gentry were well arranged, carefully executed, and thoroughly substantial. I remember my father pointing out to me the extreme care and attention with which he finished his buildings. He inserted small fragments of basalt into the mortar of the external joints of the stones, at close and regular distances, in order to protect the mortar from the adverse action of the weather; and to this day they give proof of their efficiency.

The excellence of my grandfather's workmanship was a thing that my own father impressed upon me when a boy. It stimulated in me the desire to aim at excellence in everything that I undertook, and in all practical matters to arrive at the highest degree of good workmanship. I believe that these early lessons had a great influence upon my future career.

My father, Alexander Nasmyth, was the second son of Michael Nasmyth. He was born in his father's house in the Grassmarket, on the 9th of September, 1758.

I have not much to say about my father's education. For the most part he was his own schoolmaster. I have heard him say that his mother taught him his A B C, and that he afterward learned to read at Mammy Smith's. This old lady kept a school for boys and girls at the top of a house in the Grassmarket. There my father was taught to read his Bible and to learn his Carritch (the Shorter Catechism).

My father's profession was that of a portrait-painter, to begin with; but later he devoted himself to landscape-painting. But he did not confine himself to this pursuit. He was an all-round man, with something of the universal about him. He was a painter, an architect, and a mechanic. Above all, he was an incessantly industrious man.

I was born on the morning of the 19th of August, 1808, at my father's house in Edinburgh. I was named James Hall, after a dear friend of my father. My mother afterward told me that I must have been a "very noticin' bairn," as she observed me, when I was only a few days old, following with my little eyes any one who happened to be in the room, as if I had been thinking to my little self, " Who are you ? "

When I was about four or five years old I was observed to give a decided preference to the use of my left hand. At first everything was done to prevent my using it in preference to the right, until my father, after viewing a little sketch I had drawn with my left hand, allowed me to go on in my own way. I used my right hand in all that was necessary, and my left in all sorts of practical manipulative affairs. My left hand has accordingly been my most willing and obedient servant, and in this way I became ambidexter.

In due time I was sent to school; and while attending the High School, from 1817 to 1820, there was the usual rage among boys for spinning-tops, " peeries," and " young cannon." By means of my father's excellent foot-lathe I turned out the spinning-tops in capital style, so much so that I became quite noted among my school companions. They all wanted to have specimens of my productions. They would give any price for them. The peeries were turned with perfect accuracy, and the steel-shod or spinning pivot was centred so as to correspond with the heaviest diameter at the top. They would spin twice as long as the bought peeries. When at full speed they would " sleep ; " that is, turn round without a particle of wavering. This was considered high art as regarded top-spinning.

Flying-kites and tissue-paper balloons were articles that I was also somewhat famed for producing. There was a good deal of special skill required for the production of a flying-kite. It must be perfectly still and steady when at its highest flight in the air. Paper messengers were sent up to it along the string which held it to the ground. The top of the Calton Hill was the most favorite place for enjoying this pleasant amusement.

Another article for which I became equally famous was the manufacture of small brass cannon. These I cast and bored, and mounted on their appropriate gun-carriages. They proved very effective, especially in the loudness of the report when fired. I also converted large cellar-keys into a sort of hand-cannon. A touch-hole was bored into the barrel of the key, with a sliding brass collar that allowed the key-guns to be loaded and primed, ready for firing.

The principal occasion on which the brass cannon and hand-guns were used was on the 4th of June, — King George the Third's birthday. This was always celebrated with exuberant and noisy loyalty. The guns of the Castle were fired at noon, and the number of shots corresponded with the number of years that the king had reigned. The grand old Castle was enveloped in smoke, and the discharges reverberated along the streets and among the surrounding hills. Everything was in holiday order. The coaches were hung with garlands, the shops were ornamented, the troops were reviewed on Bruntsfield Links, and the citizens drank the king's health at the Cross, throwing the glasses over their backs. The boys fired off gunpowder, or threw squibs or crackers, from morning till night. It was one of the greatest schoolboy events of the year.

My little brass cannon and hand-guns were very busy that day. They were fired until they became quite hot. These were the pre-lucifer days. The fire to light the powder at the touch-hole was obtained by the use of a flint, a steel, and a tinder-box. The flint was struck sharply on the steel, a spark of fire consequently fell into the tinder-box, and the match (of hemp string, soaked in saltpetre) was readily lit and fired off the little guns.

One of my attached cronies was Tom Smith. Our friendship began at the High School in 1818. A similarity of disposition bound us together. Smith was the son of an enterprising general merchant at Leith. His father had a special genius for practical chemistry. He had established an extensive color-manufactory at Portobello, near Edinburgh, where he produced white lead, red lead, and a great variety of colors, — in the preparation of which he required a thorough knowledge of chemistry. Tom Smith inherited his father's tastes, and admitted me to share in his experiments, which were carried on in a chemical laboratory situated behind his father's house at the bottom of Leith Walk.

We had a special means of communication. When anything particular was going on at the laboratory, Tom hoisted a white flag on the top of a high pole in his father's garden. Though I was more than a mile away, I kept a lookout in the direction of the laboratory with a spy-glass. My father's house was at the top of Leith Walk, and Smith's house was at the bottom of it. When the flag was hoisted I could clearly see the invitation to me to come down. I was only too glad to run down the Walk and join my chum, to take part in some interesting chemical process. Mr. Smith, the father, made me heartily welcome. He was pleased to see his son so much attached to me, and he perhaps believed that I was worthy of his friendship. We took zealous part in all the chemical proceedings, and in that way Tom was fitting himself for the business of his life.

Mr. Smith was a most genial-tempered man. He was

shrewd and quick-witted, like a native of York, as he was. I received the greatest kindness from him as well as from his family. His house was like a museum. It was full of cabinets, in which were placed choice and interesting objects in natural history, geology, mineralogy, and metallurgy. All were represented. Many of these specimens had been brought to him from abroad by his ship-captains, who transported his color manufactures and other commodities to foreign parts.

My friend Tom Smith and I made it a rule — and in this we were encouraged by his father — that, so far as was possible, we ourselves should actually *make* the acids and other substances used in our experiments. We were not to buy them ready-made, as this would have taken the zest out of our enjoyment. We should have lost the pleasure and instruction of producing them by means of our own wits and energies. To encounter and overcome a difficulty is the most interesting of all things. Hence, though often baffled, we eventually produced perfect specimens of nitrous, nitric, and muriatic acids. We distilled alcohol from duly fermented sugar and water, and rectified the resultant spirit from fusel-oil by passing the alcoholic vapor through animal charcoal before it entered the worm of the still. We converted part of the alcohol into sulphuric ether. We produced phosphorus from old bones, and elaborated many of the mysteries of chemistry.

The amount of practical information which we obtained by this system of making our own chemical agents, was such as to reward us, in many respects, for the labor we underwent. To outsiders it might appear a very troublesome and roundabout way of getting at the finally desired result; but I feel certain that there is no better method of rooting chemical or any other instruction deeply in our

minds.   Indeed, I regret that the same system is not pursued by the youth of the present day. They are seldom
if ever called upon to exert their own wits and industry to
obtain the requisites for their instruction.   A great deal is
now said about technical education; but how little there
is of technical handiness or head work! Everything is
bought ready-made to their hands; and hence there is no
call for individual ingenuity.

I left the High School at the end of 1820. I carried
with me a small amount of Latin and no Greek. I do
not think I was much the better for my small acquaintance with the dead languages.

By the time I was seventeen years old I had acquired a
considerable amount of practical knowledge as to the use
and handling of mechanical tools, and I desired to turn
it to some account.   I was able to construct working
models of steam-engines and other apparatus required for
the illustration of mechanical subjects.   I began with
making a small working steam-engine, for the purpose of
grinding the oil-colors used by my father in his artistic
work.   The result was quite satisfactory.   Many persons
came to see my active little steam-engine at work; and
they were so pleased with it that I received several orders
for small workshop engines, and also for some models of
steam-engines to illustrate the subjects taught at Mechanics' Institutions.

I contrived a sectional model of a complete condensing
steam-engine of the beam and parallel-motion construction.   The model, as seen from one side, exhibited every
external detail in full and due action when the fly-wheel
was moved round by hand; while on the other, or sectional side, every detail of the interior was seen, with the
steam-valves and air-pump, as well as the motion of the

piston in the cylinder, with the construction of the piston and the stuffing-box, together with the slide-valve and steam-passages, all in due position and relative movement.

I was a regular attendant at the Edinburgh School of Arts from 1821 to 1826, meanwhile inventing original contrivances of various sorts.

About the year 1827, when I was nineteen years old, the subject of steam-carriages to run upon common roads occupied considerable attention. Several engineers and mechanical schemers had tried their hands, but as yet no substantial results had come of their attempts to solve the problem. Like others, I tried my hand. Having made a small working model of a steam-carriage, I exhibited it before the members of the Scottish Society of Arts. The performance of this active little machine was so gratifying to the Society, that they requested me to construct one of such power as to enable four or six persons to be conveyed along the ordinary roads. The members of the Society, in their individual capacity, subscribed £60, which they placed in my hands, as the means of carrying out their project.

I accordingly set to work at once. I had the heavy parts of the engine and carriage done at Anderson's foundry at Leith. There was in Anderson's employment a most able general mechanic, named Robert Maclaughlan, who had served his time at Carmichael's, of Dundee. Anderson possessed some excellent tools, which enabled me to proceed rapidly with the work. Besides, he was most friendly, and took much delight in being concerned in my enterprise. This " big job " was executed in about four months. The steam-carriage was completed and exhibited before the members of the Society of Arts. Many successful trials were made with it on the Queensferry

Road, near Edinburgh. The runs were generally of four or five miles, with a load of eight passengers, sitting on benches about three feet from the ground.

The experiments were continued for nearly three months, to the great satisfaction of the members.

The chief object of my ambition was now to be taken on at Henry Maudsley's works in London. I had heard so much of his engineering work, of his assortment of machine-making tools, and of the admirable organization of his manufactory, that I longed to obtain employment there. But I was aware that my father had not the means of paying the large premium required for placing me there, and I was also informed that Maudsley had ceased to take pupils, they caused him so much annoyance. My father and I went to London ; and Mr. Maudsley received us in the most kind and frank manner, and courteously invited us to go round the works. When this was concluded I ventured to say to Mr. Maudsley that "I had brought up with me from Edinburgh some working models of steam-engines and mechanical drawings, and I should feel truly obliged if he would allow me to show them to him." "By all means," said he ; "bring them to me to-morrow at twelve o'clock." I need not say how much pleased I was at this permission to exhibit my handiwork, and how anxious I felt as to the result of Mr. Maudsley's inspection of it.

I carefully unpacked my working model of the steam-engine at the carpenter's shop, and had it conveyed, together with my drawings, on a handcart to Mr. Maudsley's, next morning, at the appointed hour. I was allowed to place my work for his inspection in a room next his office and counting-house. I then called at his residence, close by, where he kindly received me in his library. He asked me to wait until he and his partner, Joshua Field, had inspected my handiwork.

I waited anxiously. Twenty long minutes passed. At last he entered the room, and from a lively expression in his countenance I observed in a moment that the great object of my long-cherished ambition had been attained. He expressed, in good round terms, his satisfaction at my practical ability as a workman, engineer, and mechanical draughtsman. Then, opening the door which led from his library into his beautiful private workshop, he said, " This is where I wish you to work, beside me, as my assistant workman. From what I have seen there is no need of an apprenticeship in your case."

One of his favorite maxims was, " First *get a clear notion* of what you desire to accomplish, and then in all probability you will succeed in doing it." Another was, " Keep a sharp lookout upon your materials ; get rid of every pound of material you can *do without;* put to yourself the question, 'What business has it to be there?' avoid complexities, and make everything as simple as possible." Mr. Maudsley was full of quaint maxims and remarks, — the result of much shrewdness, keen observation, and great experience. They were well worthy of being stored up in the mind, like a set of proverbs, full of the life and experience of men. His thoughts became compressed into pithy expressions exhibiting his force of character and intellect. His quaint remarks on my first visit to his workshop and on subsequent occasions proved to me invaluable guides to " right thinking " in regard to all matters connected with mechanical structure.

On the morning of Monday, May 30, 1829, I began my regular attendance at Mr. Maudsley's workshop, and remained with him until he died, Feb. 14, 1831. It was a very sad thing for me to lose my dear old master, who always treated me like a friend and companion. At his death I passed over into the service of his worthy partner, Joshua Field, until my twenty-third year, when I intended to begin business for myself.

I first settled myself at Manchester, but afterwards established a large business outside of Manchester on the Bridgewater Canal. In August, 1836, the Bridgewater Foundry was in complete and efficient action. The engine ordered at Londonderry was at once put in hand, and the concern was fairly started in its long career of prosperity. The wooden workshops had been erected upon the grass, but the greensward soon disappeared. The hum of the driving-belts, the whirl of the machinery, the sound of the hammer upon the anvil, gave the place an air of busy activity. As work increased, workmen multiplied. The workshops were enlarged. Wood gave place to brick. Cottages for the accommodation of the work-people sprung up in the neighborhood, and what had once been a quiet grassy field became the centre of a busy population.

It was a source of vast enjoyment to me, while engaged in the anxious business connected with the establishment of the foundry, to be surrounded with so many objects of rural beauty. The site of the works being on the west side of Manchester, we had the benefit of breathing pure air during the greater part of the year. The scenery round about was very attractive. Exercise was a source of health to the mind as well as the body. As it was necessary that I should reside as near as possible to the works, I had plenty of opportunities for enjoying the rural scenery of the neighborhood. I had the good fortune to become the tenant of a small cottage in the ancient village of Barton, in Cheshire, at the very moderate rental of fifteen pounds a year. The cottage was situated on the banks of the river Irwell, and was only about six minutes' walk from the works at Patricroft. It suited my moderate domestic arrangements admirably.

On June 16, 1840, a day of happy memory, I was married to Miss Anne Hartop.

I was present at the opening of the Liverpool and Manchester Railway, on Sept. 15, 1830. Every one knows the success of the undertaking. Railways became the rage. They were projected in every possible direction; and when made, locomotives were required to work them. When George Stephenson was engaged in building his first locomotive, at Killingworth, he was greatly hampered, not only by the want of handy mechanics, but by the want of efficient tools. But he did the best that he could. His genius overcame difficulties. It was immensely to his credit that he should have so successfully completed his engines for the Stockton and Darlington, and afterward for the Liverpool and Manchester, Railway.

Only a few years had passed, and self-acting tools were now enabled to complete, with precision and uniformity, machines that before had been deemed almost impracticable. In proportion to the rapid extension of railways the demand for locomotives became very great. As our machine tools were peculiarly adapted for turning out a large amount of first-class work, we directed our attention to this class of business. In the course of about ten years after the opening of the Liverpool and Manchester Railway, we executed considerable orders for locomotives for the London and Southampton, the Manchester and Leeds, and the Gloucester Railway Companies.

The Great Western Railway Company invited us to

tender for twenty of their very ponderous engines. They proposed a very tempting condition of the contract. It was that if, after a month's trial of the locomotives, their working proved satisfactory, a premium of £100 was to be added to the price of each engine and tender. The locomotives were made and delivered; they ran the stipulated number of test miles between London and Bristol in a perfectly satisfactory manner; and we not only received the premium, but, what was much more encouraging, we received a special letter from the board of directors, stating their entire satisfaction with the performance of our engines, and desiring us to refer other contractors to them with respect to the excellence of our workmanship. This testimonial was altogether spontaneous, and proved extremely valuable in other quarters.

The date of the first sketch of my steam-hammer was Nov. 24, 1839. It consisted of, first, a massive anvil, on which to rest the work; second, a block of iron constituting the hammer, or blow-giving portion; and, third, an inverted steam cylinder, to whose piston-rod the hammer-block was attached. All that was then required to produce a most effective hammer, was simply to admit steam of sufficient pressure into the cylinder, so as to act on the under side of the piston, and thus to raise the hammer-block attached to the end of the piston-rod. By a very simple arrangement of a slide-valve under the control of an attendant, the steam was allowed to escape, and thus permit the massive block of iron rapidly to descend by its own gravity upon the work then upon the anvil.

Thus, by the more or less rapid manner in which the attendant allowed the steam to enter or escape from the cylinder, any required number or any intensity of blows could be delivered. Their succession might be modified

in an instant; the hammer might be arrested and suspended according to the requirements of the work. The
workman might thus, as it were, *think in blows*. He
might deal them out on to the ponderous glowing mass,
and mould or knead it into the desired form as if it were
a lump of clay, or pat it with gentle taps, according to his
will or at the desire of the forgeman.

Rude and rapidly sketched out as it was, this my first
delineation of the steam-hammer will be found to com-
prise all the essential elements of the invention. There
was no want of orders when the valuable qualities of the
steam-hammer came to be seen and experienced; soon
after I had the opportunity of securing a patent for it in
the United States, where it soon found its way into the
principal iron-works of the country. As time passed by,
I had furnished steam-hammers to the principal foundries
in England, and had sent them abroad even to Russia.

But the English Government is proverbially slow in rec-
ognizing such improvements. It was not till years had
passed by, that Mr. Nasmyth was asked to furnish hammers to government works. Then he was invited to apply
them to pile-driving. He says : —

My first order for my pile-driver was a source of great
pleasure to me. It was for the construction of some great
royal docks at Devonport. An immense portion of the
shore of the Hamoaze had to be walled in so as to exclude
the tide.

When I arrived on the spot with my steam pile-driver,
there was a great deal of curiosity in the dockyard as to
the action of the new machine. The pile-driving machine-

men gave me a good-natured challenge to vie with them in driving down a pile. They adopted the old method, while I adopted the new one. The resident managers sought out two great pile logs of equal size and length, — seventy feet long and eighteen inches square. At a given signal we started together. I let in the steam, and the hammer at once began to work. The four-ton block showered down blows at the rate of eighty a minute, and in the course of *four and a half minutes* my pile was driven down to its required depth. The men working at the ordinary machine had only begun to drive. It took them upward of *twelve hours* to complete the driving of their pile !

Such a saving of time in the performance of similar work — by steam *versus* manual labor — had never before been witnessed. The energetic action of the steam-hammer, sitting on the shoulders of the pile high up aloft, and following it suddenly down, the rapidly hammered blows keeping time with the flashing out of the waste steam at the end of each stroke, was indeed a remarkable sight. When my pile was driven the hammer-block and guide-case were speedily re-hoisted by the small engine that did all the laboring and locomotive work of the machine, the steam-hammer portion of which was then lowered on to the shoulders of the next pile in succession. Again it set to work. At this the spectators, crowding about in boats, pronounced their approval in the usual British style of "Three cheers !" My new pile-driver was thus acknowledged as another triumphant proof of the power of steam.

In the course of the year 1843 it was necessary for me to make a journey to St. Petersburg. My object was to endeavor to obtain an order for a portion of the locomotives required for working the line between that city and Moscow. The railway had been constructed under the engineership of Major Whistler, and it was shortly about to be opened.

The Major gave me a frank and cordial reception, and informed me of the position of affairs. The Emperor, he said, was desirous of training a class of Russian mechanics to supply not only the locomotives, but to keep them constantly in repair. The locomotives must be made in Russia. I received, however, a very large order for boilers and other detail parts of the Moscow machines.

I enjoyed greatly my visit to St. Petersburg, and my return home through Stockholm and Copenhagen.

Travelling one day in Sweden, the post-house where I was set down was an inn, although without a sign-board. The landlady was a bright, cheery, jolly woman. She could not speak a word of English, nor I a word of Dannemora Swedish. I was very thirsty and hungry, and wanted something to eat. How was I to communicate my wishes to the landlady? I resorted, as I often did, to the universal language of the pencil. I took out my sketch-book, and in a few minutes I made a drawing of a table with a dish of smoking meat upon it, a bottle and a glass, a knife and fork, a loaf, a salt-cellar, and a corkscrew. She looked at the drawing and gave a hearty laugh. She nodded pleasantly, showing that she clearly understood what I wanted. She asked me for the sketch, and went into the back garden to show it to her husband, who inspected it with great delight. I went out and looked about the place, which was very picturesque. After a short time the landlady came to the door and beckoned me in, and I found spread out on the table everything that I desired, — a broiled

chicken, smoking hot from the gridiron, a bottle of capital
home-brewed ale, and all the *et ceteras* of an excellent
repast. I made use of my pencil in many other ways.
I always found that a sketch was as useful as a sentence.
Besides, it generally created a sympathy between me and
my entertainers.

As the Bridgewater Foundry had been so fortunate as
to earn for itself a considerable reputation for mechanical
contrivances, the workshops were always busy. They
were crowded with machine tools in full action, and exhibited to all comers their effectiveness in the most satisfactory manner. Every facility was afforded to those who
desired to see them at work; and every machine and
machine tool that was turned out became in the hands
of its employers the progenitor of a numerous family.

Indeed, on many occasions I had the gratification of
seeing my mechanical notions adopted by rival or com-
petitive machine constructors, often without acknowledgment; though, notwithstanding this point of honor, there
was room enough for all. Though the parent features
were easily recognizable, I esteemed such plagiarisms as a
sort of left-handed compliment to their author. I also
regarded them as a proof that I had hit the mark in so
arranging my mechanical combinations as to cause their
general adoption ; and many of them remain unaltered to
this day.

My favorite pursuit, after my daily excursions at the
foundry, was astronomy. I constructed for myself a telescope of considerable power, and, mounting my ten-inch
instrument, I began my survey of the heavens. I began as a learner, and my learning grew with experience.
There were the prominent stars, the planets, the Milky
Way, — with thousands of far-off suns, — to be seen. My

observations were at first merely general; by degrees they became particular. I was not satisfied with enjoying these sights myself. I made my friends and neighbors sharers in my pleasure, and some of them enjoyed the wonders of the heavens as much as I did.

In my early use of the telescope I had fitted the speculum into a light square tube of deal, to which the eyepiece was attached, so as to have all the essential parts of the telescope combined together in the most simple and portable form. I had often to move it from place to place in my small garden at the side of the Bridgewater Canal, in order to get it clear of the trees and branches which intercepted some object in the heavens which I wished to see. How eager and enthusiastic I was in those days! Sometimes I got out of bed in the clear small hours of the morning, and went down to the garden in my night-shirt. I would take the telescope in my arms and plant it in some suitable spot, where I might take a peep at some special planet or star then above the horizon.

It became bruited about that a ghost was seen at Patricroft! A barge was silently gliding along the canal near midnight, when the boatman suddenly saw a figure in white. " It moved among the trees, with a coffin in its arms!" The apparition was so sudden and strange that he immediately concluded that it was a ghost. The weird sight was reported all along the canal, and also at Wolverhampton, which was the boatman's headquarters. He told the people at Patricroft, on his return journey, what he had seen; and great was the excitement produced. The place was haunted; there was no doubt about it! After all, the rumor was founded on fact; for the ghost was merely myself in my night-shirt, and the coffin was my telescope, which I was quietly shifting from one place to another,

in order to get a clearer sight of the heavens at midnight.

I had been for some time contemplating the possibility
of retiring altogether from business. I had got enough of
the world's goods, and was willing to make way for younger
men.

Many long years of pleasant toil and exertion had done
their work. A full momentum of prosperity had' been
given to my engineering business at Patricroft. My share
in the financial results accumulated, with accelerated rapidity, to an amount far beyond my most sanguine hopes.
But finding, from long-continued and incessant mental
efforts, that my nervous system was beginning to become
shaken, especially in regard to an affection of the eyes,
which in some respects damaged my sight, I thought the
time had arrived for me to retire from commercial life.

Behold us, then, settled down at Hammerfield for life.
We had plenty to do. My workshop was fully equipped.
My hobbies were there, and I could work them to my
heart's content. The walls of our various rooms were
soon hung with pictures and other works of art, suggestive
of many pleasant associations of former days. Our library
bookcase was crowded with old friends in the shape of
books that had been read and re-read many times, until
they had almost become part of ourselves. Old Lan-
cashire friends made their way to us when " up in town,"
and expressed themselves delighted with our pleasant
house and its beautiful surroundings.

I was only forty-eight years old, which may be considered the prime of life. But I had plenty of hobbies, perhaps the chief of which was astronomy. No sooner had I
settled at Hammerfield than I had my telescopes brought
out and mounted. The fine, clear skies with which we

were favored furnished me with abundant opportunities for the use of my instruments.   I began again my investigations on the sun and the moon, and made some original discoveries.

It is time to come to an end of my recollections.   I have endeavored to give a brief *résumé* of my life and labors.   I hope they may prove interesting as well as useful to others.   Thanks to a good constitution and a frame invigorated by work, I continue to lead, with my dear wife, a happy life.

XIII.

SIR HENRY BESSEMER.

THE AGE OF STEEL.

IN intervals of the reading meetings so many of the children's afternoons with Uncle Fritz had been taken up with excursions to see machinery at work, that their next meeting at the Oliver House was, as it proved, the last for the winter.

They had gone to the pumping-station of the water-works, and had seen the noiseless work of the great steam-engine there. They had gone to the Ætna Mills at Watertown, and with the eye of the flesh had seen " rovers " and shuttles, and had been taught what " slobbers " are. They had gone to Waltham, and had been taught something of the marvellous skill and delicacy expended on the manufacture of watches. They had gone to Rand and Avery's printing-house ; and here they not only saw the processes of printing, but they saw steam power " converted " into electricity. They had gone to the Locomotive Factory in Albany Street, and understood, much better than before, the inventions of George Stephenson, under the lead of the foremen in the shops, who had been very kind to them.

On their last meeting Uncle Fritz reminded them of something which one of these gentlemen had taught them about the qualities of steel and iron; and again of what they had seen of steel-springs at Waltham, when they saw how the balances of watches are arranged.

"Some bright person has called our time 'the Age of Steel,'" he said. "You know Ovid's division was 'the Age of Gold, the Age of Silver, the Age of Brass, the Age of Iron.' And Ovid, who was in low spirits, thought the Age of Iron was the worst of all. Now, we begin to improve if we have entered the Age of Steel; for steel is, poetically speaking, glorified iron.

"Now the person to whom we owe it, that, in practice, we can build steel ships to-day where we once built iron ships, and lay steel rails to-day where even Stephenson was satisfied with iron, is Sir Henry Bessemer. The Queen knighted him in recognition of the service he had rendered to the world by his improvements in the processes of turning iron into steel.

"It is impossible to estimate the addition which these improvements have made to the physical power of the world. I have not the most recent figures, but look at this," said Uncle Fritz. And he gave to John to read from a Life of Sir Henry Bessemer: —

"Prior to this invention the entire production of cast steel in Great Britain was only about fifty thousand tons annually; and its average price, which ranged from £50 to £600, prohibited its use for many of the purposes to which it is now universally applied. After the invention, in the year 1877, the Bessemer steel produced in Great Britain alone amounted to 750,000 tons, or fifteen times the total of the former method of manufacture, while the selling price averaged only £10 per ton, and the coal consumed in producing it was less by 3,500,000 tons than would have been required in order to make the same quality of steel by the old, or Sheffield, process. The total reduction of cost is equal to about £30,000,000 sterling upon the quantity manufactured in England during the year."

The same book goes on to show that in other nations £20,000,000 worth of Bessemer steel was produced in the same year.

"You see," said Uncle Fritz, "that here is an addition to the real wealth of the world such as makes any average fairy story about diamonds and rubies rather cheap and contemptible.

" You will like Sir Henry Bessemer, Hester, because he was happily trained and had good chances when he was a boy. And you will be amused to see how his bright wife was brighter than all the internal-revenue people. She was so bright that she lost him the appointment which had enabled him to marry her. But I think he says somewhere, with a good deal of pride, that but for that misfortune, and the injustice which accompanied it, he should have probably never made his great inventions. It is one more piece of ' Partial evil, — universal good.' "

Then the children, with Uncle Fritz's aid, began picking out what they called the plums from the accounts he showed them of Sir Henry Bessemer's life.

BESSEMER'S FAMILY.

At the time of the great Revolution of 1792 there was employed in the French mint a man of great ingenuity, who had become a member of the French Academy of Sciences at the age of twenty-five. When Robespierre became Dictator of France, this scientific academician was transferred from the mint to the management of a public bakery, established for the purpose of supplying the populace of Paris with bread.   In that position he soon became the object of revolutionary frenzy.   One day a rumor was set afloat that the loaves supplied were light in weight; and, spreading like wildfire, it was made the occasion of a fearful tumult.   The manager of the bakery was instantly seized and cast into prison.   He succeeded in escaping, but it was at the peril of his life.   Knowing the peril he was in, he lost no time in making his way to England; and he only succeeded in doing so by adroitly using some documents he possessed bearing the signature of the Dictator.   Landing in England a ruined man, his talents soon proved a passport to success.   He was appointed to a position in the English mint; and by the exercise of his ingenuity in other directions, he ere long acquired sufficient means to buy a small estate at Charlton, in Hertfordshire.   Such, in brief, were the circumstances that led to the settlement there of Anthony Bessemer, the father of Sir Henry Bessemer.   The latter may be said to have been born an inventor.   His father was an inventor before him.   After settling in England, his inventive ingenuity was displayed in making improvements in microscopes and in type-founding, and in the discovery of what his son has happily described as the true alchemy.   The latter discovery, which he made about the beginning of the present century, was a source of considerable profit to him.   It is generally known that when gold articles are made by the jewellers, there are various discolorations left on their surface by the process of manufacture; and in order to clear their surface, they are put into a solution of alum, salt, and saltpetre, which dissolves a large quantity of the copper that is used as an alloy. Anthony Bessemer discovered that this powerful acid not only dissolved the copper, but also dissolved a quantity of gold. He accordingly began to buy up this liquor; and as he was the only one who knew that it contained gold in solution, he had no difficulty in arranging for the purchase of it from all the manufacturers in London. From that liquor he succeeded in extracting gold in considerable quantities for many years. By some means that he kept secret (and the secret died with him), he deposited the particles of gold on the shavings of another metal, which, being afterwards melted, left the pure gold in small quantities. Thirty years afterward the Messrs. Elkington invented the electrotype process, which had the same effect. Anthony Bessemer was also eminently successful as a type-founder. When in France, before the Revolution of 1792, he cut a great many founts of type for Messrs. Firmin Didot, the celebrated French type-founders; and after his return to England he betook himself, as a diversion, to type-cutting for Mr. Henry Caslon, the celebrated English type-founder. He engraved an entire series, from pica to diamond, — a work which occupied several years. The success of these types led to the establishment of the firm of Bessemer and Catherwood as type-founders, carrying on business at Charlton. The great improvement which Anthony Bessemer introduced into the art of type-making was not so much in the engraving as in the composition of the metal. He discovered that an alloy of copper, tin, and bismuth was the most durable metal for type; and the working of this discovery was very successful in his hands. The secret of his success, however, he kept unknown to the trade. He knew that if it were suspected that the superiority of his type consisted in the composition of the metal, analysis would reveal it, and others would then be able to compete with him. So, to divert attention from the real cause, he pointed out to the trade that the shape of his type was different, as the angle at which all the lines were produced from the surface was more obtuse in his type than in those of other manufacturers, at the same time contending that his type would wear longer. Other manufacturers ridiculed this account of Bessemer's type, but experience showed that it lasted nearly twice as long as other type. The business flourished for a dozen years under his direction, and during that period the real cause of its success was kept a secret. The process has since been re-discovered and patented. Such were some of the inventive efforts of the father of one of the greatest inventors of the present age.

HENRY BESSEMER.

The youngest son of Anthony Bessemer, Henry, was born at Charlton, in Hertfordshire, in 1813. His boyhood was spent in his native village ; and while receiving the rudiments of an ordinary education in the neighboring town of Hitchin, the leisure and retirement of rural life afforded ample time, though perhaps little inducement, for the display of the natural bent of his mind. Notwithstanding his scanty and imperfect mechanical appliances, his early years were devoted to the cultivation of his inventive faculties. His parents encouraged him in his youthful efforts.

At the age of eighteen he came to London, "knowing no one," he says, "and myself unknown, — a mere cipher in a vast sea of human enterprise." Here he worked as a modeller and designer with encouraging success. He engraved a large number of elegant and original designs on steel, with a diamond point, for patent-medicine labels. He got plenty of this sort of work to do, and was well paid for it. In his boyhood his favorite amusement was the modelling of objects in clay; and even in this primitive school of genius he worked with so much success that at the age of nineteen he exhibited one of his beautiful models at the Royal Academy, then held at Somerset House.

STAMPED PAPER.

Thus he soon began to make his way in the metropolis; and in the course of the following year he was maturing some plans in connection with the production of stamps which he sanguinely hoped would lead him on to fortune. At that time the old forms of stamps were in use that had been employed since the days of Queen Anne; and as they were easily transferred from old deeds to new ones, the Government lost a large amount annually by this surreptitious use of old stamps instead of new ones. The ordinary impressed or embossed stamps, such as are now employed on bills of exchange, or impressed directly on skins or parchment, were liable to be entirely obliterated if exposed for some months to a damp atmosphere. A deed so exposed would at last appear as if unstamped, and would therefore become invalid. Special precautions were therefore observed in order to prevent this occurrence. It was the practice to gum small pieces of blue paper on the parchment; and, to render it still more secure, a strip of metal foil was passed through it, and another small piece of paper with the printed initials of the sovereign was gummed over the loose end of the foil at the back. The stamp was then impressed on the blue paper, which, unlike parchment, is incapable of losing the impression by exposure to a damp atmosphere. Experience showed, however, that by placing a little piece of moistened blotting-paper for a few hours over the paper, the gum became so softened that the two pieces of paper and the slip of foil could be easily removed from an old deed and then used for a new one. In this way stamps could be used a second and third time; and by thus utilizing the expensive stamps on old deeds of partnerships that were dissolved, or leases that were expired, the public revenue lost thousands of pounds every year. Sir Charles Persley, of the Stamp Office, told Sir Henry Bessemer that the Government were probably defrauded of £100,000 per annum in that way. The young inventor at once set to work, for the express purpose of devising a stamp that could not be used twice. His first discovery was a mode by which he could have reproduced easily and cheaply thousands of stamps of any pattern. "The facility," he says, " with which I could make a permanent die from a thin paper original, capable of producing a thousand copies, would have opened a wide door for successful frauds if my process had been known to unscrupulous persons; for there is not a government stamp or a paper seal of a corporate body that every common office clerk could not forge in a few minutes at the office of his employer or at his own home. The production of such a die from a common paper stamp is a work of only ten minutes; the materials cost less than one penny; no sort of technical skill is necessary, and a common copying-press or a letter stamp yields most successful copies." To this day a successful forger has to employ a skilful die-sinker to make a good imitation in steel of the document he wishes to forge; but if such a method as that discovered and described by Sir Henry Bessemer were known, what a prospect it would open up! Appalled at the effect which the communication of such a process would have had upon the business of the Stamp Office, he carefully kept the knowledge of it to himself; and to this day it remains a profound secret.

More than ever impressed with the necessity for an improved form of stamp, and conscious of his own capability to produce it, he labored for some months to accomplish his object, feeling sure that, if successful, he would be amply rewarded by the Government. To insure the secrecy of his experiments, he worked at them during the night, after his ordinary business of the day was over. He succeeded at last in making a stamp which obviated the great objection to the then existing form, inasmuch as it would be impossible to transfer it from one deed to another, to obliterate it by moisture, or to take an impression from it capable of producing a duplicate. Flushed with success and confident of the reward of his labors, he waited upon Sir Charles Persley at Somerset House, and showed him, by numerous proofs, how easily all the then existing stamps could be forged, and his new invention to prevent forgery. Sir Charles, who was much astonished at the one invention and pleased with the other, asked Bessemer to call again in a few days. At the second interview Sir Charles asked him to work out the principle of the new stamping invention more fully. Accordingly Bessemer devoted five or six weeks' more labor to the perfecting of his stamp, with which the Stamp Office authorities were now well pleased. The design, as described by the inventor, was circular, about two and a half inches in diameter, and consisted of a garter with a motto in capital letters, surmounted by a crown. Within the garter was a shield, and the garter was filled with network in imitation of lace. The die was executed in steel, which pierced the parchment with more than four hundred holes; and these holes formed the stamp. It is by a similar process that valentine makers have since learned to make the perforated paper used in their trade. Such a stamp removed all the objections to the old one. So pleased was Sir Charles with it that he recommended it to Lord Althorp, and it was soon adopted by the Stamp Office. At the same time Sir Henry was asked whether he would be satisfied with the position of Superintendent of Stamps with £500 or £600 per annum, as compensation for his invention, instead of a sum of money from the treasury. This appointment he gladly agreed to accept; for, being engaged to be married at the time, he thought his future position in life was settled. Shortly afterwards he called on the young lady to whom he was engaged, and communicated the glad tidings to her, at the same time showing her the design of his new stamp. On explaining to her that its chief virtue was that the new stamps thus produced could not, like the old ones, be fraudulently used twice or thrice, she instantly suggested that if all stamps had a date put upon them they could not be used at a future time without detection. The idea was new to him; and, impressed with its practical character, he at once conceived a plan for the insertion of movable dates in the die of his stamp. The method by which this is now done is too well known to require description here; but in 1833 it was a new invention. Having worked out the details of a stamp with movable dates, he saw that it was more simple and more easily worked than his elaborate die for perforating stamps; but he also saw that if he disclosed his latest invention it might interfere with his settled prospects in connection with the carrying out of his first one. It was not without regret, too, that he saw the results of many months of toil and the experiments of many lonely nights at once superseded; but his conviction of the superiority of his latest design was so strong, and his own sense of honor and his confidence in that of the Government was so unsuspecting, that he boldly went and placed the whole matter before Sir Charles Persley. Of course the new design was preferred. Sir Charles truly observed that with this new plan all the old dies, old presses, and old workmen could be employed. Among the other advantages it presented to the Government, it did not fail to strike Sir Charles that no Superintendent of Stamps would now be necessary, — a recommendation which the perforated die did not possess. The Stamp Office therefore abandoned the ingenuous and ingenious inventor. The old stamps were called in, and the new ones issued in a few weeks; the revenue from stamps grew enormously, and forged or feloniously used stamps are now almost unheard of. The Stamp Office reaped a benefit which it is scarcely possible to estimate fully, while Bessemer did not receive a farthing. Shortly after the new stamp was adopted by Act of Parliament, Lord Althorp resigned, and his successors disclaimed all liability. When the disappointed inventor pressed his claim, he was met by all sorts of half-promises and excuses, which ended in nothing. The disappointment was all the more galling because, if Bessemer had stuck to his first-adopted plan, his services would have been indispensable to its execution; and it was therefore through his putting a better and more easily worked plan before them that his services were coolly ignored. " I had no patent to fall back upon," he says, in describing the incident afterward. " I could not go to law, even if I wished to do so ; for I was reminded, when pressing for mere money out of pocket, that I had done all the work voluntarily and of my own accord. Wearied and disgusted, I at last ceased to waste time in calling at the Stamp Office, — for time was precious to me in those days, — and I felt that nothing but increased exertions could make up for the loss of some nine months of toil and expenditure. Thus sad and dispirited, and with a burning sense of injustice overpowering all other feelings, I went my way from the Stamp Office, too proud to ask as a favor that which was indubitably my right."

GOLD PAINT.

Shortly after he had taken out his first patent for his improvement in type-founding, his attention was accidentally turned to the manufacture of bronze powder, which is used in gold-work, japanning, gold-printing, and similar operations. While engaged in ornamenting a vignette in his sister's album, he had to purchase a small quantity of this bronze, and was struck with the great difference between the price of the raw material and that of the manufactured article. The latter sold for 11 2s. a pound, while the raw material only cost 11d. a pound. He concluded that the difference was caused by the process of manufacture, and made inquiries with the view of learning the nature of the process. He found, however, that this manufacture was hardly known in England. The article was supplied to English dealers from Nuremberg and other towns in Germany. He did not succeed, therefore, in finding any one who could tell him how it was produced. In these circumstances he determined to try to make it himself, and worked for a year and a half at the solution of this task. Other men had tried it and failed, and he was on the point of failing too. After eighteen months of fruitless labor he came to the conclusion that he could not make it, and gave it up. But it is the highest attribute of genius to succeed where others fail, and, impelled by this instinct, he resumed his investigations after six months' repose. At last success crowned his efforts. The profits of his previous inventions now supplied him with funds sufficient to provide the mechanical appliances he had designed.

Knowing very little of the patent law, and considering it so insecure that the safest way to reap the full benefit of his new invention was to keep it to himself, he determined to work his process of bronze-making in strict secrecy; and every precaution was therefore adopted for this purpose. He first put up a small apparatus with his own hands, and worked it entirely himself. By this means he produced the required article at 4s. a pound. He then sent out a traveller with samples of it, and the first order he got was at 80s. a pound. Being thus fully assured of success, he communicated his plans to a friend, who agreed to put £10,000 into the business, as a sleeping partner, in order to work the new manufacture on a larger scale. The entire working of the concern was left in the hands of Sir Henry, who accordingly proceeded to enlarge his means of production. To insure secrecy, he made plans of all the machinery required, and then divided them into sections. He next sent these sectional drawings to different engineering works, in order to get his machinery made piece-meal in different parts of England. This done, he collected the various pieces, and fitted them up himself, — a work that occupied him nine months. Finding everything at last in perfect working order, he engaged four or five assistants in whom he had confidence, and paid them very high wages on condition that they kept everything in the strictest secrecy. Bronze powder was now produced in large quantities by means of five self-acting machines, which not only superseded hand labor entirely, but were capable of producing as much daily as sixty skilled operatives could do by the old hand system.

To this day the mechanical means by which his famous gold paint is produced remains a secret. The machinery is driven by a steam-engine in an adjoining room ; and into the room where the automatic machinery is at work none but the inventor and his assistants have ever entered. When a sufficient quantity of work is done, a bell is rung to give notice to the engine-man to stop the engine ; and in this way the machinery has been in constant use for over forty years without having been either patented or pirated. Its profit was as great as its success. At first he made 1,000 per cent profit ; and though there are other pro-ducts that now compete with this bronze, it still yields 300 per cent profit. " All this time," says the successful inventor thirty years afterward, " I have been afraid to im-prove the machinery, or to introduce other engineers into the works to improve them. Strange to say, we have thus among us a manufacture wholly unimproved for thirty years. I do not believe there is another instance of such a thing in the kingdom. I believe that if I had patented it, the fourteen years would not have run out without other people making improvements in the manufacture. Of the five machines I use, three are applicable to other processes, one to color-making especially; so much so that notwithstanding the very excellent income which I derive from the manufacture, I had once nearly made up my mind to throw it open and make it public, for the purpose of using part of my invention for the manufacture of colors. Three out of my five assistants have died; and if the other two were to die and myself too, no one would know what the invention is." Since this was said (in 1871), Sir Henry has rewarded the faithfulness of his two surviving assistants by handing over to them the business and the factory.

BESSEMER STEEL.

Sir Henry Bessemer was first led to turn his attention to the improvement of the manufacture of iron by a remark of Commander Minie, who was superintending certain trials of the results of Sir Henry's experiments in obtaining rotation of shot fired from a smooth-bore gun. "The shots," said Minie, "rotate properly; but if you cannot get stronger metal for your guns, such heavy projectiles will be of little use."

At this time Sir Henry had no connection with the iron or steel trade, and knew little or nothing of metallurgy. But this fact he has always represented as being rather an advantage than a drawback. "I find," he says, "in my experience with regard to inventions, that the most intelligent manufacturers invent many small improvements in various departments of their manufactures, — but, generally speaking, these are only small ameliorations based on the nature of the operation they are daily pursuing; while, on the contrary, persons wholly unconnected with any particular business have their minds so free and untrammelled to new things as they are, and as they would present themselves to an independent observer, that they are the men who eventually produce the greatest changes." It was in this spirit that he began his investigations in metallurgy. His first business was to make himself acquainted with the information contained in the best works then published on the subject. He also endeavored to add some practical knowledge to what he learned from books. With this view he visited the iron-making districts in the north, and there obtained an insight into the working merits and defects of the processes then in use. On his return to London he arranged for the use of an old factory in St. Pancras, where he began his own series of experiments. He converted the factory into a small experimental "iron-works," in which his first object was to improve the quality of iron. For this purpose he made many costly experiments without the desired measure of success, but not without making some progress in the right direction. After twelve months spent in these experiments he produced an improved quality of cast iron, which was almost as white as steel, and was both tougher and stronger than the best cast iron then used for ordnance. Of this metal he cast a small model gun, which was turned and bored. This gun he took to Paris, and presented it personally to the Emperor,[1] as the result of his labors thus far. His Majesty encouraged him to continue his experiments, and desired to be further informed of the results.

As Sir Henry continued his labors, he extended their scope from the production of refined iron to that of steel;

---

[1] Napoleon III., under whose protection Bessemer had been experimenting in projectiles when his attention was turned to the manufacture of iron.

and in order to protect himself, he took out a patent for each successive improvement.   One idea after another was put to the test of experiment; one furnace after another was pulled down, and numerous mechanical appliances were designed and tried in practice.   During these experiments he specified a multitude of improvements in the crucible process of making steel; but he still felt that much remained to be done.   At the end of eighteen months, he says, " the idea struck me " of rendering cast iron malleable by the introduction of atmospheric air into the fluid metal.   His first experiment to test this idea was made in a crucible in the laboratory.   He there found that by blowing air into the molten metal in the crucible, by means of a movable blow-pipe, he could convert ten pounds or twelve pounds of crude iron into the softest malleable iron.   The samples thus produced were so satisfactory in all their mechanical tests that he brought them under the notice of Colonel Eardley Wilmot, then the Superintendent of the Royal Gun Factories, who expressed himself delighted and astonished at the result, and who offered him facilities for experimenting in Woolwich Arsenal.   These facilities were extended to him in the laboratory by Professor Abel, who made numberless analyses of the material as he advanced with his experiments.   The testing department was also put at his disposal, for testing the tensile strength and elasticity of different samples of soft malleable iron and steel.   The first piece that was rolled at Woolwich was preserved by Sir Henry as a memento.   It was a small bar of metal, about a foot long and an inch wide, and was converted from a state of pig iron in a crucible of only ten pounds.   That small piece of bar, after being rolled, was tried, to see how far it was capable of welding; and he was surprised to see how easily it answered the severest tests. After this he commenced experiments on a larger scale. He had proved in the laboratory that the principle of purifying pig iron by atmospheric air was possible ; but he feared, from what he knew of iron metallurgy, that as he approached the condition of pure soft malleable iron, he must of necessity require a temperature that he could not hope to attain under these conditions. In order to produce larger quantities of metal in this way, one of his first ideas was to apply the air to the molten iron in crucibles ; and accordingly, in October, 1855, he took out a patent embodying this idea. He proposed to erect a large circular furnace, with openings for the reception of melting-pots containing fluid iron, and pipes were made to conduct air into the centre of each pot, and to force it among the particles of metal. Having thus tested the purifying effect of cold air introduced into the melting iron in pots, he labored for three months in trying to overcome the mechanical difficulties experienced in this complicated arrangement. He wondered whether it would not be possible to dispense with the pipes and pots, and perform the whole operation in one large circular or egg-shaped vessel. The difficult thing in doing so, was to force the air all through the mass of liquid metal. While this difficulty was revolving in his mind, the labor and anxiety entailed by previous experiments brought on a short but severe illness ; and while he was lying in bed, pondering for hours upon the prospects of succeeding in another experiment with the pipes and pots, it occurred to him that the difficulty might be got over by introducing air into a large vessel from below into the molten mass within.

Though he entertained grave doubts as to the practicability of carrying out this idea, chiefly owing to the high temperature required to maintain the iron in a state of fluidity while the impurities were being burned out, he determined to put it to a working test; and on recovering health he immediately began to design apparatus for this purpose. He constructed a circular vessel, measuring three feet in diameter and five feet in height, and capable of holding seven hundred-weight of iron. He next ordered a small, powerful air-engine and a quantity of crude iron to be put down on the premises in St. Pancras, that he had hired for carrying on his experiments. The name of these premises was Baxter House, formerly the residence of old Richard Baxter; and the simple experiment we are now going to describe has made that house more famous than ever. The primitive apparatus being ready, the engine was made to force streams of air, under high pressure, through the bottom of the vessel, which was lined with fire-clay; and the stoker was told to pour the metal, when it was sufficiently melted, in at the top of it. A cast-iron plate — one of those lids which commonly cover the coal-holes in the pavement — was hung over the converter; and all being got ready, the stoker in some bewilderment poured in the metal. Instantly out came a volcanic eruption of such dazzling coruscations as had never been seen before. The dangling pot-lid dissolved in the gleaming volume of flame, and the chain by which it hung grew red and then white, as the various stages of the process were unfolded to the gaze of the wondering spectators. The air-cock to regulate the blast was beside the converting-vessel; but no one dared to go near it, much less deliberately to shut it. In this dilemma, however, they were soon relieved by finding that the process of decarburization or combustion had expended all its fury; and, most wonderful of all, the result was steel!

The new metal was tried. Its quality was good. The problem was solved. The new process appeared successful. The inventor was elated, as well he might be !

The new process was received with astonishment by all the iron-working world. It was approved by many, but scoffed at by others. As trials went on, however, the feeling against it increased. The iron so made was often "rotten," and no one could tell exactly why.

Bessemer, however, continued to investigate everything for himself, regardless of all suggestions. Some ideas of permanent value were offered to him, but were set at nought. It was not till another series of independent experiments were made that he himself discovered the secret of failure. It then appeared that, by mere chance, the iron used in his first experiments was Blaenavon pig, which is exceptionally free from phosphorus; and consequently, when other sorts of iron were thrown at random into the converter, the phosphorus manifested its refractory nature in the unworkable character of the metal produced. Analyses made by Professor Abel for Sir Henry showed that this was the real cause of failure. Once convinced of this fact, Sir Henry set to work for the purpose of removing this hostile element. He saw how phosphorus was removed in the puddling-furnace, and he now tried to do the same thing in his converter. Another series of costly and laborious experiments was conducted ; and first one patent and then another was taken out, tried, and abandoned. His last idea was to make a vessel in which the converting process did not take place, but into which he could put the pig iron as soon as it was melted, along with the same kind of materials that were used in the puddling-furnace. He was then of opinion that he must come as near to puddling as possible, in order to get the phosphorus out of the iron. Just as he was preparing to put this plan into operation, there arrived in England some pig iron which he had ordered from Sweden some months previously. When this iron, which was free from phosphorus, was put into the converter, it yielded, in the very first experiment, a metal of so high a quality that he at once abandoned his efforts to dephosphorize ordinary iron. The Sheffield manufacturers were then selling steel at £60 a ton; and he thought that as he could buy pig iron at £7 a ton, and by blowing it a few minutes in the converter could make it into what was being sold at such a high price, the problem was solved.

But there was yet one thing wanting. He had now succeeded in producing the purest malleable iron ever made, and that, too, by a quicker and less expensive process than was ever known before. But what he wanted was to make steel. The former is iron in its greatest possible purity; the latter is pure iron containing a small percentage of carbon to harden it. There has been an almost endless controversy in trying to make a definition that will fix the dividing line that separates the one metal from the other.[1]

For our present purpose, suffice it to quote the account given in a popular treatise on metallurgy, published at the time when Bessemer was in the midst of his experiments.

---

[1] In Grüner's text-book on steel, he says: "In its properties, as well as in its manufacture, steel is comprised between the limits of cast and wrought iron. It cannot even be said where steel begins or ends. It is a series which begins with the most impure black pig iron, and ends with the softest and purest wrought iron. [Karsten stated this in these words in 1823.] Cast iron passes into hard steel in becoming malleable (natural steel for wire-mills, the ' Wildstahl' of the Germans); and steel, properly so called, passes into iron, giving in succession mild steel, steel of the nature of iron, steely iron, and granular iron."

"Wrought iron," it says, "or soft iron, may contain no carbon ; and if perfectly pure, would contain none, nor indeed any other impurity. This is a state to be desired and aimed at, but it has never yet been perfectly attained in practice. The best as well as the commonest foreign irons always contain more or less carbon. . . . Carbon may exist in iron in the ratio of 65 parts to 10,000 without assuming the properties of steel. If the proportion be greater than that, and anywhere between the limits of 65 parts of carbon to 10,000 parts of iron and 2 parts of carbon to 100 of iron, the alloy assumes the properties of steel. In cast iron the carbon exceeds 2 per cent, but in appearance and properties it differs widely from the hardest steel. These properties, although we quote them, are somewhat doubtful ; and the chemical constitution of these three substances may, perhaps, be regarded as still undetermined." Now, in the Bessemer converter the carbon was almost entirely consumed. In the small gun just described,[1] there were only 14 parts of carbon for 1,000,000 parts of iron. Bessemer's next difficulty was to carburize his pure iron, and thus to make it into steel. "The wrought iron," says Mr. I. L. Bell, " as well as the steel made according to Sir Henry Bessemer's original plan, though a purer specimen of metal was never heard of except in the laboratory, was simply worthless. In this difficulty, a ray of scientific truth, brought to light one hundred years before, came to the rescue. Bergmann was one of the earliest philosophers who discarded all theory, and introduced into chemistry that process of analysis which is the indispensable antecedent of scientific system. This Swedish experimenter had ascertained the

---

[1] A small cannon cast by Sir Henry, the description of which we have omitted.

existence of manganese in the iron of that country, and connected its presence with suitability for steel purposes." Manganese is a kind of iron exceptionally rich in carbon, and also exceptionally free from other impurities. Berzelius, Rinman, Karsten, Berthier, and other metallurgists had before now discussed its effect when combined with ordinary iron ; and the French were so well aware that ferro-manganese ores were superior for steel-making purposes that they gave them the name of *mines d'acier*. So Bessemer, after many experiments, discovered a method whereby, with the use of ferro-manganese, he could make what is known as mild steel. The process of manufacture, when described by Sir Henry Bessemer at Cheltenham in 1856,[1] was so nearly complete, that only two important additions were made afterwards. One was the introduction of the ferro-manganese for the purpose of imparting to his pure liquid iron the properties of "mild steel." The other was an improvement in the mechanical apparatus. He found that when the air had been blown into the iron till all the carbon was expelled, the continuance of "the blow" afterward consumed the iron at a very rapid rate, and a great loss of iron thus took place. It was therefore necessary to cease blowing at a particular moment. At first he saw no practical way by which he could prevent the metal going into the air-holes in the bottom of the vessel below the level of the liquid mass, so as to stop them up immediately on ceasing to force the air through them ; for if he withdrew the pressure of air, the whole apparatus would be destroyed for a time. Here, again, his inventive genius found a remedy. He had the converter holding the molten iron mounted on an

---

[1] Immediately after his first successful experiment at St. Pancras, described above.

axis, which enabled him at any moment he liked to turn it round and to bring the holes above the level of the metal; whenever this was done the process of conversion or combustion ceased of itself, and the apparatus had only to be turned back again in order to resume the operation. This turning on an axis of a furnace weighing eleven tons, and containing five tons of liquid metal, at a temperature scarcely approachable, was a system entirely different from anything that had preceded it; for it he took out what he considered one of his most important patents, "and," he says, "I am vain enough to believe that so long as my process lasts, the motion of the vessel containing the fluid on its axis will be retained as an absolute necessity for any form which the process may take at any future time." The patent for this invention was taken out about four years after his original patent for the converter.

Uncle Fritz showed them a picture of this gigantic kettle, which holds this mass of molten metal and yet turns so easily.

"But," said Helen, "you have a model of it here, Uncle Fritz." And she pointed to her Uncle Fritz's inkstand, which is something the shape of a fat beet-root, with the point turned up to receive the ink. Uncle Fritz nodded his approval. These inkstands, which turn over on a little brazen axis, were probably first made by some one who had seen the great eleven-ton converters.

Uncle Fritz showed the children the picture in the "Practical Magazine," and they spent some time together in looking over the pages of the volume for 1876.

The Bessemer process was now perfect. Nearly four years had elapsed since its conception and first application; and in addition to the necessary labor and anxiety he had experienced, no less than £20,000 had been expended in making experiments that were necessary to complete its success. It only remained to bring the process into general use.

The young people asked quite eagerly whether they could see the processes of "conversion" anywhere, and were glad to be told that Bessemer steel is made in many parts of America. One of their young friends, who was educated at the "Technology," is in charge of a department at Steelton, in Pennsylvania, and they have all written letters to him.

The American steel-makers have a great variety of ores to choose from, and they have found it possible, by using different ores, to avoid the difficulties which Mr. Bessemer first met in using the ores of England.

And so far are the processes now simplified, that in many American establishments the molten iron is received liquid from the blast furnaces, and does not have to be reduced a second time in a cupola furnace, as was the iron used by Mr. Bessemer. There is no cooling, in such establishments, between the ore and the finished steel.

XIV.

THE LAST MEETING.

GOODYEAR.

WHEN the day for the next meeting came, Uncle Fritz had a large collection of books and magazines in the little rolling racks and tables where such things are kept. But no one of them was opened.

No. The young people appeared in great strength, all at the same moment, and notified him that he was to put on his hat and his light overcoat, and go with them on what they called the first "Alp" of the season. For there is a pretence in the little company that they are an Alpine Club, and that for eight months of the year it is their duty to climb the highest mountains near Boston.

Now, the very highest of these peaks is the summit hill of the Blue Hills, to which indeed Massachusetts owes its name. For "Matta" in the Algonquin tongue meant "great," and "Chuset" meant "a hill." And a woman who was living on a little hummock near Squantum, just before Winthrop and the rest landed, was the sacred Sachem of the Massachusetts Indians. Hence the name of Mattachusetts Bay; and then, by euphony or bad spelling, or both, Massachusetts.

Uncle Fritz obeyed the rabble rout, as he is apt to do. He retired for a minute to put on heavier shoes, and, when he reappeared, he took the seat of honor in the leading omnibus. And a very merry expedition they had to the summit, where, as the accurate Fergus told them, they were six hundred feet above the level of the sea. There was but little wood, and they were able to lie and sit in a large group on the ground just on the lee side of the hill, where they could look off on the endless sea.

"Whom should you have told us about, had it rained?" said Mabel Fordyce.

"Oh! you were to have had your choice. There are still left many inventors. I had looked at Mr. Parton's Life of Goodyear, and the very curious brief prepared for the court about his patents. Half of you would not be here to-day but for that ingenious and long-suffering man."

"Should not I have come?" said Gertrude, incredulously.

"Surely not," said Uncle Fritz, laughing. "I saw your water-proof in your shawl-strap. I know your mamma well enough to know that you would never have been permitted to come so far from home without that ægis, or without those trig, pretty overshoes. You owe water-proof and overshoes both to the steady perseverance of Goodyear and to the loyal help of his wife and daughters. Some day you must read Mr. Webster's eulogy on him and them. Indeed, he is the American Palissy. You hear a good deal of woman's rights; but, really, modern women had no rights worth speaking of till Mr. Goodyear enabled them to go out-doors in all weathers.

"I meant we should have an afternoon with the Good-years. Then I meant that you should know, Gertrude, where that slice of bread came from."

"Well," said she, "I do not know much, but I do know that. It came out of the bread-box."

"Very good," said the Colonel, laughing. "But some-body put it into the bread-box. And it is quite as well that you should know who put it in. American girls and American boys ought to know that men's prayer for 'Daily Bread' is answered more and more largely every year. They ought to know why. Well, the great reason is that reaping and binding after the reapers, nay, that sowing the corn, and every process between sowing and harvest, has been wellnigh perfected by the American inventors. So I had wanted to give a day or two to reapers and binders, and the other machinery of harvesting. Indeed, if our winter had been as long as poor Captain Greely's was, and if you had met me every week, we should have had a new invention for each one. Here are the telephone and the telegraph. Here is the use of the electric light. Here is the sewing-machine, with all its nice details, like the button-hole maker. Nay, every button is made by its own machinery. Here are carpets one quarter cheaper than they were only four years ago ; cotton cloths made more by machinery and less by hand labor ; nay, they tell us that the cotton is to be picked by a machine before long.

"But these are things you must work up for yourselves. You are on a good track now, and have learned some of the principles of such study.

"Go to the originals whenever you can. Read what you understand, and fall back on what you did not under-stand at first, so as to try it again."

"Do you not think that all the great things have been invented, Uncle Fritz?"

This was John Angier's rather melancholy question.

"Not a bit of it, my boy. Certainly not for as keen eyes as yours and as handy hands. Let me tell you what I heard President Dawson say. He is President of McGill University, and is counted one of the first physical philosophers in America.

"He said this in substance : 'What will future times say of us, the men of the end of the nineteenth century? They will say, "What was the ban on those men, what numbed them or held them still, as if in fear? Why did they not apply in daily life their own great discoveries of the central laws of Nature? They were able to work out principles. Why could they not embody them in useful inventions? They discovered the Ocean of Truth, but they stood frightened on its shore. They found the great principles of science, and for their application they seem to have been satisfied when they had built the steam-engine, had devised the telegraph, the telephone, the phonograph, and when they had set the electric light a blazing."'

"You see, John, that he thinks there is enough more for you and the rest to invent and to discover."

Then Uncle Fritz took from his ulster pocket Mr. Parton's volume of biographical sketches.

"It is all very fine for you, Miss Alice," he said, "to lie there on your waterproof, and to be sure that even mamma will not scold when you go home. But take the book, and read, and see who has wept and who has starved that you might lie there."

And Alice read the passages he had marked for her.

The difficulty of all this may be inferred when we state that at the present time it takes an intelligent man a year to learn how to conduct the process with certainty, though he is provided, from the start, with the best implements and appliances which twenty years' experience has suggested.   And poor Goodyear had now reduced himself, not merely to poverty, but to isolation.   No friend of his could conceal his impatience when he heard him pronounce the word " India-rubber."   Business-men recoiled from the name of it.   He tells us that two entire years passed, after he had made his discovery, before he had convinced one human being of its value.   Now, too, his experiments could no longer be carried on with a few pounds of India-rubber, a quart of turpentine, a phial of aquafortis, and a little lampblack.   He wanted the means of producing a high, uniform, and controllable degree of heat, — a matter of much greater difficulty than he anticipated.   We catch brief glimpses of him at this time in the volumes of testimony.   We see him waiting for his wife to draw the loaves from her oven, that he might put into it a batch of India-rubber to bake, and watching it all the evening, far into the night, to see what effect was produced by one hour's, two hours', three hours', six hours' baking.   We see him boiling it in his wife's saucepans, suspending it before the nose of her tea-kettle, and hanging it from the handle of that vessel to within an inch of the boiling water.   We see him roasting it in the ashes and in hot sand, toasting it before a slow fire and before a quick fire, cooking it for one hour and for twenty-four hours, changing the proportions of his compound and mixing them in different ways.   No success rewarded him while he employed only domestic utensils.   Occasionally, it is true, he produced a small piece of perfectly vulcanized India-rubber ; but upon subjecting other pieces to precisely the same process, they would blister or char.

Then we see him resorting to the shops and factories in the neighborhood of Woburn, asking the privilege

of using an oven after working hours, or of hanging
a piece of India-rubber in the " man-hole " of the boiler.
The foremen testify that he was a great plague to them,
and smeared their works with his sticky compound ; but
though they regarded him as little better than a troublesome lunatic, they all appear to have helped him very
willingly.   He frankly confesses that he lived at this time
on charity ; for although *he* felt confident of being able
to repay the small sums which pity for his family enabled
him to borrow, his neighbors who lent him the money
were as far as possible from expecting payment.   Pretending
to lend, they meant to give.   One would pay his butcher's
bill or his milk-bill ; another would send in a barrel of
flour ; another would take in payment some articles of the
old stock of India-rubber ; and some of the farmers allowed
his children to gather sticks in their fields to heat his
hillocks of sand containing masses of sulphurized India-
rubber.   If the people of New England were not the
most " neighborly " people in the world, his family must
have starved, or he must have given up his experiments.
But, with all the generosity of his neighbors, his children
were often sick, hungry, and cold, without medicine, food,
or fuel.   One witness testifies : " I found, in 1839, that
they had not fuel to burn nor food to eat, and did not
know where to get a morsel of food from one day to another, unless it was sent in to them."   We can neither
justify nor condemn their father.   Imagine Columbus
within sight of the new world, and his obstinate crew
declaring it was only a mirage, and refusing to row him
ashore.   Never was mortal man surer that he had a fortune in his hand, than Charles Goodyear was when he
would take a piece of scorched and dingy India-rubber
from his pocket and expound its marvellous properties

to a group of incredulous villagers. Sure also was he that he was just upon the point of a practicable success. Give him but an oven and would he not turn you out fire-proof and cold-proof India-rubber, as fast as a baker can produce loaves of bread? Nor was it merely the hope of deliverance from his pecuniary straits that urged him on.　In all the records of his career, we perceive traces of something nobler than this. His health being always infirm, he was haunted with the dread of dying before he had reached a point in his discoveries where other men, influenced by ordinary motives, could render them available.

By the time that he had exhausted the patience of the foremen of the works near Woburn, he had come to the conclusion that an oven was the proper means of apply-ing heat to his compound. An oven he forthwith de-termined to build. Having obtained the use of a corner of a factory yard, his aged father, two of his brothers, his little son, and himself sallied forth, with pickaxe and shovels, to begin the work; and when they had done all that unskilled labor could effect towards it, he induced a mason to complete it, and paid him in brick-layers' aprons made of aquafortized India-rubber. This first oven was a tantalizing failure. The heat was neither uniform nor controllable. Some of the pieces of India-rubber would come out so perfectly "cured" as to demonstrate the utility of his discovery; but others, pre-pared in precisely the same manner, as far as he could discern, were spoiled, either by blistering or charring. He was puzzled and distressed beyond description; and no single voice consoled or encouraged him. Out of the first piece of cloth which he succeeded in vulcanizing he had a coat made for himself, which was not an ornamental garment in its best estate ; but, to prove to the unbelievers that it would stand fire, he brought it so often in contact with hot stoves, that at last it presented an exceedingly dingy appearance. His coat did not impress the public favorably, and it served to confirm the opinion that he was laboring under a mania.

In the midst of his first disheartening experiments with sulphur, he had an opportunity of escaping at once from his troubles. A house in Paris made him an advantageous offer for the use of his aquafortis process. From the abyss of his misery the honest man promptly replied, that that process, valuable as it was, was about to be superseded by a new method, which he was then perfecting, and as soon as he had developed it sufficiently he should be glad to close with their offers. Can we wonder that his neighbors thought him mad?

It was just after declining the French proposal that he endured his worst extremity of want and humiliation. It was in the winter of 1839–40 ; one of those long and terrible snowstorms for which New England is noted, had been raging for many hours, and he awoke one morning to find his little cottage half buried in snow, the storm still continuing, and in his house not an atom of fuel nor a morsel of food. His children were very young, and he was himself sick and feeble. The charity of his neighbors was exhausted, and he had not the courage to face their reproaches. As he looked out of the window upon the dreary and tumultuous scene, — " fit emblem of his condition," he remarks, — he called to mind that a few days before, an acquaintance, a mere acquaintance, who lived some miles off, had given him upon the road a more friendly greeting than he was then accustomed to receive. It had cheered his heart as he trudged sadly by, and it now returned vividly to his mind. To this gentleman he determined to apply for relief, if he could reach his house. Terrible was his struggle with the wind and the deep drifts. Often he was ready to faint with fatigue, sickness, and hunger, and he would be obliged to sit down upon a bank of snow to rest. He reached the house and told his story, not omitting the oft-told tale of his new discovery, — that mine of wealth, if only he could procure the means of working it. The eager eloquence of the inventor was seconded by the gaunt and yellow face of the man. His generous acquaintance entertained him cordially, and lent him a sum of money, which not only carried his family through the worst of the winter, but enabled him to continue his experiments on a small scale. O. B. Coolidge, of Woburn, was the name of this benefactor.

On another occasion, when he was in the most urgent need of materials, he looked about his house to see if there was left one relic of better days upon which a little money could be borrowed. There was nothing but his children's school-books, — the last things from which a New Englander is willing to part. There was no other resource. He gathered them up, and sold them for five dollars, with which he laid in a fresh stock of gum and sulphur, and kept on experimenting.

Alice and Hester looked over the rest of the story while the others packed up the wrecks of the picnic and prepared to go down the hill. Then they joined Uncle Fritz in the advance, and thanked him very seriously for what he had shown them.

"Such a story as that," said Hester, "is worth more than anything about cut-offs or valves."

"I think so too," said he.

"I should like," said the girl, "to write to those children of his a letter to thank them for what they have done, and what he did for me, and a million girls like me."

"It would be a good thing to do," said he, "and I think I can put you in the way."

"And I do hope," said Alice, eagerly, "that if we are ever tested in that way we shall bear the test."

"Dear Uncle Fritz, if we cannot invent a flying-machine, and have not learned how to close up rivets this winter, we have learned at least how to bear each other's burdens."